WHERE LEGENDS DIE

To Katelynn,
Live Your Dream.
~Catie Cordero

BOOKS BY CATIE CORDERO

Ramble and Roar

Marvel and Mayhem

Standing Lost (A Memoir)

Where Legends Die

WHERE LEGENDS DIE

CATIE CORDERO

FLYWHEEL
BOOKS

Published by Flywheel Books
Zeeland, MI 49464
www.catiecordero.com

Printed in the United States of America

ISBN: 979-8-218-24837-6

Cover Design by Justin Heap
Cover Photography by Kari Dunham
Featured Historical House: The Felt Estate
Formatting by Polgarus Studio

Book Reference: How Girls Can Help Their Country, Handbook for Girl Scouts, 1913
Song Reference: After You've Gone by Henry Creamer, Turner Layton, Mario (Kobalt Music Publishing)

DISCLAIMER: Some of the content in this novel displays the mindsets and prejudices prevalent in the 1900s. The derogatory language and expressions have been used to depict historical accuracy and do not reflect the views of the author. This novel was critiqued by sensitivity reader, Author Toni Shiloh.

For my children, Isabella and Gabe.
Let the world hear your laughter.

ACKNOWLEDGMENTS

This book has been a journey to write. I had the initial idea in 2019 for a ghost story, something I had always wanted to write. However, due to personal health issues, job changes, a worldwide pandemic, and raising kids, this project was shelved several times. But thanks to my family and friends (aka cheer squad)–I didn't give up.

First, thank you to my mother Cindy Overbeek, who has read all my manuscripts, even those I wrote through grade school! You're long-suffering. Thank you for always believing in me. Thank you for your support, encouragement, and love. I'm so grateful.

Second, thank you to my husband, Jonathan Cordero for pushing me to keep writing books. When I doubt myself, you remind me of the gift God has given and to never squander it. And you make me smile! I love you.

To all my critique partners–Connie Alvero, Carol Graft, Jonathan, and Cindy—you all make me better. Thank you for the honest and creative feedback.

To my kids, Isabella and Gabriel, thanks for being patient when I work long hours, for encouraging my ideas, and your unconditional love. Go Team Cordero!

Thank you to Author Toni Shiloh for being my sensitivity reader, giving honest critique, and helping me tell the story accurately for my non-white characters.

Thank you to Julie Moes for being my cover model and making June Flynn come to life. Kari Dunham, you nailed it on the cover photography! Gorgeous images. And Justin Heap, you know how to take all my ideas and mold them into the perfect cover design. You amaze me. Also, a big thank you to The Felt Estate for allowing me to feature this historic house on my cover.

To all my friends and family, thank you for your prayers, book purchases, and continued support of my writing.

Last but far from least, I thank you, God, for co-writing with me, day after day. I tried to do it without you (when I was mad), and we both know how that went. Thanks for being faithful. Thanks for wooing me. And thanks for being the first one who said, "Catie, I believe in you."

JUNE

CHAPTER ONE

Most people go their whole lives without witnessing a murder. For those who do, I imagine it changes them. Makes them paranoid. Makes them lie awake at night listening to every howl against the windowpane or creak of the walls. They refuse to sleep for fear of depicting dreams.

I'd imagine this is the normal response.

I found out that I, June Flynn, was not normal.

CHAPTER TWO

Saturday, April 12, 1919
12:30 PM

Desperate situations make people do desperate things. Was I desperate? Very.

Fighting through overgrown trees and brush, I wondered if the listed property was in fact a myth.

"Should be just ahead," said Mr. Ennis, swinging his clipboard like a hatchet trying to fight his way through.

Another branch of briars caught my blouse, fraying the ivory threads. "Goodness, Mr. Ennis. You never mentioned we'd be hiking through a jungle."

"Terribly sorry, Ms. Flynn. It's a bit more overrun than I remembered."

"A bit?" My sixteen-year-old daughter, Alice, groaned behind me.

Trying to stay optimistic, I called back to Alice. "Just up ahead, dear."

"Mom, what kind of house sits in a thicket?"

"I suspect we'll see."

She wrestled her skirt from a thornbush. "If we don't bleed out first."

I shook my head. Alice had a flair for the dramatic. Though I had to admit neither of us were fans of physical fitness or the great outdoors. We were Manhattan girls. Our idea of exercise was walking through Siegel and Cooper's Department Store. Glancing skyward, I saw dark clouds forming that warned of rain. I hoped we would find the house quickly.

"Aha! There it is," said Mr. Ennis pointing forward.

My heart plummeted. It didn't match the picture in the advertisement which showed a cozy wooden cottage nestled among beautiful oak trees. What sat before me was a weathered box of boards whose siding had darkened to black. Like gnarled fingers, branches of the surrounding trees reached out, twisting and coiling around the roof before curling into the broken windows. I held my breath for fear that one solid sneeze would send the whole thing crashing to the ground. For the love of Pete, I had fought a hostile forest of foliage and sacrificed one of my favorite middies for *this.* I wanted to scold Mr. Ennis for the advert's false representation and storm away, but the status of my bank account made me inhale a breath of composure. Maybe the inside would be better? Forcing a smile, I turned to my daughter. "Looks like an adventure."

She frowned. "Looks haunted."

"It's rough around the edges," said Mr. Ennis, "but this cabin has good bones."

"See, Alice, it has good bones." Reaching out, I patted the post connected to a wooden awning. It shuddered at my touch. My hand snapped back.

"Good bones, huh?" Alice propped a hand on her hip.

"No need to worry, those posts are merely cosmetic." Mr. Ennis gave us a reassuring nod, as if his word was gold. "The interior beams are strong, believe me. Let's have a look inside." He wrestled away a couple of branches obstructing the door. "I think you'll find it more spacious than the outside's appearance." The knob turned, but the door didn't open. "It sticks sometimes." He pushed harder. Still, it didn't budge. Inhaling a breath, he drove his full weight into the door, forcing it open. "There we go. It's a cinch."

Like a wave of pure evil, the smell that hit us would have sent any sane person running. I was not that person. I coughed, trying to rid my throat of the warm taste of rotten eggs. "Quite the aroma."

"I apologize." Mr. Ennis supplied a sheepish smile. "It needs a good airing." Moving inside, he gestured for us to follow. "This main area is the parlor with the kitchen at the rear."

I paused at the doorway, taking a cautious peek inside. Alice stood behind me, gagging.

A loud boom of thunder broke through the sky, making me jump across the threshold. The house was small. I could probably cross the expanse of the parlor and kitchen in under fifteen steps.

Another crack of thunder, and the rain came down, driving Alice inside.

"Cover your face with your shirt, sweetheart. That should help." The floor creaked as I walked through the shadowed room. Draperies of cobwebs filled each corner and spread across the ceiling. Scattered across the floor were little piles of pebbles that I surmised to be rat droppings. The rain sounded like a growl through the threadbare walls. Droplets trickled from the ceiling. I cringed at the sight before me. My heart squeezed with the same familiar ache that started the day Niall left. "It definitely needs a good cleaning."

Alice stared at me. Her shirt covered her nose and mouth, but the incredulous look in her eyes said it all. Though muffled, her words carried a distinct amount of force. "Mother, there are enough rat turds here to fill a wheelbarrow."

I tilted my head thinking about that. "We might have to buy one."

She huffed.

Breezing past her, I entered the kitchen area, trying to sidestep the pebbles which was a failing feat. Reaching the other side of the house, I inspected a dusty cast iron stove. It had two burners on the range. "Does this work?" I pulled open the stove door. A little mouse jumped out, grazing my hand. Shrieking, I scurried in a circle stomping my shoe.

Alice screamed in unison.

"Did I get him?" I yelled.

"I don't know!" She hugged her arms around her body, looking like a frozen flamingo balancing on one leg.

I spun toward Mr. Ennis. "Did I?"

"I think he got away."

I shuddered, thinking of his little mouse toes running across my hand.

"But it looks like we found the culprit for the various deposits." Mr. Ennis lifted a finger in the air like he'd made a grand discovery.

I flung my hand toward the floor. "One mouse couldn't do all of this."

He cleared his throat, averting his gaze. "The stove still works, I believe. *And* there's a bit of furniture."

Resting nearby was a round table and two chairs, also adorned with webs. The only other visible furnishing in the house was a sofa missing its front legs. I hardly considered these items a selling point. "How long has this house been abandoned?"

"18 years," he said. "Unfortunately, with the broken windows, unwanted pests have come in."

"18 years? Why so long?"

His face grew solemn. "Thing is…this is the house where Albin and Irena Krall used to live. They were servants of Mr. Whitaker, the original owner of this property. After the tragedy in 1901, the residence remained vacant."

The word tragedy struck me. I stepped closer to him. "What kind of tragedy?"

"Well, it's said that Irena fell into a deep depression while carrying her first child. No one knows why. Halfway through her term, she walked out to Stony Point in Esopus Creek. She entered the water until it was well over her head and never came up for air." Mr. Ennis paused, shaking his head. "Albin was wracked with grief and died in the house four days later. No one has lived here since."

I placed a hand over my heart. "How awful."

"I told you this place was haunted," muttered Alice.

"The townspeople think so too." Mr. Ennis' tone held a slight edge. Shifting his stance, he faced the parlor fireplace and pointed to the set of doors flanking it. "Through the door on the left is a bedroom and the door on the right leads to a washroom."

My mind lingered on his comment, but I didn't ask for clarification. Entering the tiny bedroom, my breath caught in my throat. The wall before me had streaks of marks engraved into the wood from the floor to the height of my hip. Were those animal scratches? I walked closer. The gouges weren't thin like animal claws. They must have been carved with a blade of some sort. Like a repetitive dragging against the grain. The notion sent a shiver up my spine.

"Ick!" Alice gasped. "What made those marks?"

My mind raced to create a plausible story, for her and for myself. "I'm sure it was an animal. See how the scratches only reach halfway up the wall?" As the words left my mouth, I pictured a grief-stricken Albin lying on the floor, scraping his pocket knife against the wall, over and over again. I swallowed hard. "Only animals would be able to scratch that high."

Alice crossed her arms. "Mother, don't sell me a dog. Little raccoon nails couldn't do that."

I swallowed. "Sandpaper and paint. That's all it needs."

"What about the image seared in my mind?"

"Look at a picture of Wallace Reid. His face can heal anything." Linking my arm with hers, I dragged her along. "Let's check out the washroom." One glance around the space showed only a rusted metal tub on the cracked tiled floor. "Ah, Mr. Ennis, where is the toilet?"

"Please, call me Lloyd." He rubbed a hand over his thick

beard. "There isn't any indoor plumbing, but the water pump outside works." He shifted away, adding, "And there is an outhouse."

"An outhouse?" Alice squeaked.

"It should be behind the house, probably no more than 100 feet."

"A hundred feet?" Her mouth hung open. "What are we, marathon runners?"

Cringing, I looked up at the ceiling. "What about electricity?"

"Ms. Flynn, you're in the country. There isn't electricity, but the kitchen stove will operate by making a fire in the hearth. And in the winter—," he gestured to the brick fireplace which was missing a few bricks, "—you'll want to keep the main fire going."

Make a fire? Did I look like a pioneer woman?

Alice's forehead creased. "Mom, do you know how to make a fire?"

Of course not (but I couldn't say that). I cast her an optimistic smile. "I can learn."

She tossed a hand in the air. "We're going to freeze and starve."

It was highly likely (but she didn't need to know that). "No we're not. We will be fine."

"You can't possibly be considering buying this place. It's ridiculous. We don't belong in—what town is this again?" Alice directed the question to Mr. Ennis.

"Saugerties."

"Yes, Sausage-ties. We don't belong here. We're meant to be home in Manhattan," she pleaded. "Our friends are there. We don't know anyone here. I understand we can't afford our current apartment, but we can find something else. Something less expensive."

Looking into her beseeching hazel eyes, my chest tightened. She had Niall's eyes. "I already found a better paying job here. Manhattan is over an hour's train ride away." Tugging her aside,

I lowered my voice. "Your father didn't leave us much. This is what I can afford."

"Please. This house"—she looked around— "is the stuff of nightmares."

She was right. I trembled thinking about sleeping here, but my options were few. The gravestone had cut a deep trench into the funds I had. "Mr. Ennis, I mean Lloyd, tell me again what the owner is asking for this house?"

"Four hundred dollars."

Alice's fingers dug into my sleeve. "You cannot be serious. There is no way we can live here."

Swallowing, I surveyed the decay of the house. Broken shards of glass lay on the warped wood floors. Black stains dripped down the walls probably from the leaky roof. The thought of hunting down the outhouse made my stomach churn. This place was a disaster. It looked irreparable. And much more, I was a woman with almost no skills or funds to fix it. Yet, I felt drawn to this house. It had been left. Abandoned and unloved.

At that moment, my heart knew what I had to do. It was illogical. This house smelled of defeat. But it was meant for me, and I was meant for it. Lifting my chin high, I pronounced, not so much to Lloyd, but to the world itself, "I'll take it."

An audible whoosh of air left his mouth. "Really? You want to buy it?"

With eyes the size of walnuts, Alice took both of my hands. "No, Mom. Please. We can't live here."

Freeing myself from her grip, I squared my shoulders and stood tall (which wasn't hard since I was in fact a tall woman). "This place deserves a second chance."

"Goodness, it's not a person! It's a building!" Alice turned to Lloyd. "Tell her that this is madness. We're just two women. We can't live in a house like this. There's no way."

He sighed. "Ms. Flynn, your daughter is right. When you asked to see this place, I only agreed because you were so persistent, but I never thought you'd buy it."

I crossed my arms, studying him. With the thick beard, it was hard to tell his age. I guessed he was near to my own. "Well, I've seen it, and I'm going to buy it."

"But you're alone. You don't have a husband to help you."

His words struck like a hand. Then and there, I despised him. I despised all men like him. I knew I was alone. I knew that buying this house was irrational, but I was done being told what a woman could or couldn't do. When my husband went to war, I found a job. It was women like me who kept this country running while our men fought overseas. I'd be damned if someone told me that I couldn't do this. "I'm buying it." The words left my lips with force. "For one hundred dollars."

"Are you crazy?" He huffed. "That's *well* below the asking price."

I stepped closer, narrowing my eyes. "War makes us all a little crazy. Put in the offer, Lloyd." With that, I strode out the door into the rain.

CHAPTER THREE

Monday, April 14
10:00 AM

The day I met Niall replays in my mind often.

Being 16, with zero prospects, I was stuck courting Arthur Meade, a boy with a personality equivalent to mold.

On this particular day, Arthur suggested we go to the soda shop. It was a mile from my house, no great distance, unless you're Arthur. After five minutes of his slow stride, it took all my will not to load him on my back and run to the shop. When the brick building of Hogget's Drug Store was in view, I left Arthur in my dust, bolted into the shop and collapsed on a stool. Putting my head in my hands, I tried to regain my strength to tolerate another minute of Arthur's dull stories.

"Looks like ya need a milkshake," said a voice, smooth as honey.

I lifted my chin, meeting the hazel eyes of a boy with a black bow tie and white vest. "Hello." A smile lifted the corners of my mouth.

He smiled back. "Hello, lass."

Then Arthur plonked down on the stool beside me. "Goodness, June. What's the rush?"

My eyes remained fixed on Mr. Soda Shop. "I was thirsty."

As Arthur launched into another tale about the time he

caught a fish, I watched soda boy making the shakes. His movements were effortless, propelled with a sort of fluidity. And when he spoke to the other customers—glory be—he had the kind of accent that replaced his i's with the sound "oy" and didn't pronounce the h's. I hadn't heard it before, but I knew then and there, I liked it. To my utmost surprise, the boy kept glancing in my direction.

Setting a shake in front of me (he somehow forgot Arthur's), he leaned his elbows on the counter and asked, "What be yer name?"

"June Mitchell."

"Mighty fine name. Sunny like yer hair."

My fingers instinctively touched my blond braid. "Thank you."

Arthur looked between me and the boy. "Hey fella, I didn't receive my shake."

"What's your name?" I ask the boy.

"Niall Flynn."

Mercy, even his name sounded adventurous. "I haven't seen you here before."

"Started a week ago. Me family be new to this here town."

He was new. I liked that. "Where are you originally from?"

"Dublin, Ireland. But me Da moved us to Jersey a few years back. Then he got a job in Brooklyn 'bout a month ago. So here I be."

Ireland. He was foreign. I didn't know why that made me flush with excitement, but it did. I was certain I didn't stand a chance, especially once he caught sight of the other Brooklyn girls, but at this particular moment, all I could see was his hazel eyes looking at me as if I were interesting.

Arthur cleared his throat. "Say June, I think it's about time we head back to your house."

I would rather cut off my big toe than walk home with Arthur, but of course I would do the ladylike thing, the what-my-dad-expected-of-me-thing, and walk home with the dud.

Arthur paid for my shake. We were almost out the door, when Niall appeared at my side, lightly touching my arm. "June, I be wonderin' if I could call on ya sometime?"

Arthur's freckled face reddened. "Hey fella, can't you see that—"

"I'd like that," I said to Niall. "I live on the corner of President and Hoyt."

"Tomorrow around two?"

"That'll work."

"I be countin' down the minutes." Niall walked back to the soda counter.

And I floated out the door. Arthur didn't speak to me for the entire walk home. I thanked the Lord for that.

The next day, Niall called on me. And the day after that. And the day after that. Soon, we were officially courting. My father was not a bit delighted. He didn't want me courting an Irish immigrant, but he allowed the charade to go on because he fully expected the shine to wear off. If I was honest, I expected Niall to lose interest in me too. But he didn't. After a year, Niall asked my father for his blessing to marry me. My father refused.

So, late one night, I snuck out with one suitcase, and we eloped. Without money for a proper honeymoon, we stayed three days at a cheap hotel. The faucet dripped and the bed sheets smelled musty, but being punch-drunk in love, I could have sworn I was in Paris. Lying in the arms of Niall, my fears eased. I wasn't a disappointment. I wasn't unwanted. I was Mrs. June Flynn.

If only I could turn back time to those carefree days, when we thought we'd chase our dreams and live forever.

A time before war took away our husbands and left widows penniless.

Wrapping a dinner plate in a sheet of newspaper, I paused, staring at a picture of clean-faced soldiers. So young. So much future ahead of them. I wondered how many had a chance to live it.

When Niall went off to fight, I had bought every newspaper, from every stand, every day. I read each page, hoping for news, wanting assurance that he was safe. These precious papers gave me a tangible connection to him during those long months. I yearned to read that the 3rd Battalion 5th Marines were triumphant and coming home, but such words were never printed. Instead, the words on June 7, 1918 read *Marines Met with Heavy Fire in Belleau Wood.* I held that issue in my hands for hours. The black ink smeared under my tears. After months of reading and hoping, my beloved newspapers had let me down. They had reported my worst fears. Angry, I had shoved them all into a potato sack and threw them into the back of the closet.

Until today, they had remained in the dark, practically forgotten. Now, they had a new purpose. These papers held my heart during those months of waiting and now, these papers would hold my possessions as I moved on.

A knock sounded on my apartment door. Drawing in a strong breath, I knew who would be standing on the other side. I swung it open. "Hello, Loretta."

My neighbor, who was a good deal older than I, saw my face and shook her head. "Darling, have you been crying again? For heaven's sake, of course you have." Brushing past me, she paused in front of a stack of boxes. "I feel this is all too soon. It's causing you added grief."

I sighed. "I can't afford to stay here."

"But you don't know anyone in Saugerties. Your friends and family are here."

"Some friends, yes."

"Don't you have an aunt?"

"She hasn't talked to me in years. Her heart is so calloused, it's a wonder it still beats."

"Are Niall's parents still in New York?"

"No, they returned to Ireland years ago. Would you like me to move there?"

"Goodness no. But couldn't they send you financial support?"

"They haven't the extra to give."

Loretta crossed her arms. "June, I'm concerned. This is moving too quickly. First you tell me that you've accepted a job in Saugerties and next you're buying a house there. That's a lot of change, especially since it hasn't been a year—" she stopped flat, dropping her gaze to the floor.

"I know it's fast. But I need to do this."

"Why?"

Walking into the kitchen, I pulled another plate out of the cupboard. "I have to learn to live on my own. I have to make a living for Alice."

"Why can't you make a living in Manhattan?" She pulled off her gloves, tucking them into her purse.

"I can't afford the rent here. Besides, I am buying a house in Saugerties."

"How can you afford a house if you can't afford this apartment?"

"I'm getting a good deal."

Loretta's brow pinched. "Is something wrong with it?"

I avoided her scrutinizing gaze. "It needs some work."

"Who's going to work on it?"

"Alice and I."

She sniffed. "Are you serious?"

I placed a hand on my hip. "Yes."

"You know how to do handy work?"

"I'll figure it out."

"What kind of work are we talking? A good spring cleaning or repairs?"

"Both."

Loretta folded her arms. "You know, dear, you're an attractive gal. I don't think it would be hard to land a new husband."

"It's only been 10 months since Niall died!"

"Ten months is plenty long. I think it's high time you moved on."

My hands clenched at my sides as heat bubbled in my chest. "I would rather move upstate and live in a scrapheap, than be rushed into another marriage."

Loretta shook her head. "I always knew you were a bit odd."

If mercy was a tangible presence, I willed it to come now. I breathed in. Mercy didn't come. "Loretta, you have a big mouth. If I had wanted your opinion, I would have asked for it. Since your arrival today, you've done nothing beneficial. At the very least, you could have helped me wrap my belongings, but instead you've stood there beating your gums."

She blinked three times in quick succession. "You must still be on phase one of the grief work."

"What?"

"Sigmund Freud has a three-step plan to overcome grief."

"What are the steps?"

"Letting go of the ties with the deceased, readjusting to current life, and building new relationships."

Just the thought of letting go caused my eyes to gloss over. "I doubt I'll be reaching the end anytime soon."

Loretta held still for a moment, then she sat her purse on the kitchen table, picked up a plate, and folded a newspaper around it.

As she placed it into a box, my guilt set in. "I'm sorry. I shouldn't have said all that."

"I deserved it. I do have a big mouth, but you've always endured me. I'm going to miss you." Her wrinkled lips parted in a smile. "One thing I know for certain. If anyone can move upstate, buy a scrapheap, and support her daughter…it's you June Flynn, it's you."

CHAPTER FOUR

Saturday, April 19
8:45 AM

A week later, I had our life boxed up. We didn't own many belongings since our apartment came fully furnished. Our net worth was summed up by a mismatched set of plateware, a few knick-knacks, linens, clothing, a dusty gramophone, and a bank account with $43 dollars.

Rain poured down on my Model T as we rumbled along Main Street. Like any sane widow of 35, I got the heck out of Manhattan, leaving behind its plaguing memories. There wasn't a better way to move on than to jump ahead with two feet. That's what I was doing. Jumping. Unfortunately, Alice was dragging. While I saw this as a fresh beginning, she saw it as her life ending. "It's all going to work out, dear. We are going to make a great life here." I parked alongside the curb by the three-story hotel called The Exchange. "We'll stay here until our house is more live-able."

"That'll be the day," she replied in a flat voice.

"Glad you're coming around." Popping open my umbrella, we exited the car with two suitcases and sidestepped puddles along the road. We strode through the hotel's double doors into a mediocre lobby. The floral upholstery on the sofas and chairs had faded to muted colors. The front desk sat on the right side of the room with two gentlemen in blue uniforms behind it. One of the men spoke quietly on the telephone while the other filed cards.

"Hello," I said, approaching the desk. "I'm June Flynn. I spoke with someone on the phone about renting a room."

"Hello, Ms. Flynn," said the desk clerk. "We have a few rooms available right now. How many nights will you be staying?"

"Maybe a week? Possibly more. The house I purchased isn't ready to move into, but my job begins on Monday."

His bushy gray brows raised a smidgen. "By any chance, are you the new typist for the Daily Journal?"

I placed a hand to my chest in surprise. "I am. How did you know?"

"I had heard they had hired a new typist from out-of-town." He tilted his head. "Where are you ladies from?"

"Manhattan."

"Well I'll be. Now that's a big city. Never got over there myself, but I've always thought about it."

"If you ever do, be sure to dine in at the River Pier Café. Great food, and it overlooks the Hudson."

"Much obliged for the advice. I also heard that you purchased the old Krall place. Is that true?"

I nodded. "It is."

"My, my." His brows lifted higher. "Was it Lloyd Ennis that brokered the sale?"

I nodded.

He leaned forward with a conspiratorial expression. "Did he tell you what happened there before selling it to you?"

"If you mean the story of Irena and Albin Krall, then yes, I know."

"You certainly are brave. Folks 'round here won't step a foot near that place. Legend has it that Irena's spirit still lingers there. After the recent *incident*, people are convinced it's true. We never thought we'd see the day when someone would be desperate enough to—"

"How much is your nightly rate?" I cut him off.

He cleared his throat running a finger down the cards on the rack in front of him. "That depends on what kind of room you would like. If you need a room with two beds and a bathroom, that will cost $2.50 a night. If you want a room with one full-sized bed and a shared bathroom, that will cost $1.50 a night."

I inhaled a sharp breath. My job only paid $23.00 a week. "I'll take the bedroom with a single bed and shared bathroom. Mark me down for eight days."

Alice touched my arm. "That won't be long enough."

The desk clerk didn't hide the concern on his face. "Are you sure, Ms. Flynn?"

I dusted Alice's fingers off my arm. "Eight days, please. At that time, I'll decide my next steps."

"Very well." He plucked a white card from the rack behind him and wrote my name next to room number 15. Picking a bell off the desk, he rang it. Another gentleman arrived from the hallway. The desk clerk handed him a key. "Please assist our guests to room 15."

The bellhop carted our suitcases to the room and handed me the key. "Is there anything else you need, ma'am?"

"Is there a local hardware store nearby?"

"Martin's Hardware is a couple stores down from us. Swell place, too. They have everything."

"Wonderful, thank you."

"Enjoy your stay."

We had a simple room. Wooden bed frame with a pale blue quilt. Matching end tables and one armchair in the corner next to an armoire. I set the suitcases on the bed.

Alice propped her hands on her hips. "Eight days won't be enough. A month wouldn't suffice. Didn't you hear that desk clerk? The house is haunted!" If her eyes could emit rays of fire, I would be burning. "And what did he mean by incident?"

"He's merely a busybody. I don't believe in superstitious

stories and neither should you." I unclasped the luggage. "Once we get the house clean enough, then we can live there while we fix it up."

"Mother, it smells putrid in there. How are we going to breathe?"

Lifting a blue frock from the suitcase, I crossed over to the armoire. "I'm sure someone at the hardware store will know what to do. As soon as I unpack, I'm going to Martin's. We can't waste time. Do you want to unpack your suitcase?"

She sank onto the bed. "No."

Her downcast frame pricked my heart. "I think this town will be good for us. It's small and feels cozy."

"It must be small if word has spread about you buying that creepy house."

I shifted toward the window that overlooked the street. Across the hotel was a brick building called Grand Union Market Place. Signs in the windows boasted prices on bread, laundry soap, and other goods. Down the street, rows of white and red striped awnings perched over the shop doors. Lampposts dotted the sidewalks with an occasional bench staggered between. The town looked charming. Hanging the rest of my clothes, I closed the armoire doors. "I'm leaving. Would you like to join me?"

"No thanks. I'm going to read my book before the rats eat it."

"Good idea." I left the room with her gaping at me. It was a short walk to Martin's Hardware. Swinging open the door, I entered what could only be deemed as a dream-come-true. Floor to ceiling shelves lined the walls stocked with cookware, candlesticks, paint cans, and rows and rows of boxed items. Sitting on the floor were cast iron heaters, metal toolboxes, and petite wooden tables bearing pretty lamps. I passed by glass cabinets filled with things from gold plated hair brushes to embroidered hand towels. At the rear of the store were displays of hammers and tools beside mini drawers holding nuts, bolts, and nails. My heavens, what didn't this store sell?

"Hello there," said a voice behind me.

I spun around to find a man in a white long-sleeved shirt tucked into brown tweed trousers and matching vest. "Hello."

"Can I help ya find anythin'?"

I heard it. The same Irish accent as Niall. Sweet mercy. My throat knotted. I found it hard to breathe as I stared at this random employee.

He stared back at me waiting for an answer.

Why, even the hint of caramel outlining his pupil reminded me of Niall. This fella had darker brown hair though. Tears filled my eyes.

Lickety-split, the employee yanked a handkerchief from his pocket. "There now, lass. Did I upset ya?"

I shook my head, dabbing at the trailing tears. "It's not you, it's your accent."

"Me accent? Does it offend ya?"

"No, no." I waved the handkerchief. "It reminds me of my late husband."

He plucked off his cap, placing it to his chest, "Me sincere condolences."

"He died nearly a year ago, fighting in the war. Now, here I am crying in a hardware store."

With a tone so tender, he said, "Don't ya fret a minute. Ya earned the right to cry."

My chin tipped downward as I wiped at the tears. "Time has helped, but grief is a tricky thing. It creeps up when least expected."

"That it does." He tucked his hands in his pockets. "I too fought in the war."

"You did? What division?"

"I served in the 47th Infantry Regiment."

"My husband served in the 5th Marines."

"Belleau Wood?"

I nodded.

"'Twas a horrible battle fer sure."

"Were you there for it?"

"Not that one, no."

"That's a good thing. Too many men were lost. I'm glad that you returned."

"Most of me." He lifted his pant-leg to reveal a steel and leather prosthetic. "Second Battle of Marne. Hand grenade landed behind the berm where me troop be defendin'."

My hand went to my mouth. "I'm sorry."

"Me too." He gave a small shrug. "The war takes pieces of us all."

"I wonder if we even gained what was promised?"

He released a heavy sigh. "That be the question."

We stood in silence for a moment. Both of us with our own thoughts.

Another hardware employee surfaced, looking at us with a question on his face. Embarrassment sent a wave of heat up my neck. "I apologize for taking up your time like this."

He held up his hand. "It be time well spent."

I extended the handkerchief to him with a sheepish smile. "It's a little wet now."

"Keep it. Many do be brought to tears in hardware stores." He gave me a gentle wink.

"I'm June Flynn by the way."

"Me name's Elex O'Keefe."

"Believe it or not, I actually did come here to buy supplies." I extracted a written list from my purse and handed it to him.

"Quite a long list." He read it silently, until he reached one item. "Rat traps?"

"I bought a house."

"And ya need rat traps?"

"I think so. They might still be in there."

His forehead creased. "Sounds like a wee bit of work."

"It's more than wee."

The creases in his forehead deepened. "Hirin' any workers?"

I shifted my weight from one heel to the other. "My daughter will help me. She's sixteen."

"If ya don't mind me askin', where be this house?"

Part of me didn't want to say, since Elex seemed to be outside the gossip loop. I shrugged, trying to play it off. "It's near Esopus Creek."

"The creek? Yer not referrin' to that dilapidated house near Stony Point, are ya?"

Bugger. He guessed it. "That's the one."

His eyes widened. "Ya bought the old Krall cabin?"

"I did."

"Fer the love of Mary, why?"

I fidgeted with my sleeve. "It was in my price range."

"Last time I saw that place it looked overtaken by trees and brush."

"Hence the pruning shears."

"It be takin' more than shears." The side of his mouth curved up. "Ya mean to tell me that yous two are goin' to fix this house up on yer own so?"

"That's the plan."

"Have ya ever done this kind of work before?"

"No."

His mouth now lifted into a full smile. "Yer quite the darin' woman. Don't know many a man who'd step foot in that house, let alone live there. Especially now."

My head inclined in confusion. "What do you mean?"

Now he looked confused. "Ya haven't heard?"

I shook my head.

"Cripes." He rubbed a hand against the back of his neck. "A man disappeared. Behind yer house. They say his tracks went into Esopus Creek, near Stony Point, but a body hasn't been found. It be like he vanished."

My mouth gaped in shock. "When did this happen?"

"Week ago. The whole town's been in uproar."

"There must be an explanation. People don't just vanish."

The expression on my face must have matched my inner worry because Elex quickly tapped my shoulder in a reassuring way.

"I do be sure he'll show up. Probably a misunderstandin'." He looked down at my list. "Let me fetch some boxes from the back, then we can load up yer supplies."

I nodded as he walked away. A man vanished in the creek behind my house. I trembled at this thought. How could that happen? Why would that happen? Unless, as Elex said, it was a misunderstanding. Maybe the man chose to leave. Maybe he wanted it to look like he disappeared. People do strange things all the time. I assured myself that everything was fine. There wasn't anything to fear. I almost had myself convinced.

After paying for my supplies, my net worth dropped another 12 dollars. Leading Elex to my car parked outside the Exchange, I asked, "Do you sell windows at Martin's?"

"We can order and install."

"Is it possible to make payments? I'm a bit short on funds."

"That can be arranged."

"Ah good. Will you send someone to measure the windows? Not sure what I'll need."

"I be seein' to it personally. Mighty grand to meet ya."

Feeling flattered, my hand brushed my throat. "Nice meeting you as well."

Tipping his cap, he walked away.

CHAPTER FIVE

Saturday, April 19
11:00 AM

As our Ford putted down Main Street, Alice peered at me from behind the boxes covering her lap. "Can't we hire some men to fix it up for us?"

"I wish we could. But the funds aren't there." Turning off Main, I slowed on narrow Oakledge Dr. "Think of it like this…we're adventurers exploring the great unknown."

"Does the great unknown look like it's going to collapse and kill us?"

"Lloyd said that the house has good bones. It's not going to kill us."

"The rats might."

I waved my hand in dismissal. "I bought rat traps." We rounded the bend until we arrived at the driveway of the Whitaker Estate. The gravel drive was well kept until it forked in the direction of our house. That's when weeds and grass became more visible than the gravel itself. We drove until the weeds and brush became too dense, making it impossible to see any fallen trees or limbs. I shifted the lever into park. "Look's like we're walking from here. But this time, I have this." With a triumphant smile, I lifted the long primitive blade that was laying by my feet. "This beauty is called a machete. It can cut through anything!"

Alice looked at my tool in horror. "You're going to cut a limb off with that."

"I will not." My voice held a note of indignance. "Elex showed me how to swing it."

"Who's Elex?"

"A worker from the hardware store."

"Who does he think you are, queen of the Amazons?"

"We're about to find out. Come on. Carry a box of supplies and the broom with you." Swinging the blade back and forth, I watched in wonder as the brush fell over. "Ha! I'm doing it." I glanced back to see if Alice was witnessing this miracle.

She stood behind the car door, watching.

"Why aren't you following me?"

"I'm waiting until you are a good distance ahead."

Rolling my eyes, I returned to hacking at the thorns and brush. When the cabin came into view, sweat coated my entire body causing my garments to stick to my skin. But, I had done it. "Victory is mine!" I hollered, slicing through the last twiggy branches obstructing the entrance. Opening the door, the same awful smell and sight welcomed us.

"It's as bad as I remembered." Alice grimaced, plugging her nose.

"Yes, but this time, it's ours!" I set the machete on the moth-eaten sofa. "I'll start sweeping, and you can bring in the last box of supplies."

Alice let the box in her hands drop to the floor with a thud before trudging back out of the house.

My shoulders sank at her apparent frustration. Alice and I had always been close. When Niall left for war, we grew even closer. As I worked outside the home, she picked up the slack around the house. We were a team. After Niall's death, we clung to each other. She couldn't see it now, but I knew we would get through this.

"Here's the last." She dropped the box on the floor.

"Darling, will you start on the cobwebs? There is a duster in one of the boxes."

She didn't move.

"What's the problem?"

"I can't believe we're going to live here."

"You need to try and think positively. I know this place is dirty, but it will be beautiful when it's done."

"Mother, look around you. Don't you see how bad it is?"

"Of course I see it, but together, we can fix it."

She exhaled a heavy breath. "You might want to, but I don't. I don't want anything to do with this house."

I stopped sweeping. "I realize that this place is overwhelming to look at, I do, but it is ours now. That's the end of it."

She glared at me. "If Dad were here he'd be—"

"Well he's not here." The words came out sharper than I intended.

Her surprise morphed into anger. "Every day I'm reminded of that. Every morning I wake up and he's not here. At least in Manhattan, I had a piece of his presence in the apartment, but now that's gone too." Her voice rose. "Now, I've lost my father, my city, and my friends! And what do I get in return? A strange town, with strange people, and this pigsty!"

"You think I wanted this?" My voice matched her volume. "You think I wanted to leave my friends behind? You think I wanted to leave Manhattan and our apartment? I had to buy this dump because your father, God rest his soul, didn't plan for the future!" I threw the broom to the ground.

"Don't talk about him like that!"

"I will talk about it, Alice! I will because you need to understand. You seem to think I have other choices. But I don't. Your father chose to fight in that war. He didn't have to enlist. He was an Irishman. He could have avoided the draft. But he chose to go. He wanted to go, and now he's gone! So what do you want me to do, huh? What? I'd like to know."

Her lower lip trembled, followed by tears falling down her face.

Seeing her pain diluted my fury. I wrapped my arms around

her and wept too. None of it was fair. The loss. The grief. The loneliness.

"I'm sorry, Mom," she managed to say through sobs. "I just miss him."

"I know, sweetheart. I do too."

"I wish he were still here."

"So do I. I wish it everyday, but somehow, we have to find a way to live on." I brushed wet strands of hair from her cheek. "We just have to."

"I know. At least we have each other."

"Always."

Three knocks sounded on the front door. We both jumped.

"June, are ya in there?" It was a man's voice. Thank goodness, it wasn't Irena Krall.

"Yes. Who is it?"

"Elex O'Keefe. From Martin's Hardware."

Great, this man was going to find me crying again. I rubbed the tears off my face with my sleeve, hoping my eyes weren't too red.

Alice looked at me with an arched brow.

"Come in." I called out.

As he stepped inside, his eyes grew bigger. His gaze traveled from the floor to the ceiling. A look of disgust stretched across his face. Like an intrinsic response, he took a step backward. His left boot slipped.

Alice and I followed his eyes downward to the smeared batch of droppings.

He swallowed. "Right. Grand little house, so it is."

I laughed out loud. "Oh yes, the grandest."

"See now why ya wanted those traps." He grinned.

"They're essential," said Alice.

"True enough." Elex nodded to her. "Sorry, don't believe I done had the pleasure of meetin' ya yet."

I clapped a hand to my cheek. "Where's my head? Elex, this is my daughter, Alice."

He pulled off his newsboy cap. "Hello, lass."

"Hello."

"Right so, as promised, I come to measure the dimensions of yer windows. Thought ya be wantin' those sooner than later."

"Yes, thank you. As you can see, the front window is shattered, the kitchen and bedroom windows are cracked, but I think the washroom window will suffice for now."

"Grand so. Will set to it then." He proceeded into the kitchen, taking a measuring tape from his jacket pocket.

Alice leaned close to me and whispered, "He sounds like Dad."

"He is Irish." I whispered back.

"How do you know?"

"He told me at the hardware store."

"Did you ask him?"

"Yes, and then I cried."

"You cried in the store?"

I pressed a hand to my chest. "I couldn't stop."

"What did he do when you started crying?"

"He gave me his handkerchief."

"That was kind."

"He was very nice to me." We paused, both studying him.

Alice crossed her arms. "Did you notice that he has a limp?"

"A grenade blew off part of his leg. He has a prosthetic."

"Really?" She looked impressed. "I never saw a prosthetic before, I wonder what it looks like."

"He showed it to me. It's steel with leather wrapped around it."

Her eyes enlarged. "How much of it's gone?"

"From the knee down."

"Better than the whole thing, I guess."

"I would say so."

She rubbed a hand over her chin. "Do you think he's good-looking?"

"For Pete's sake. Why ask me that?"

"It's a legitimate question. Do you?"

I shrugged, trying to appear nonchalant, though I knew full well that I thought him attractive. "He's got a nice face."

"His backside isn't bad either." She winked at me.

"Alice Mae!"

Elex cleared his throat. "Just thought I be lettin' ye ladies know that I can hear everythin' ya be sayin'."

Alice and I exchanged glances of horror.

"Say Alice, let's see if we can find the water pump outside, shall we?"

"Good idea. Better bring the machete." She pointed to the sofa.

Grabbing it off a cushion, I hurried after her. She giggled as we fled the house. Even though I was mortified, it felt good to hear my daughter laugh.

CHAPTER SIX

Sunday, April 20
8:30 AM

After a quick breakfast in the hotel's café, Alice and I returned to the house. Many people adhered to the philosophy that work shouldn't be done on God's holy day. Again, I was desperate. My job started tomorrow, and I couldn't afford the hotel. I hoped word wouldn't spread about me working on a Sunday. But I knew better. Word would definitely spread.

Yesterday, we discovered the water pump behind the house. Unfortunately, we couldn't get the lever to move. Thankfully, Elex was around. He managed to clear away the grime and grease up the parts until it started moving again. The water came out sludge brown for several minutes. Eventually, it flowed clear. After fixing our pump and measuring our windows, he packed up and left.

All in all, our first day of fixing the house proved to be a success. I had swept the floors clean, and Alice had cleared away most of the cobwebs. Upon our return today, I had a specific mission—find the outhouse. We headed out armed, me with my machete and Alice with a broom. Fighting our way through, we searched for a crescent moon.

"I think I see it." Alice pointed to a tiny building a ways to our right.

I hacked at branches until I could pry the door ajar. It creaked open. The sight before me was one out of an Edgar Allen Poe horror story. Webs hung all around. Floorboards were warped and rotten. More droppings littered the space. A nest of some kind sat in the corner. It might have moved or squeaked. Worst of all was the smell. An aroma of decay mixed with urine. I stepped back, gasping. Behind me, Alice dry heaved.

"I can't do that." I kicked the door shut with my boot.

Alice backed away. "We need help. You should ask Elex."

"Good idea. I'll stop at the hardware store tomorrow." Heading back to the house, I surveyed the living room. "Would you like to mop the floor or wash the walls?"

Her upper lip curled. "I guess I'll mop the floors."

"I'll fetch some water." I filled two metal pails with water and soap. Unfortunately, the water wasn't hot because I didn't know how to make a fire in the stove. One day, I'd learn that as well.

Dunking a towel into the pail, I scrubbed the living room walls. Water mixed with the dust and dirt, forming a loose paste. It oozed down the walls in brown streaks. I groaned. This was going to take forever. Tossing my bucket of water against the wall, I trekked out to the pump for a refill. Sweat beaded on my forehead as I worked the lever. Water gushed into the pail, filling it to the brim. I hefted it up by the handle when a shrill cry cut through the air. Alice! My fingers released the pail splashing water on my boots. I raced back to the door with my heart thumping in my chest. Before I entered, Alice barreled out of the house, nearly colliding with me.

"What's wrong?" we both said in unison.

"Didn't you scream?" I asked her.

"No, I thought it was you."

"It wasn't me." My eyes darted around. "Where did it come from?"

"I don't know."

"Maybe it wasn't a scream. It sounded like a shriek. Maybe it was an animal."

"An animal?" She shook her head. "That didn't sound like an animal. It sounded human. Like a woman's scream."

I shuttered. "What direction did it sound like it came from?"

"That way." Alice pointed toward the old Whitaker mansion.

Though we lived on the grounds of the estate property, we hadn't met the current owner. Even at the bank, while signing our sale documents, the owner never showed up. Lloyd told me they had signed their portion earlier. On the papers, I had noted their scrawled initials, I.L.J. "Maybe we should check the mansion to see if someone is there."

Alice's forehead creased. "What if it's dangerous?"

"What if there is a girl in need of help?"

"How are we going to help her?"

"We won't know until we check it out. Come on." Hiking up my skirt, I jogged through the precarious path I had pruned until we reached the gravel drive. Oddly enough, the Whitaker residence didn't look run-down, though I was told it was vacant. Maybe a groundskeeper was maintaining it? But why would someone pay to keep up a place they didn't visit? Unless—he secretly did. Creeping up to the brick house, I peeked into a side window. No lamps were lit inside, although with the sunlight, I could see white sheets draping the furniture. This had to be the parlor.

"Do you see anything?" whispered Alice.

"Doesn't look like anyone's here. We should look in a few more windows, just to be sure." I walked around the back of the house, peering into window after window. They all showed dark rooms with abandoned furnishings.

Alice hastened ahead to a couple of large wooden doors angled against the house. She lifted a handle, flinging one of the doors open. "This must lead to a cellar." She threw open the second door. "There are steps."

I followed her outstretched finger down the stairs. At the

base of the steps was a doorway. From this viewpoint, I couldn't see into the room.

Below, we heard a rustle of movement. A lump formed in the center of my throat. "Someone's home." I wanted to grab Alice's hand and run. I wanted to flee this strange place with its strange legends and go back to Manhattan. We weren't country girls. We weren't thrill seekers. Goodness, what was I thinking moving here? I looked at my daughter. As a mother, I would do anything to protect my girl. Staring at the cellar opening, a holy anger filled my soul. What if that scream was in fact someone else's little girl? I couldn't stand by and allow that. My Niall had given his life for justice, and I would see justice met here today. "Dash it all, I should have brought the machete." Grabbing a fallen tree branch, I pointed it at Alice. "Stay here." I proceeded down the steps.

"Mom, we should go for help," she hissed. "You can't go in there!"

I held up a hand to silence her. Taking a deep breath, I ran into the cellar, branch extended. A rush of movement came at me in a fast flutter. I screamed, swinging the branch in defense.

Alice screamed too.

A barn owl shrieked as it flew in a frenzy around the cellar, knocked a bottle off the shelf, and then escaped through the open door. The bottle broke upon the packed dirt floor. Red wine splashed on a picture propped against the base of shelves. It was a framed picture of a young woman. She had long blond hair that hung over her shoulders. Set in a very pale face was a stark pair of deep blue eyes, so dark they looked black. The eyes stared directly at me as if they were alive.

Alice grabbed my arm. "Why is there a picture of a woman down here?"

"Who knows." I grimaced. "How did an owl get in?"

"Maybe through a chimney."

Inhaling, I focused on calming my heart rate. "No one's here. Let's head back." We climbed the stairs out of the cellar and closed the doors.

Alice trembled as we walked away. "That cry sounded human though, didn't it?"

"I told you from the start that it was an animal." I was lying (but she didn't need to know that).

She stopped, crossing her arms. "You mean to tell me that you barged into that cellar to save an animal?"

"What can I say, Alice, I love animals."

"Tell that to the mouse you almost stomped to death."

I waved my hand in dismissal. "A mere misunderstanding. The mouse misunderstood that he didn't belong in my house."

CHAPTER SEVEN

Monday, April 21
7:15 AM

A large red brick school sat before us. It had white doors and English Ivy growing up the walls. "Looks swanky."

Alice fidgeted with her braid.

"I bet you'll make lots of friends."

She sighed. "I hope so."

Leaning over, I hugged her goodbye. There was a slight tremble to her shoulders. If only I knew the magic words to relieve her nerves. "Will you be okay?"

"I've made it this far. Only God knows how," she shrugged. "I'll be fine."

"Have a good day, sweetheart."

"Thanks, Mom." She strode up the sidewalk into Saugerties High School, disappearing behind the doors.

"Please be good to her." I said softly.

Passing several downtown shops, I spotted the striped awning of Harmon's Corner Pharmacy which sat directly next to my place of employment, *The Saugerties Daily Journal.* My previous postman, Nico Zanneti, had told me about this newspaper needing another typist. With my last year's work as a secretary, the paper hired me.

Parking alongside the curb, I stepped out of my car. A gust

of wind tugged my hat. I clamped the brim to hold it in place. Inside my white gloves, my palms were sweating. I paused outside the front door, looking at the large window. Here we go. Inhaling a breath, I entered the newsroom already in full swing—men walked around the tables waving papers, typewriters clinked, and others chatted on telephones. In an instant, I fell in love with the electric atmosphere. As I maneuvered through the maze of people and tables, several workers glanced up at me. I could hear them talk as I passed by.

"Is that her?"

"It must be."

"She's not what I expected."

"Goodness, she's tall."

More faces and eyes peered from all around the room, trained in my direction. I saw a mixture of curiosity and skepticism. Their scrutiny made me feel uncomfortable. I was an average blonde with an average figure, but in one area I did excel—my height, which the onlookers had latched onto immediately. I'd rather they notice my nice blue frock (it had a ruched waistband). I even polished my black pumps.

Walking to the door that led into the office of my new boss, Mr. Saviano, I tapped lightly.

"Did someone knock?" a voice called from within.

I stepped closer, trying to make my voice loud enough to be heard through the door. "Yes, sir. It's me, June Flynn."

"Come in." He called back.

I turned the knob, stepping inside. I found Mr. Saviano's seat filled, but not by him. Weeks ago, I had interviewed with Carmine Saviano. He had offered me the job days later. Today, a younger man with shiny, slicked black hair lounged in the chair with a telephone in one hand and a coffee in the other. He had several newspapers splayed across the desk. Upon my entry, he looked over. His deep brown eyes met mine with an inquisitiveness that made me halt in place. "I need those numbers, Sammy," he spoke into the phone. "We go to print in two hours. I need those numbers." As he listened to Sammy's response, he continued to study me.

Unsure of what to do, I stood there, looking back at him. It wasn't an unpleasant view. The label of handsome didn't do him justice. This man had film star good looks. Wallace Reid good looks. Make a girl weak in the knees good looks. Our eyes remained fixed in a standoff, while Sammy's voice mumbled through the receiver.

"Excuses help no one, Sam. Two hours. Okay? Good." He hung up the phone, drank a swig of coffee and gestured to me. "You say your name is Jane?"

"No, sir." Gripping my purse between nervous fingers, I hurried closer. "It's June. June Flynn."

"Ah, June. How can I help you?"

"I'm the new typist. Mr. Saviano hired me. Today is supposed to be my first day."

He slapped a hand to his forehead. "Forgive my forgetfulness. He did mention you. He left me in charge while he's working on important business in New York City. You're from there, right?"

"I am."

"Love Manhattan. Great stores. Great food. Loads of entertainment." His gaze journeyed upward like he was picturing it. "Who knows, maybe someday…" His voice drifted off in wonder.

I too found myself wondering. Who was this man? He had the same sing-song Italian cadence as my postman Nico. I cleared my throat, "And you are?"

Snapping back to reality, he bounced off the chair. "I'm Salvatore Saviano." He wore a double-breasted gray suit with silk stripes. This kind of suit could set a man back more than twenty dollars. "My father is Carmine. The Saugerties Daily Journal has been in our family for fifty years. Long time, eh? My grandfather won the press off some fella in a poker game.

Can you believe that? What luck, huh?" He extended his hand to me. "Welcome to our crew."

I shook his hand, now intrigued. "Your grandfather decided to use the press to start his own paper?"

"He did. My Nonna thought him mad. She told him to sell it, but he had a vision. It goes to show you that anything is possible." He circled around, leaning against the front of the desk. His shoes were only four feet from mine. His were shinier.

From this close proximity, I saw a scar cutting through his left eyebrow. On his tanned face, it wasn't unattractive.

He rubbed his fingers against his chin. "You ever work at a paper before?"

"No, I haven't."

"There's nothing like it." He smiled (the kind that could win awards). "The excitement of a breaking story, the rush of a deadline—" he tipped his head back— "I'll never tire of it. Did my father show you around when you were here last?"

I shook my head. "It was only an interview."

"Right. Follow me. I gotta make my rounds." He lightly placed a hand on my elbow, ushering me out of his office. Glancing over, he met my eyes directly. "You're quite a tall gal, huh?"

"Maybe you're short." The words slipped out before I could filter them.

He laughed out loud. "You got a sense of humor. I like that." Gesturing to the newsroom, he said, "Everyday, we go to print by 9 AM. We put out the afternoon dailies, see. In order to make that deadline, we have several departments. Each department depends on the others." He stopped as we reached the first long table below hanging lamps. The table bore three typewriters. Two women sat plunking on the keys. The third typewriter remained unoccupied. "This is our typing department." He gestured to a woman with sharp features and slanted eyebrows. "This here is our senior typist, Martha. She's been with us for four years, but she'll be leaving us soon, due to the arrival of her first child."

Martha placed a hand on top of her growing belly, granting me a curt nod.

"This is our other typist, Frieda." Salvatore motioned to a petite brunette seated beside Martha. "This is June Flynn. She'll be joining yous dolls."

"Hello." I said to the women.

"This will be your spot." He touched the third typewriter.

My pride rose as I looked at the typewriter. It had beautiful black keys, each marked with white letters. As I reached out to touch it, Salvatore paraded me onwards to the next department where one man engaged in an excited conversation over the phone and another man flipped through handwritten notes. There was also a younger fella reviewing telegraph dispatches.

"This is our reporting section," he said. "We have three reporters who handle all our stories." He rattled through introductions, then steered me through sales and accounting, before proceeding down a hall into another room. "This is composing, printing, and circulation." We stopped first at a table under bright lights where a man stood assembling metal letters inside a small tray. "Tony here is making today's featured article," he said. "Each small tray is put into a large metal tray for printing. Which is over here." He walked to a long iron press with all sorts of wheels, pulleys, and moving parts.

An operator threaded paper into the first revolving cylinder. As it spun around the loops, ink pressed on the white page in the form of words.

"This is our rotary printing press. She's a beauty." Salvatore marveled at the machine. "It never gets old, watching a blank sheet transform into a masterpiece of literature." He turned to me, his face alight. "It's magical, don't you think?"

Caught up in his enthusiasm, I found myself nodding. Prior to this moment, I wouldn't have deemed a press *magical.* Inventive engineering, yes. Magical, no. Now as I looked in his sparkling brown eyes, I thought, sure why not.

"Though," he lifted a finger, "every machine comes with its challenges. There is always maintenance to keep it running smoothly. Just this morning, we had an issue with the ink coverage, but," he gestured to a man who collected a printed paper out of the end of the press, "we oughta be back in business before the second edition." He called out to a man in overalls, shielded behind a paper. "How's it looking, Ishmael?"

The man lowered the page in his hands. I saw that he was a black man.

Ishmael glanced at me then returned his focus to Sal. "We're in good shape." He brought over the sample.

Salvatore reviewed the page. "Much better." He placed a hand on Ishmael's shoulder. "This is Ishmael Davis. He's only been an engineer for our paper for two months, but I don't know how we got along without him before that."

Ishmael smiled. "Glad to be here."

"This is Ms. June Flynn." Salvatore gestured to me. "She's a new typist."

He pulled off his cap, not meeting my gaze. "Pleasure to meet you, ma'am."

I stuck out my hand. "You as well."

His eyes widened at my outstretched hand. He shook it once, then dropped his hand back to his side.

Knowing that Ishmael had a large role at the paper told me unspoken things about the Saviano's. Good things.

"Over here, our pressmen will read through the first edition in order to catch any defects." Salvatore ushered me to the end of the press. "Then all corrections will be made for our final edition. As the folded papers come off the conveyor, they are tied into packages and circulation delivers them to retailers, newsstands, and houses. All in time for lunch."

"You run quite the operation."

"We give it our best. Come on, let's get you settled at your table."

As I followed him back into the newsroom, the front door flung open and a mostly bald man with bottle-shaped glasses burst inside. "There's been another vanishing!"

At this the newsroom fell silent, attuned to whatever he would say.

"It's Stuart Ellsworth. He's disappeared." He pushed up the brim of his glasses. "His mother discovered him missing this morning. No sign of him anywhere. They contacted the police, who found his car stuck in the hedges off Esopus Drive. The authorities found tracks leading toward Stony Point."

"Stony Point?" Salvatore's voice sounded excited. "You sure, Clyde?"

"Positive."

He looked at the clock on the wall. "We gotta hour to get this story on the press. James and Thomas—get Ellworth's picture and ask the neighbors if they heard or witnessed anything. Clyde, I need you to personally talk with Ellworth's parents. Get the full story. With any luck, we'll get this out before The Telegraph. This is big, people. Big!" He clapped his hands. "Back to work!" The newsroom roared to life, with people scurrying around and telephones ringing.

As Salvatore rushed off in a frenzy, I stood agape at the suddenness of this news. Another disappearance. Near my house. Wandering to my table, I sank into my chair facing my typewriter.

Frieda sat next to me, typing at the speed of sound.

I leaned toward her, lowering my voice. "I don't know what I'm supposed to do."

She didn't look at me. "Don't worry. The papers will start piling on your desk at any minute."

"Oh." I sat back, staring at my typewriter. In Manhattan, we had plenty of crime. That was a thing of normal proportions, but in a small town like this I was surprised. And the fact that it was all occurring behind my house, left me anxious. I leaned near Frieda again. "There's been two disappearances, near Stony Point?"

"That's right." Her finger clinked the keys—typing, typing, typing.

"Who was the first?"

"Henry Brickmore." The way she said his name seemed like she had a bad taste in her mouth.

"Did you know him?"

"Everyone in town knew him. Old money. He is a member of the Whitaker family line. They were a part of the establishment of this town. They've made a fortune with their iron mills and bluestone quarries. They love their wealth. And love flaunting it all the more."

"Have the police searched the creek?"

"Of course. They dragged it, but his body wasn't found."

"Goodness." I sighed. "Right behind my house."

"Your house?" Frieda's voice held an eerie edge. "Five days after Lloyd Ennis showed you through *the house*, Henry Brickmore vanished. Coincidence?" She threw me a probing look. "Maybe or maybe not." She flipped a page and continued typing. "There is a theory though."

Martha groaned. "Frieda, stop with the gossip. You have a job to do."

"Can't you see me typing, Martha?" Frieda rolled her eyes. "As I was saying—Charles Whitaker was the original owner of the entire property that you now live on. He owned the mansion, surrounding acres, and the servants' cabin that you bought. Albin and Irena Krall lived in the cabin. Albin actually died there. Did Lloyd tell you that before he sold you the place?"

"Yes, he did."

"Oh." Frieda looked surprised by this. "Well, what you may not know is that Whitaker took advantage of the Kralls. He paid them cheap wages and made them live outside the mansion because they were German immigrants. It's said that all Irena ever wanted was to be a mother. Year after year, she didn't conceive. Finally after three years of marriage, she was pregnant. Sadly, six months later, she drowned herself. Albin died days later in the house. It was a terrible tragedy."

My forehead creased. "Why would she drown herself? That doesn't make any sense."

"I know," said Frieda. "Which is why I tend to believe the other story. Irena didn't commit suicide. She was murdered. But that's not all."

"Of course not," mumbled Martha. "There's always more with Frieda Duffy."

"Did anyone ask you, Martha?" She snorted.

"What does any of this have to do with the disappearances?" I asked.

"I'm getting there." Frieda organized her typed papers into a tidy pile. "Shortly after the deaths of Irena, her unborn child, and Albin, the infant of Charles Whitaker became seriously ill. Even with medical attention, he didn't improve and days later, he died. Weeks after that, the next two youngest sons met their end by strange accidental deaths. Then, Mrs. Whitaker suffered a mental episode, causing her to have fits of rage. The doctors couldn't help her, and so, Charles sent her to an asylum. She died there a month later. But that didn't end the bad luck. Charles Whitaker himself took ill. He died that same year, leaving only his eldest son, Felix, and daughter, Julianne, behind."

"Oh my."

"Tragic, I know." She loaded another sheet of paper into her typewriter. "Rumor spread that Irena Krall was taking her revenge and wouldn't stop until every member of the Whitaker household was dead. Felix was afraid, being a man of superstition, and sold his father's estate to an unknown buyer. Lloyd Ennis brokered the sale and met with a representative of the new buyer. No one knows where Felix and Julianne Whitaker moved to, *and* no one knows who owns the old Whitaker estate. Both the Whitaker mansion and the Krall house have remained vacant, until three months ago when someone phoned in a listing for the sale of the servant's house for $400.00. Saugerties residents didn't believe the house would sell, but then you came into our city." She paused, looking straight into my eyes. "The day you entered that cabin, you re-awakened the wrath of Irena. She is once again seeking out the Whitaker blood-line."

I drew back in surprise. "You can't be serious?"

"I most certainly am. Henry Brickmore is the third cousin of Charles Whitaker. And Stuart's mother is Charles' half sister. Irena is continuing her revenge. You shouldn't go back to that house. It's not safe."

The very thought that these people could believe such nonsense irritated me. "That's ridiculous. I own the house. Not Irena. Not Albin. Me. And furthermore, I don't believe in ghost stories."

Frieda's eyes narrowed. Her words came out with a peculiar reverence. "Maybe you ought to start."

A shiver rippled through my spine. I hated that her words had my palms sweating. It wasn't true of course. It was all conjecture.

Martha let out a throaty grunt. "Ugghhh."

Frieda released an annoyed sniff. "Now what, Martha? You disagree with me?" She shifted in her seat to look at the other typist who was now hunched over holding the sides of her stomach. "Goodness, Martha! Are you having a contraction?"

Martha's eyes were squeezed shut in her beet-red face. "Ohhh."

"What is it?" said Frieda.

"My—my—" Martha cringed.

At the same time, Frieda and I noticed that Martha's skirt looked like a glass of water had been poured in her lap.

Frieda shot to her feet. "Martha's having her baby right here!" She called out to the entire newsroom.

Martha grabbed her by the skirt. "Sit down."

I circled around the table, kneeling at Martha's side. "How long have you been feeling contractions?"

"All day. But I'm not due for three weeks."

Salvatore showed up at my side. "Martha, you okay?"

"I need to go to the hospital."

"Sure thing." He helped her to her feet. "My car's just outside. June, you come along and help Martha." As we shuffled toward the door, he called back. "Frieda, send someone to Martha's husband and tell him to meet us there."

We hurried to his car, an emerald Stutz Bearcat.

My mouth gaped. This wasn't a run-of-the-mill-vehicle. A Stutz was fancy. By golly, the newspaper business must be good for him to afford his swanky suit and ritzy car. Unfortunately, his sports car had step-over sides instead of doors. Poor Martha. The other downfall, his car wasn't spacious. We squeezed onto the single leather seat, with me snug between Martha and Salvatore.

Every time Martha twisted or turned with a contraction, my body was pushed into his. He didn't make a peep. His eyes remained glued to the road and he drove, fast. Which was good because I was counting in my head and Martha's contractions were coming about every four minutes. Sweet mercy, that baby would be crowning soon.

In the line-up of first day concerns, this one never crossed my mind.

Martha groaned again.

Sal came to a jarring halt in front of Hudson City Hospital. He jumped over the side and ran into the building. As I helped Martha from the car, he reappeared with a nurse, who didn't miss a beat in placing her into a wheelchair.

We trotted after the nurse, as she wheeled Martha inside the lobby.

"Are you the husband?" the nurse asked him.

"No, I'm her employer."

"Where's her husband?"

"He oughta be arriving any minute."

"Okay. You can wait here." The nurse pushed Martha

through a set of double doors and out of view.

Salvatore stared at the doors in stunned silence.

I looked at his blanched face. "Are you alright?"

He blinked, but his gaze didn't leave the doors. "Yeah. I think so." He smoothed a hand over his slick hair. "Geez Louise, she's really having that baby."

I smiled. Poor fella. He was in shock. "She'll be okay." I patted his arm. "She's a woman after all."

At this, he turned to me. His expression was serious, contemplative. "I never thought about it before, but you're right. Us men," he opened his hands, "we can build things, run companies, heck, we can create newspapers, but that,"—he gestured to where Martha had been wheeled away— "bringing a kid into the world, that is something else."

A man ran into the building. "I'm here for Martha! Martha Bixby! She's having our baby!"

The front desk nurse ushered him through the doors.

Salvatore smoothed a hand over his hair again, releasing a soft chuckle. "Quite the first day, huh?"

"Mr. Saviano, I'm from New York City." I crossed my arms. "I'm still waiting for the day to get eventful."

He released a full laugh. "I'm glad my father hired you." His lips spread with a wide smile. "Please, call me Sal."

CHAPTER EIGHT

Monday, April 21
2:30 PM

"How was your first day of school?"

A sigh heavy with sadness escaped Alice's mouth. "Not great. The only people who talked to me were those that wanted to know if my mother bought the old Krall cabin and is it really haunted?"

"That good, huh?"

She wasn't amused. "It's embarrassing."

"I had a similar experience at my job. I didn't realize how big of a deal this legend of Albin and Irena is around here. People take it quite seriously."

"You're telling me."

"Maybe once the house is fixed up, people will forget the legend ever existed." I drove away from the school. "Are you hungry?"

"No."

"Well I am. I hear the meatloaf at our hotel is the stuff of dreams."

"I doubt that."

"Me too."

Our hotel café had a large crowd for four o'clock on a weekday. In Manhattan, things didn't start picking up until about seven. Patrons turned curious glances in our direction as we zigzagged between the tables, selecting one in the rear corner of the room.

A young red-haired waitress in a simple dress and apron came to our table. She bore a nice smile. "Afternoon, ladies. Me name is Etta. Can I get ya something to drink while yous look over the menu?"

There it was again. That cheerful Irish brogue. At least this time, I didn't start to cry. Instead, I smiled and nodded to the waitress. "Thank you. I'll take a water."

"Coca-Cola," said Alice.

"Be back in a snap." Etta spun around.

We perused the diner menu in silence. "What are you going to have?"

"French fries," said Alice.

"That's it?"

She nodded.

I didn't feel like arguing. When Etta returned with our beverages, we gave our order. I decided to go with the meatloaf and baked potato. Instead of leaving to put in our order, Etta tucked her notepad into her apron. "Don't believe I be seein' yous here before. Are ya new to the area?"

"Yes, we are," I replied. "We moved here on Saturday."

Her eyes widened like she was having an epiphany. "By any chance, are ya June Flynn?"

I nearly sighed. "Yes."

She snapped her fingers. "Ya look exactly like what me uncle described."

I tipped my head to the side. "Is your uncle Elex?"

"Ah, the very one. He's been bangin' on about yer project." She gestured to Alice. "Ya must be, Alice."

"I am."

A waitress called from the kitchen, "Etta, your next order's up!"

"Right so, better get that." She strolled to the kitchen at a nonchalant pace.

I sipped my water. "She seems like a nice girl. Perhaps, you could be friends."

"Mom, it's not that simple. I can't just say, 'Hey, you want to be friends?'"

"Why not?"

"Because that would be odd."

"It would be efficient."

"I'll pass." Alice swirled her straw in her Coca-Cola. "What happened at work?"

I closed my eyes, shaking my head. "From the moment I walked in, I heard people talking about me." I thought about what Frieda had told me. It seemed like superstitious hype, but the fact that people were disappearing behind our house made me uneasy. I certainly didn't want to worry Alice with such details. "On a different note, I almost delivered a baby in a car today."

"What?" She leaned toward me. "Who?"

"My co-worker, Martha, went into labor in the newsroom. I went with my boss's son, Salvatore, to rush her to the hospital."

"You made it in time?"

"Just. We pulled up to the hospital, and the nurse wheeled her away. Thirty minutes later, the baby was born."

Etta returned, setting our plates in front of us.

"This looks delicious," I said. "Say Etta, if you don't mind me asking, how old are you?"

"Fifteen."

"Do you attend Saugerties High School?"

"No ma'am. When me uncle went off to war, I stopped attendin' school. Had to work in order to help pay the bills. As it were, me Ma has a problem with the drink and half the time she don't be makin' it to her job. Curse of the Irish, the drink. Now that Uncle Elex is back from war, he be helpin' us out. Taken a load off me, that has."

I blinked twice at her unsolicited honesty. "I'm glad that your uncle's back. Maybe now you'll be able to return to school."

She shrugged. "Aye, perhaps."

"Etta," called the other waitress, "Quit lollygagging and get back to work."

"Hold yer horses, Blanche!" Etta shot back. "Ya know, me uncle be real handy. Can do just about anythin'."

"Can he fix an outhouse?" asked Alice.

Etta threaded her pen behind her ear. "Ach, ya got an outhouse?"

Alice nodded.

"What a bleedin' nightmare. That do be a cold pee come this winter."

"Etta! You're needed on the register!" Blanche hollered again.

"Jeepers, does it look like the place be burnin'?" Etta rolled her eyes. "I let me uncle know yer in need of his help. Pleasure meetin' yous." Spinning around, she ambled to the register.

Cutting into the meatloaf, I popped a bite into my mouth.

"Is it everything you hoped for?" asked Alice.

I pushed the dry meat down my throat with a swig of water. "If this meatloaf is an indication of *Saugerties' best*, we might be in for a rude awakening."

Alice laid her head back. "Dear sweet, Manhattan. How I miss you."

Under my breath, I agreed with her.

Meal finished, we walked to the counter to pay. I noticed a board hanging on the wall bearing several flyers and pictures. One advert in particular caught my eye. On it was a group of girls wearing uniforms and scarves. The words *Girl Scouts of the United States* were printed at the top of the flyer. Below, it said *Start A Troop in Your City*. Unpinning the brochure, I opened it.

Alice peered over my shoulder. "What's that?"

"Some sort of club, I think."

A heading stood off the page in bold letters—BE PREPARED. Below it read,

> *A Girl Scout learns to swim, not only as an athletic accomplishment, but so that she can save a life. She passes her simple tests in childcare, home nursing, and household efficiency in order to be ready for the big duties when they come. She learns the important facts about her body, so as to keep it the fine machine it was meant to be. She makes a special point of woodcraft and camp lore, not only for the fun and satisfaction they bring, but because they are the best emergency course we have today. A Girl Scout is trained so that she is ready to help herself, her home, and her Country. A girl who meets or can meet membership requirements shall not be denied admission or access to the Girl Scout program because of class, race, ethnicity, or disability.*

I waved the pamphlet at Etta. "Is there a troop here?"

"Not yet. Myrtle Mellus hung that up months ago."

Alice took the brochure in her hands. "Looks interesting. Too bad there isn't a group here."

Too bad, indeed. It would be a great way for Alice to meet some girls.

"Are ya outdoorsy, Ms. Flynn?" said Etta.

"Hardly." I grinned. Though it piqued my curiosity, I knew I could never lead something like this. I was a single mother with a rundown house to fix up. I didn't have time to teach a group of young ladies stuff that I didn't know myself.

Etta rang up my order. "Yer total is forty-five cents."

I dug into my purse to fetch the coins. I handed her money along with an extra nickel for a tip.

"Thank you," said Etta. "'Twas nice meetin' ya today."

"It was nice to meet you too." Alice hung the brochure back on the board.

I glanced at it one more time as we left the restaurant.

CHAPTER NINE

Tuesday, April 22
7:35 AM

Frieda slapped yesterday's edition on the table. "June, did you see this?"

I picked it up. "No, I haven't." The headline jumped off of the page.

Another Mysterious Vanishing

—

Car Found Abandoned

—

By Clyde Lockwood

The Saugerties police projected themselves into yet another disappearance case today, making this the second in less than three weeks' time. Mr. Stuart Ellsworth, son to Mr. Ernest and Theodora Ellsworth was pronounced missing early this morning.

Ellsworth was last seen by his three friends dining at Ziegler's Café and Barroom on Partition, until Ellsworth complained of fatigue, hence withdrawing in his two-seater. When

Ellsworth was discovered absent this morning by Mrs. Ellsworth, she inquired of his friend, Paul Harmon. Harmon reported that Ellsworth had left the café shortly after 9 o'clock.

Patrol searched the surrounding area for Ellsworth's car, finding it wedged in a hedge on Esopus Drive. Boot tracks led from the vehicle toward the creek. A search of the vehicle provided a driving license that identified it as belonging to Stuart Ellsworth.

So far, no body has been found. The police department is no nearer a solution. With this being the second vanishing by Esopus Creek, it is speculated that these disappearances are connected. Are they a product of an actual abduction or is the ghost of Irena Krall to blame?

Huffing, I set the paper down. Why would Sal print such a thing? "This is a newspaper. Speculations shouldn't be printed."

"It's more than speculation." Frieda leaned in, eyes large. "Irena Krall is back."

"Oh?" I donned an awestruck expression. "From where is she returning? A vacation, perhaps?"

She recoiled with a snort. "This is serious business. Two men from the Whitaker bloodline are missing. How do you explain that?"

It did seem like someone was targeting the Whitaker family. But why? I thought of the vacant estate, and the noise from the cellar. Though the shrill cry must have come from the owl, I couldn't shake an eerie feeling. Goose pimples surfaced on my skin. The woman in the photo filled my mind, staring at me with her dark, piercing eyes. "You're right, Frieda. People disappearing is a dire matter and should be taken seriously."

She straightened her blouse, looking pleased with herself. "Exactly."

"Say," I leaned forward. "Have you ever seen a picture of Irena?"

Frieda nodded. "Once, in the paper, 18 years ago. It was Irena's obituary. It gave a brief detailing of her life and death. Nothing more was ever printed. I was five when that paper came out, but I still remember her photo clear-as-day. That image burnt into my mind."

"They printed a picture of her?"

"It felt like it was looking at me from out of the page."

My skin prickled. "Do we keep files of our old papers here?"

"Of course. Every paper that has ever been printed with The Saugerties Daily Journal is stored in the morgue."

My eyebrows shot up. "The morgue?"

She waved off my alarm. "That's what we call the file room."

"I'd love to see that. Can you show me?"

She crossed her arms. "Why?"

"I'm curious. I'd like to know what Irena looked like…as a precaution."

"Now, you're seeing reason." She glanced around the newsroom. Only a couple people from editing were at their table. "Come with me."

I hurried after her to the end of the hall past the printing room. We took a staircase that led into the basement. Ten steps down, and the temperature felt like it dropped ten degrees.

"Normally typists aren't allowed in the morgue because it's not our job to look up old files. Only reporters and editors do that." Frieda pulled a hanging cord, which filled the basement with a soft glow of light. Rows of metal filing cabinets lined the walls. Each cabinet drawer was labeled with a month and the year and various topics.

I rubbed a hand against my shirtsleeve. "In what month did she die?"

"June, 1901." Frieda shuffled around the room. Opening a drawer, she riffled through the folders inside. "This should be it." Tugging the full issue out, she opened it to the obituaries and grimaced. "Ugh. Here it is." She extended it to me.

As I took the paper from her, the hairs on my arms stood up. It was the same picture from the cellar. The white blond hair. The pale face. Those haunting eyes. "Goodness."

"Freaky, huh?"

Beside the picture was her obituary.

IRENA LOUISE KRALL

As a result of a tragic drowning, Irena Louise Krall, age eighteen, passed away yesterday, the eleventh of June. She was survived by her husband, Albin Krall. In addition to her husband, the following relatives survive her in New Paltz: her parents, Mr. and Mrs. Daniel Jansen, and her brothers, Otis, Roland, and Ivon.

A sudden laugh, followed by loud talking pulled our attention toward the stairs.

Frieda grabbed the edition from my fingers, stuffing it back into the drawer. "Let's go." She snapped off the light, and we tiptoed up the stairs. Sal followed a press operator from the hall into the printing room. Hustling past, we reached our department table and sank into our chairs.

One of the reporters walked over, dropping a stack of handwritten notes next to Frieda. She didn't miss a beat. Loading a sheet of paper into her typewriter, she keyed the words on the page.

My heart pounded faster in my chest. Why would a wealthy estate owner have a framed picture of his servant in his cellar? It didn't make sense.

The reporter with bottled-shaped glasses halted in front of my table. "It's June, right?"

I knew I hadn't met him officially, but my name wasn't hard to come by. "Yes. You're Clyde, right?"

"That I am." He smoothed a hand against a small patch of hair above his ear. "Top reporter for The Saugerties Daily Journal."

Frieda snorted.

His nose scrunched. "You got something to say, Frieda?"

Her fingers paused. She looked up with an expression of supreme innocence. "Not at all."

"Good." He extended me a stack of papers. "These need to be typed up and given to editing pronto. You're new. Can I trust you to do this?"

I removed the pages from his grasp. "I can do my job."

"See that you do." He walked away, shoulders swaying.

"Clyde Lockwood," said Frieda in a bland tone. "Mr. All-Important. It doesn't help that he married into money and lives in some big house."

I threaded a paper into my typewriter. "If you ask me, he's much too bald to be so arrogant."

Her mouth gaped. Removing her fingers from her typewriter, she rotated toward me. "Goodness, you're nothing like Martha."

"Is that good or bad?"

"I like it. Martha holds to the belief, like most of the women around here—be seen and not heard." She frowned. "I haven't quite figured out how to do that."

With her guard down, I saw Frieda. Young. Vulnerable. Trying to find her way like the rest of us. "It's okay. Life is a web. We're all striving to make sense of the tangles."

"Thanks, June."

"You're welcome." Looking down at Clyde's notes, I typed the first three words.

"By the way," Frieda leaned nearer to me, "I think he oils it."

My eyebrows lifted. "Oils what?"

"His bald spot," she added in a hushed voice. "It's always shiny. Unless," she paused, "Can a bald spot sweat?"

I considered this. "Perhaps, but probably not that much." The image of Clyde trying to make his hairless scalp more appealing struck me as hilarious. I burst into laughter.

She joined in, inciting glares from editing. "I'm glad you're here."

"I am too." Smiling, I returned to typing. It didn't take me long to finish Clyde's update on the Spanish flu. It seemed a cruel fate to have a horrible war and world-altering sickness within the same years. Rising from my seat, I delivered the papers to editing.

Sal poked his head out of his father's office and waved at me, "June, can you come here for a moment?"

My first instinct said, 'Oh, dear? Have I done something wrong?' Swallowing down my angst, I entered the office.

He gestured to the door. "Go ahead, close the door and have a seat."

I did as I was told.

"I wanted to apologize for the chaos of yesterday." He spread his hands on the top of the desk. "What with Clyde's breaking story and then Martha. It was bananas, but you handled it all with such confidence. I was impressed."

My shoulders straightened. "Thank you."

"This business means the world to my family." He looked past me, with a reflective glimmer. "I'd do anything for it. Someday, it will become my own. I hope to pass it on to my future son or daughter." He refocused on my face. "How would you like to have lunch today?"

I startled. "Lunch?"

"I was thinking maybe The Maxwell Hotel or Lorna's Cafe? What do you like to eat? Lorna's has great sandwiches."

I couldn't sort out how we had gone from *family reflection* to *having lunch*. "I only get a thirty-minute lunch break."

"Not if you're with the future boss." He winked at me.

My stomach fluttered. I wasn't sure if this was normal protocol or if he had other intentions. "I brought lunch to work."

"You can save it for tomorrow. Let me treat you as a way of

welcoming you to our staff. It's something we do all the time."

Oh. This was protocol. "Will other employees be joining us?"

"Nah."

Lunch was simple enough, but if the other staff wasn't present, a passerby could get the wrong impression. All I needed was gossip to spread about me courting my boss' son. I didn't need any more bad press. "With Martha gone, I don't think it's a good idea for me to be away. Thank you for the offer. Very generous. I better get back to work." I rose to my feet, exiting before he could utter another word. The moment I was out, I chided myself for acting hastily. What if he had other matters to discuss? I should have waited for him to dismiss me. Goodness, June. Sweat made my hands clammy.

"Got called into the boss' office, huh," said Frieda. "Everything okay?"

"Yes. Fine." I kept my voice level, hiding my internal anxiety. Sal was my current boss, and he was only being thoughtful. Why did I overreact? I looked down at a new stack of handwritten sheets beside my typewriter. At the top was the scrawled headline, "Allied Negotiations and Forthcoming Peace Treaty." Even though the armistice had ceased the fighting, the war wasn't officially over. Many soldiers had yet to return home. With every mention of the war, it triggered a picture of Niall and the pain of his absence. This was why I couldn't go to lunch with Sal. I wasn't ready to move on.

For the next couple of hours, I acted like a child and avoided contact with Sal. When I had to deliver papers to editing, I went the long way around to keep from walking past his office.

By eleven, today's edition was completed and out the door. Frieda stood up. "It's time for my lunch. I'll be back in thirty."

I bent my wrists in and out, giving them a short stretch before returning to typing. I hadn't seen Sal since he'd gone to the print room. I wondered if he was lunching alone.

"June," said a voice behind me.

I jolted in my chair, my finger hitting the wrong letter. Fiddlesticks, I'd have to fix that.

"Didn't mean to scare ya."

I spun around. "Elex, what're you doing here?"

"Just on me break. Etta tells me yer outhouse be needin' some help."

"Yes!" I pressed a hand to my chest, relieved that he didn't ask me to join him for lunch too. "The outhouse. It's awful. I don't know if it's even usable."

"It mightn't be. Me shift is over at five. I could take a look then."

"That would be wonderful."

Out of the corner of my eye, I saw Sal enter the newsroom holding a paper. He paused outside his office, looking directly at Elex.

Elex noticeably stiffened.

"Anything the matter, June?" asked Sal.

I shifted in my seat to face him. "Everything is fine, thanks."

Sal bore a stern expression, but his gaze wasn't on me. "All right then." He entered his office. His door shut louder than necessary.

Elex cleared his throat. "Won't take up any more of yer time. Be seein' ya later."

"I appreciate it."

"Not a worry. Least I can do fer a fellow soldier's wife." He tipped his cap and departed.

When the clock struck 2:30 PM, I collected my handbag and exited the front door. I had made it without talking to Sal the rest of the day. That was a feat, though I would have to see him tomorrow. What was I going to do? Continue to avoid him? A guilty sensation churned in my stomach. It was silly to be acting this way. The wind tugged on my dress as I scurried down the sidewalk. It was only lunch, after all. I had passed the second lamppost when I heard someone call out my name. Halting, I turned around. Sweet mercy, it was Sal.

He jogged over to me in a five-piece suit. "Glad I caught you. Feels like I owe you an apology," he rushed on, "Thinking I made you uncomfortable by inviting you to lunch. Seems like you avoided me the rest of the day. I might've read that wrong, but if I offended you in any way, please," he pressed a hand over his heart, "accept my apology."

Darn it. He had noticed. My throat tightened with humiliation. "Thank you," I managed to squeeze out.

"So I did offend you?"

I released a shaky sigh. "No, you surprised me."

His head tilted. "How so?"

I contemplated how to answer. It would be easier to make a blanket statement, but that would be cowardly. "My husband, Niall, died in the war. Now, I'm trying to figure out how to live life as a single mother of a sixteen-year-old daughter. It's tough learning how to live under new circumstances. And yes, I'm still young enough for—," I cleared my throat, "—and when you asked me to lunch, it felt like a gesture of—" I couldn't bring myself to finish the statement.

"Courtship?" he filled in.

"Yes." I exhaled, letting myself relax. "But now, I know it wasn't that, and I overreacted."

His lips twitched with a smile. "Actually, it was."

I blinked. "You were pursuing me?"

He opened his hands with a shrug. "Being squished together in my car and seeing you in action, not to mention that you're an absolute doll—I figured I better spring at the chance before someone else does."

My mouth gaped. "You've only known me for a day."

"True but" he lifted a finger, "I don't know, it seemed like we bonded. I'm sorry 'bout your husband. I understand if it's too soon. Mourning takes time. When my mother passed, my father couldn't move on. He said, 'A great love can never be rediscovered.' Not that I'm hoping you'll agree with his theory. He is considerably older, and you've got much more life ahead of you. Saugerties would be crestfallen if such a lovely gal like yourself chose to remain single."

I arched a brow. "Saugerties?"

"Well, the general male population therein."

At this, I smiled. Salvatore was charming.

"But on my honor," he pressed a hand to his chest, "I will not ask you out again, until you decide you are ready for such an invitation."

"I appreciate that."

"Would you permit me one question?"

I nodded.

"Does your choice not to dine with me have anything to do with that man who came to see you today?"

"No. I just met Elex at the hardware store. He's helping me with some repairs. That's all."

"I'm relieved to hear that." He looked intently into my eyes. "Because that man has a reputation. You oughta tread carefully with him."

"What do you mean?"

"The war can change a person, this I know, but before he left, Elex O'Keefe was not an honorable man. He spent his time drinking, gambling, and brawling. Two years ago, he nearly beat a man to death. Spent a night in jail for it too. It wasn't long after that he enlisted in the army. I didn't think he'd turn up again."

I listened to this news, stunned. Elex seemed kind and gentle. The way he comforted me in the hardware store as I cried, I couldn't picture him ever hurting anyone.

"Please, promise me that you'll be careful."

"Of course. Thank you for telling me."

"I'll see you tomorrow, June." Pivoting on the ball of his shiny shoe, he walked away.

CHAPTER TEN

Tuesday, April 22
2:40 PM

As I walked to Alice's school, Sal's admonition looped through my head. *Be careful. He nearly beat a man to death.* Why would Elex harm another man? Did the man deserve it? There had to be more to the story.

From the way Alice plodded toward me across the lawn, I detected trouble.

"Hello, sweetheart. How did today go?"

"Terrible." She heaved a sigh. "The girls in my class aren't talking to me, even though I hear them whispering behind my back. If it wasn't for this boy named George, I would have eaten alone at lunch, again."

My heart ached. In Manhattan, she had plenty of good friends. Starting over was tough, especially with young ladies. "Have you tried to introduce yourself to the other girls?"

"A couple, but they weren't interested in getting to know me." Folding her arms, she walked ahead.

I stepped in line beside her, wondering what to do. It was my decision to move us, and I had to figure out a way to make this work. "What if we start a Girl Scout group here? It could be a good way for you to meet girls your age, and for me to connect with their mothers."

"But you don't know anything about first aid, woodworking, making fires, swimming—"

I held up my hand. "I know. My skills are severely limited. But I'm sure they have manuals. We'll all learn together."

Alice turned a skeptical eye to me. "Where will we host the meetings?"

"Our house."

"It's a mess."

"It has walls and a roof." I scooped her hand into mine. "I learned something after your father passed away—I can't depend on a man to save me. I have to learn to fend for myself. I believe that joining the Girl Scouts is what we need. Together we will grow stronger, wiser, and more prepared for whatever life has ahead."

Alice's features relaxed. She leaned into me. "I never thought of myself as a Girl Scout, but I kind of like the sound of it."

I wrapped an arm around her. "So do I. Let's go to the hotel and call that number on the brochure."

She turned up her chin, giving me a grin. "Does this mean we're going to skip working on the house today?"

"No."

I sprinkled baking soda on the warped floors of our *beloved* house, hoping to neutralize the odor. We had to hurry up the process, now that we were going to be setting up our own troop. The Girl Scouts coordinator, Ms. Thelma Parker was only too happy to help us get started. Apparently, a girl named Myrtle Mellus had been bugging the headquarters for quite some time, requesting a club to be formed in Saugerties. Until I reached out, there was no one willing. Thelma didn't seem phased by my lack of know-how. Instead she assured me that with a sense of curiosity and adventure, anything could be learned. Curiosity I had, but I worried about skill (and the lack thereof).

In order to expedite the application process, Thelma offered to come to Saugerties this weekend via the train from New York City, the very place we had left. I couldn't believe I had never heard of this organization while living there. Though I doubted I would have been quite as intrigued as I was now. Desperation continued to lead me in new directions.

Thelma said we should hold a public forum during her visit and invite all interested parties to learn about the Girl Scouts. Which meant there was no going back.

"Alice, what color do you think we should paint the walls?"

She looked around the parlor. "Anything is better than this."

Hearing a car drive up outside, we peered out the broken front window. Due to the dense weeds and brush, the car had to stop about four car lengths away from our front door. Elex and, to my surprise, Etta exited the Ford.

We walked out of the house and waved hello.

Etta marched across the matted down path (thanks to my machete). "Hi-ya, Alice. I tagged along hopin' ya would show me around yer house."

Alice shrugged. "There's not much to see."

"I doubt that." Etta's eyes grew wider. "Yer livin' in a legend."

"More like a nightmare."

"Even better." Etta linked her arm with Alice like they'd been friends for years.

A grin lifted the corners of Alice's mouth. "All right then." She pulled Etta into the house. "I'll show you our bedroom first. There's this spot on the wall with knife marks."

Etta gasped. "Ya don't be serious?"

"It was probably Albin."

Etta squealed.

I smiled as I watched them disappear into the house. This was the first time my daughter was happy to show it off.

"Hope ya don't mind Etta comin'," said Elex as he approached me, carrying a toolbox and shovel.

"Not at all. I'm glad. It's nice for Alice."

"It be good for Etta too. Havin' time with girls her age. She don't get much of that."

"Etta mentioned that at the restaurant. She said she had to drop out of school when you enlisted because she needed to support her mother."

He flinched. "I never wanted her to stop school."

"I'm sure you didn't." My thoughts went to Niall. "But even righteous choices can have harmful effects on loved ones."

His forehead creased. "I don't be holdin' her back. Etta can return to school anytime."

Oh dear. Did he sound hurt? I quickly backtracked. "Oh well, that's good. I'm sure she'll be glad of it."

"Right so." He gave a brief nod. "Where be yer outhouse?"

"It's in the back. I'll show you." I hastened onward, feeling flustered. I shouldn't have brought up school or Etta's mother. I said too much. I know I did, but didn't Elex see that he was partially to blame? He needed to realize that his actions had consequences. Stopping short of the outhouse, I gestured to it. "Here it is."

He passed by me, setting his shovel and box on the ground. He peered inside. "Ach, what a bleedin' mess." Entering, he looked into the hole. "The pit needs to be shoveled and lined with new wood. Also, the floorboards be rotten. They need to be replaced. Needs a new roof too." He rapped on the walls. "The walls still be in decent shape, but ya might want a new bench."

My shoulders drooped. This sounded expensive. Why did I think buying this place was a good idea? I sighed. "I didn't properly weigh out the costs involved in this project before buying it."

He studied me. "Why did ya buy it?"

"It sort of spoke to me." I scuffed the toe of my boot against a patch of weeds. "I felt like it deserved better. Like it hadn't been given a fair shot. I thought maybe I was the person who could give this house a second chance." I tucked my clenched hands into my skirt pockets. "I was being too optimistic. I should re-list it."

"We both know it won't sell."

I groaned. "I wish I could go back in time. I wish I was still in my mouse-free apartment that had running water and a toilet *indoors*."

"Wishing won't help ya." He shrugged. "Perhaps, yer not the savior of this here house. Maybe, it be you that needs the savin'."

I drew back. "That's an odd thing to say. You don't even know me."

"I be good at readin' people."

"Well," I crossed my arms. "I know plenty about you too."

His lips curved into an amused smirk. "I can guess who filled ya in."

"If you're referring to Salvatore Saviano, yes. He warned me to be careful because you have a temper."

"That all he said?"

I lifted my chin. "Is there more to it?"

"Me thinks ya think there is, but I can assure that ya don't know the facts. Salvatore is a liar."

"He's my boss."

He shrugged. "Yer boss is a liar."

"I don't appreciate you calling him a liar."

"I don't care."

"I think you should leave now."

Releasing a heavy sigh, he picked up his toolbox and shovel. As he walked away from me, he muttered. "Ya can't believe everythin' ya hear."

I followed after him. "I don't, but sometimes, a person has to dig in to find the truth."

"I wonder if ya'd know the truth if it slapped ya in the arse."

I huffed. "Well I never—," my words dropped off as Lloyd Ennis, my broker, materialized from out of the foliage. Sweet mercy, another intolerable man.

"Is everything okay?" asked Lloyd.

"I was just sending Elex on his way," I said with a bite to my words.

"I be leavin', thank ya very much." Elex bit back.

"Ah, well." Lloyd nodded, like that cleared it all up.

Elex stopped at the front door, calling out, "Etta! Get out here. We leavin' now."

She yelled back, from somewhere inside, "But we done just arrived!"

He exhaled in exasperation. "Fer the love of Mary, Joseph and the wee donkey, get out here."

She sauntered outside, looking entirely put out.

Elex didn't exchange any more words. He marched to his car, threw in the tools and drove off before Etta could close her passenger door.

I glared after the departing vehicle. Sure, I wanted Alice to have friends, but I was having second thoughts on Etta if it came with the price tag of her uncle.

A throat cleared behind me.

I turned to Lloyd. Inhaling, I grasped for composure. "What brings you by, Lloyd?"

"I came to see how you were settling in." He managed a half-hearted smile.

"Is that right?" I propped a hand on my hip. "Well not very good, considering this place is a dump." (So much for composure).

His eyebrows jolted up. "You did get a steal on it, though."

"Tell that to the outhouse you never showed me. Or the water pump you never showed me. This place is a hole!"

He held up his hands in surrender. "Hey, now. I told you not to buy this house."

I heaved an exhale. He was right about that.

"He did tell us, Mom," said Alice.

I glanced over my shoulder. Where did she come from?

"Listen, I know this house needs a lot of repairs," said

Lloyd. "That's why I came over to offer my help. I do think this house has potential."

Help. That word sounded good. "Are you a handy-man, Lloyd?"

"I know some things. For starters, I can bring over a mower to cut down the weeds on your driveway and in front of your house. Then you'd have a sort of lawn."

Hmmm, maybe I was wrong about Lloyd. Maybe he wasn't such a nincompoop after all. "I like the sound of that."

"I'll come by tomorrow if that's good."

"That will work fine."

He gave me another weak smile and left in his car.

I didn't know if it was because I was a war widow or simply single, but every time I turned around men were coming out of the woodwork.

CHAPTER ELEVEN

Wednesday, April 23
7:45 AM

I knocked twice on Sal's office door.

"Come in," he called.

I found him mulling over typed notes. Exchanging morning pleasantries, I got to the point. "I have a question for you."

He folded his hands. "Do ask."

"I wondered if I could place an advertisement in our paper today. I'm willing to pay for it."

"An advertisement about what?"

"The Girl Scouts. I'm starting a troop here in Saugerties for young ladies. This program teaches them how to grow into efficient and successful adults. I'm going to help them do that."

"Sounds like a big undertaking. You have the time?"

"I'll make time. The library has agreed to allow me to hold it there this Saturday." I handed him a sheet of paper. "That's why I need this published today."

He read my advertisement aloud.

> **Girls 13 to 18 years of age! You can be a part of something big. It's called the Girl Scouts of the United States. A special meeting will be held at the library at 1:00 PM this Saturday. Hear all**

about how you can be part of this enthusiastic group of girls trained in outdoor activities, domestic skills, and groomed with the highest standards of community service and patriotism. All girls are welcome—no matter their race, class, or disability.

Sal set the paper down on his desk. "Interesting." He tented his fingertips. "You realize there's gonna be opposition to this kind of equality in a group of girls."

"I'm prepared to handle that."

"Are you?" His left brow arched. "June, when I hired Ishmael, I had four staff quit on the spot. Two were press operators. They refused to work with him because he was a man of color. If you open up this club to everyone, you might not have much of a club. And there will be constant heat on you. Personally, you have my stamp of approval. We'll print your ad, but I warn you, this won't be an easy venture."

I looked at my handwritten note lying atop the mess of papers on his desk. I inhaled a slow breath. "Thank you for being honest with me." I lifted my chin to meet his questioning gaze. "Let's print it."

He nodded, handing me the advertisement. "Type it up and turn it into editing. Tell them I said it goes in today's paper."

"How much do I owe for it?"

He waved his hand in dismissal. "Consider it a donation to the Girl Scouts."

I smiled. "Thank you, Sal."

"Anytime, doll."

I turned to leave.

"Wait June, one more thing."

I spun back to him.

"What are you gonna do about that house of yours?"

I tipped my head to the side. "You know that I bought a house?"

He gave me a look that said, 'Please, everyone knows that you bought a house.'

I clutched my hands in front of my skirt, sighing. "My daughter and I are fixing it up, but it's in worse shape than I first thought."

He nodded, as if he expected as much. "It's been abandoned for a long time. I figured it would require some heavy repairs. Have you hired any workers?"

"No but Elex got my water pump working, and Lloyd says he'll help me too."

Sal's brows lifted at the mention of these men.

I wasn't certain, but I thought I detected jealousy on his face.

"Ah." He paused. "Well, I know a thing or two about carpentry myself."

"You do?" Given his dapper appearance, I couldn't picture him working with any tools other than a comb.

"Yeah, nuttin' to it. I tell you what, how about I come over this evening and look the place over? Then I can assess what needs doing."

I thought he might have alternative motives, but my budget said I needed all the help I could get. "Okay. Tonight."

At 11:30 AM, I walked down the hall toward the restroom before taking my lunch break. Passing by the printing press area, I was about to open the door to the ladies' room when I heard voices drifting up the stairs from the morgue.

"You certain no one saw you there?" asked Sal.

"Positive. I was careful," said Clyde.

Though I knew I shouldn't eavesdrop, I drew closer to the banister.

"We gotta beat out The Telegraph," said Sal. "This month is our month to do it. With these disappearances, our paper is getting the attention it deserves. We need more articles about

Henry and Stuart. If we're lucky, another Whitaker will vanish."

Clyde agreed.

"Dig up anything you can about Irena Krall."

"There's not much to be found."

"Talk with James, he wrote two stories about her following her death. He'd told my father that he was onto something bigger 18 years ago, but that got shut down."

"Well, perhaps it's time to resurrect Irena." Clyde chuckled.

Hearing their footsteps approaching, I darted into the bathroom. My mind spun. I didn't like how Sal was talking about these disappearances. How could he hope another Whitaker would vanish? Where did Clyde go that Sal didn't want him to be seen? And to my utter surprise, how did Frieda, of all people, not know about the second story on Irena?

I had to talk to James. Seemed odd that Sal hadn't assigned him the current stories since he'd done previous research on Irena. Perhaps it was because James' story had been shunned.

I should have gone straight to my desk and eaten my packed lunch, but there weren't any voices coming from the morgue. I had to find the other story. Creeping down the stairs, I snapped on the overhead light. I went straight to the filing cabinet with the June 1901 stories. I sifted through the drawer, finding the edition with Irena's obituary and the haunting picture of her. Folding it, I pushed it back into the file. I opened a second paper. There wasn't a single article on Irena in the whole edition. I scanned the third. No story. Paper after paper, I searched for anything that mentioned Irena or the Whitakers, but I found nothing. Where was it? Sal had said there were two. I opened the next copy, dated June 28th and traced over it with my finger. On the third page was a short column. The headline jumped off the page.

Was It An Accident?

Friend Believes Foul Play

By James Hayes

On the 11th of June, tragedy befell Irena Krall.

According to Mr. Charles Whitaker, Irena entered the creek alone and never came up for air. With this eyewitness account, Irena's death seemed a tragic end brought on by grief. But was it?

A friend of Irena's came to tell us otherwise. Said friend, who wishes to remain nameless, emphasized that Irena wouldn't have willingly died. Irena was a fighter. Never would she have purposefully marched into the river to her death. This person believes Irena was pulled into the river against her will, contradicting the eyewitness account.

Was her death the result of remorse or was it more sinister?

A throat cleared behind me.

My fingers crinkled the edge of the page. Turning, I found Clyde frowning at me.

"What are you doing down here?"

"Ah, well…you see I bought the Krall cabin and with the disappearances, I've been a bit worried, and I thought maybe there would be some articles that might help me better understand the legend."

"How did you know where the file room was?"

Frieda showed me, but he didn't need to know that. "I've seen you come up from the basement with papers in your hands. I was curious, so I checked it out."

He shook his head. "Curiosity is for reporters, Ms. Flynn. Which you are not." He plucked the paper out of my hands. "You should be at your desk typing. That's your job. Stick to that instead of worrying about a ghost story."

"So, you believe it's fake?"

"I'm not sure what or who is behind the disappearances. As a reporter, it's my job to dig into it, not yours. I don't know why you bought that house. Lloyd never should have allowed you to purchase it."

"He's a broker. He can't control my decisions. And neither can you." I strode away, acting composed and collected, but inside my heart raced. There was something bigger going on. I knew it. James knew it too. For some reason, he wasn't speaking up anymore. I had to talk to him personally, but it couldn't be around Sal or Clyde.

For the rest of the day, I typed my articles all the while keeping an eye on James. It wasn't hard. He didn't move fast. He meandered about the newsroom, chatting with fellas in editing and then bantering with the copy boy over telegraph messages. He had dialed someone on the phone and talked over the latest sports scores, and then he went out for a smoke. (Apparently, Carmine had a rule about not smoking in the building for the sake of the ladies.) James' laissez-faire attitude didn't strike me at all like the kind of person who would dig deeper into a story.

Finally at 2:00 pm, after Sal and Clyde had left for lunch, my moment of opportunity presented itself. James exited the building for a smoke. Clasping his notes on a recent baseball game, I excused myself from my station, pretending to have a work-related question. I hurried out the front door.

James stood under the next-door awning of Harmon's Pharmacy puffing on a cigarette.

"Uh, James, I don't mean to bother you, but I had a quick question."

He turned to me with a frown. "Can't it wait until I'm done with my break?"

"Well, no. I don't want to ask you in the office." I realized that sounded shady, and so I hurried on to explain. "See, Frieda's been telling me about the disappearances and how they're all connected to the Whitakers."

James rolled his eyes. "I wouldn't put much stock in what Frieda tells you."

"The thing is that people are saying it has to do with Irena Krall and some nonsense about her ghost seeking revenge. Well, I don't believe that. I think someone else is behind it. They are using Irena as a scapegoat."

James paused with his cigarette burning between his lips, studying me through dull eyes. "Aren't you a typist? Why do you care anyway?"

"Didn't you hear? I bought the old Krall house."

His droopy lids opened wider. "You bought it? I heard rumors, but I didn't believe a word."

"They're true. I bought it, and I'm fixing it up. It'll be a marvelous little house when I'm done." I nodded to assure myself more than James. "Anyway, I wanted to speak to you because you covered the piece on her death, didn't you?"

He blew out a gust of smoke. "That was 18 years ago."

"Yes, but men in the line of the Whitakers are disappearing. Our own paper is blaming Irena for it. Don't you care about that? After the work that you've invested into her story?"

"How do you know that I invested time in it?"

"You wrote two pieces on her. That takes time, doesn't it?"

He grunted below his breath. "More than you know."

"In your second article, you ended with the question—'Was her death the result of remorse or was it more sinister?' Did you ever discover the answer?"

He rubbed a hand over the gray stubble on his chin. "I'm 53-years-old. It's been 18 years since I covered those stories. I'm not the same person I was then. Nowadays, I'm content to do my sports column."

"James, people are missing. They're vanishing behind my

house!" I opened my hands in petition. "Like it or not, this involves me. Have you told the police anything that you've discovered along the way?"

He flicked ash to the ground. "I told them things, but Charles Whitaker knew everyone. If Whitaker said he saw Irena drown, they believed him. As for me, I was told to let it rest."

"Did you? Did you let it rest or did you keep digging?"

"Spirited little thing, aren't you?" He shook his head. "Guess you'd have to be to buy a hovel like the Krall cabin."

"You didn't answer my question."

"I tried to hunt down some leads, but once the Whitakers were gone, it seemed like it no longer mattered."

"Are you going to share your past research with Clyde? In case it could help with these current disappearances."

"Clyde can come to me if he wants, but he won't. He doesn't want my help. He's looking to make his own big break." He sniffed. "Anyway, I'd rather be left out of it."

"What about Irena's picture? Where did you get it?"

"From Albin. I was able to talk with him before he passed away."

Of course, Frieda had said that Albin had died days later. He would have been the one to give James the picture and obituary information. "Well, what about the person that came to you to testify in Irena's defense? That is valuable information. Don't you think our reporters should talk to this person again?"

"That would be impossible." He dropped the cigarette butt and stamped it out. "That person is dead."

My eyes widened. "How?"

"Influenza." He gave me a hard look. "Let me give you a piece of advice. Drop it. You don't want to be anywhere near this. Trust me." Without a nod of goodbye, he left me on the sidewalk.

CHAPTER TWELVE

Wednesday, April 23
3:30 PM

I slathered another stroke of white paint on the dark wood walls. "I think the room is already looking brighter."

Alice dipped her brush into the paint. "How can you tell? We haven't completed one wall."

"I see it in my head."

"I hope the paint quenches the smell."

"It should help." I bent down, painting along the side of the brick fireplace. My brush grazed a loose brick. It slid further out of place. I shook my head. "These bricks. I should pluck out the loose ones. Then we'll know what needs to be fixed."

"Is Elex returning to help us?"

My top lip curled back as I recalled our last conversation. "Doubtful."

She stopped mid-stroke. "Why? What happened?"

"We had a disagreement." I plucked out a loose brick.

"How? You just met him."

"He was being defensive. I barely said anything." I pulled out another brick.

"What did you say?"

"He mentioned that Etta didn't have a chance to be with girls her own age. I replied that it was probably due to him leaving for the war, which caused Etta to drop out of school to get a job to support her mother."

Alice huffed. "You said that?"

"Yes. It was the truth."

"Mother, you implied that it was his fault that his niece dropped out of school."

"Well it kind of is his fault."

Alice propped a hand on her hip. "Here the poor fella goes to war to fight for our country, and you make him feel guilty for leaving his sister and niece behind."

"He did leave. That was his choice." Squatting lower, I worked on another brick.

"There was no reason that Etta's mother couldn't work to support them. It wasn't Elex's fault."

"He left Etta in the care of an alcoholic mother." I tugged at the brick. "He shouldn't have done that. He is an Irishman. He had a choice to enter the war for America. He left because he wanted to go." As I pulled harder on the stubborn brick, my voice rose in frustration. "He should have known that Etta would have to drop out of school and become the caretaker. That she would have to give up her friendships and the life she loved just to pay the bills. He was being selfish." One final yank and the brick popped out, causing me to fall back on my rear. Four more bricks tumbled out of place without the other one supporting them.

Alice stared at me. "Are we still talking about Etta?"

I looked at the fireplace to avoid her probing gaze. With all the gaping holes, it looked worse than before.

"Hey what's that?" She reached her hand into the cracked mortar of the fireplace, pulling out a rolled sheet of paper. Unfurling it, she said with surprise, "It's a letter."

Rising to my feet, I dusted off my skirt. "What does it say?"

She read it aloud.

Dearest Irena,

After your last letter, I am convinced that I must take you home. You don't belong there. I fear that if you stay your soul will wither, and you will die. He doesn't love you. He never will. You can come back and start fresh. I worry for you, my sister. I worry every day. As soon as the harvest season is through, I will come for you.

With fondest affection, your brother, Ivon.

Collecting the letter into my hands, I read it again. "Ivon must not have made it in time."

Alice's face fell. "That's so sad."

I thought about Irena's obituary picture. The dreary look in her eyes was sadness. For the first time, the story became true to me. Irena had lived. She had a brother who wrote to her, who loved her. She must have written to him as well. He wanted to help her, to rescue her from a life of sadness. But he didn't arrive in time. Or had he? Had he come, and she chose not to go? As I studied this faded sheet of paper, my heart ached for a woman I had never met.

Alice ran her fingers over the bricks. "Do you think there are more letters hidden?"

"Maybe."

We searched the crevices of the mortar and wiggled other bricks but found nothing. Irena had kept only this one. What made this letter special?

Alice sighed. "I wished we had found others. It would have been nice to know more about her. It's strange, but finding this note makes this house feel less...creepy."

"I was thinking the same thing." I wrapped an arm around her shoulders, leaning my head against hers. "Do you think I should apologize to Elex?"

She sniffed. "I should think so. We need to be in his good graces." She gestured to the room. "Look at this place."

"I have two other men coming over tonight."

She tilted her head. "Who?"

"Lloyd and Salvatore."

"They're coming to help us?"

I nodded.

"I can imagine why." She smirked.

"What do you mean?"

"I can sum it up in three words: Single. Pretty. Woman."

I laughed. "Oh, for Pete's sake."

"I'm serious. I see the way men look at you. They'd all love to come courting."

"Well, I'm not looking to be courted."

"Good, I'm not ready for another father."

Until now, I didn't know where she stood on me courting. Sure, I wasn't looking for love, but what if it did strike? What would I do then? "I think we'd better get back to painting before it dries out."

Before we could resume, a knock sounded on the door, followed by Lloyd looking through the broken glass window. "Hello, June. You're painting, huh?" He peered inside, surveying our progress.

"Yes."

He nodded. "White. Good choice."

"Alice chose it. You want to come in?"

"Nah, I better set to cutting the grass."

"Okay thanks."

"What happened to your fireplace?" He pointed at it.

"Loose bricks."

"You pulled them out?"

"I was assessing what needs to be fixed and…" I trailed off as Sal appeared in the window beside Lloyd.

The men turned and looked at one another.

"Didn't know I'd find you here, Lloyd," said Sal with a slight chill in his tone.

"I'm cutting the grass for June. Figured she could use some help."

Sal stood taller. "That's why I'm here. To assess the work and help out."

Lloyd crossed his arms. "There's plenty of work to go around."

"Maybe you shoulda thought of that before selling her the joint."

"I didn't force her hand."

"Didn't stop the sale either."

I looked between them, wondering how I found myself in this strange town with two men arguing outside my broken window.

"I'm perfectly capable of doing the repairs here," said Lloyd. "Why don't you take your fancy car and drive home."

"Ha, you'd love that," retorted Sal.

Alice crossed her arms. "I don't care who helps if it means getting this heap fixed up."

Both men spun to face her.

"Who're you?" asked Sal.

I placed a hand on her shoulder. "This is my daughter, Alice."

He hit his forehead. "Alice. Of course. I completely forgot that you had a daughter. My apologies." He nodded to her. "Pleasure meeting you."

She didn't smile at him. "And you are?"

I was certain that she knew who he was but wanted to make him squirm.

"I'm Salvatore Saviano. Your mother's current boss at the paper."

"Oh." She continued to stare, deadpan.

He shifted his body to look at me. "How's about we survey the damage?"

"Come on in."

Lloyd lifted his chin in all manner of importance. "I'll get to cutting the grass."

"You do that." Sal brushed past him.

When he entered the house, Alice made herself busy painting.

Crossing the room, he rubbed his chin. "Looks like you've got warped and rotted floorboards. The fireplace is a disaster. Probably needs new mortar and bricks." His eyes drew up the wall to the ceiling. "You definitely have a leaky roof. Not sure if it's salvageable. Probably need to get up there to look. Do you have a ladder?"

"No."

"Right, well I can probably shimmy up one of the nearby trees."

I had a hard time imagining Sal climbing a tree. Though he wasn't wearing his usual five-piece suit. Instead, he wore a simple pair of trousers and a collared shirt rolled at the elbows, exposing his tan arms. He had come to work. "The outhouse is in complete disrepair as well."

His nose scrunched. "Outhouse, huh?"

"Not that you have to do it. I know that I'm your father's employee, but you're not required to help me."

"I'm not here 'cause you're an employee." He grinned before bending down to inspect a floorboard.

Alice cast me a glance over her shoulder.

With a hand on my hip, I stepped closer to him. "Then why are you helping me?"

He met my eyes and smiled. "That's how a friendship works, June."

I blinked, feeling a surge of heat. "Right, friends."

His smile widened. "I certainly hope so."

I saw Alice flinch. My cheeks grew warmer. I was fairly sure that Sal was flirting with me.

"Why don't we have a better look at that roof?"

We walked outside and saw Lloyd struggling to push through the brush.

"That'll keep him busy for a while." Sal winked at me.

I blinked again. Did *friends* wink at each other like that?

Sal shielded his eyes from the sun, inspecting the roof.

"With the overgrowth of trees, I'm guessing there's been tension on the roof. Probably making cracks. Let's see if I can get a closer look." He chose a tree close to the side of the house and began his ascent.

I watched with fascination. He moved with an agility that I didn't expect. From this angle, I could see his whole physique—and it wasn't bad at all.

"Mom, look who showed up," said Alice, catching me off guard.

I spun around to find Elex beside her.

"I came back to finish the outhouse, since I be a man of me word. But it seems ya found yerself plenty of help." When he said the word *help*, his eyes narrowed on Salvatore. "Can't say I be surprised." He turned, walking toward his car.

I hurried after him. "What is that supposed to mean?"

"Yer a lovely woman with no husband. Ya do the math."

"Are you saying that the only reason men want to help me is because they're hoping to woo me?"

"Seems a fair assessment."

I let out an exasperated breath. This man—he was so unlike Niall, who refused to argue with me. Instead, Niall would get quiet and bottle all his feelings. "It's not fair at all. Lloyd wants to help because he sold me this place, and Sal is my boss."

He halted mid-step. "That be their reasons, eh?"

"More or less."

"And ya believe it?"

"Why shouldn't I?"

"Because no man does hard labor unless it be worth it."

I crossed my arms. "And helping me isn't worth it?"

He met my eyes. His words came out softer, "Why'd ya think I came back?"

Oh. My face flushed. I locked onto his face, seeing him. Really seeing him. How his eyes dipped down at the corners. The straight slant of his nose. The sharp angle of his jaw. The smooth edge of his lips…

"My lawn mower is stuck," said Lloyd, interrupting us. He gestured in the general direction. "Elex, could you give me a hand?"

Elex audibly sighed. "That I can."

"June!" Sal's voice carried over from the tree. "I can see the problem with your roof."

As I walked to Sal, I stole a glance at Elex. He was looking my way.

CHAPTER THIRTEEN

Friday, April 25
3:15 PM

A horn erupted as we walked across the platform of Saugerties train station. Passengers descended the train with their luggage in hand. I searched the crowd, wondering how I'd know which one was Thelma. I had forgotten to ask for her description.

A mother and child descended the steps followed by a woman in a khaki uniform with a black scarf tied under the collar of her jacket.

"That must be her," I said, tapping Alice's arm. "She's dressed like the scouts in the brochure."

Thelma walked with a swift stride and keen expression on her face. Faint creases touched the corners of her eyes and mouth. Some black and gray hair peeked out from below her leather hat. She looked like a woman of the great outdoors. Bold. Rugged. Confident. At that moment, I hoped to be like her.

Waving her over, I made introductions and led her to my car.

"You own a car?" said Thelma, looking surprised.

"It was my late husband's. He was determined to have one. It cost a pretty penny."

"I'm sure it did. And he taught you how to drive?"

"He did. You should see the looks I get when people see me behind the wheel."

"Ah yes, leave the driving to the men." Thelma shook her head. "Such a load of nonsense. We have a Packard Touring at headquarters, and I've been taught to drive it for scouting trips. It's a valuable skill."

"I agree."

She studied me with a smile. "I can tell you have spirit. This will be fun."

On the way to the hotel, we discussed tomorrow's meeting.

"Do you think we'll have many in attendance?" asked Thelma.

"Most likely. This town is very curious. They'll come to sit and watch, although, I don't know how many will actually join."

"That portion will be left up to me then, but I think our program speaks for itself." Thelma pulled two books from her handbag. "I've brought along our handbook and training manual for you. These books contain most everything you need to know about our organization. Before a girl can be sworn in as a scout, she must attend meetings for at least a month, during which time she must pass the Tenderfoot Test." She riddled off the test requirements like they were as easy as breathing.

I, however, felt the urgent need to beseech God for mercy. How was I supposed to teach a troop of young women to do any of this? I was in over my head, and I hadn't even begun.

"Where do you plan to hold your weekly meetings?" she asked.

"At my house."

"I thought you were staying at the hotel?"

"Yes, but I bought a house. We've been renovating it."

"Can we take a look at your home? Part of the formal application is location. I need to make sure your locale will be conducive to Girl Scout meetings."

Alice coughed in the back seat like she'd just choked on her saliva.

I inhaled a breath. "I would love to show you. As a precaution though, I'd like to say that I can readily change locations, if our house doesn't meet the standards."

"I'm sure it will be fine," said Thelma with a wave of her hand.

I wasn't so sure.

When we arrived at our house, I said a silent prayer. Luckily, Lloyd and Elex had nearly cleared the weed-ridden driveway. That was a victory. Trouble was that the complete hideousness of the house could now be seen—sludge black exterior with a tilted wooden awning above the door. The moth-eaten sofa had been tossed outside just shy of the entryway. It still remained upside down in the grass with its two peg legs reaching up to the sky in surrender.

Parking, I peeked at Thelma to witness her initial reaction. She remained straight faced. Not a single twitch or frown.

Entering the living room, Thelma slowly rotated to take it in. Though the walls were painted a coat of white, the dark wood shined through. Since it had rained the night before, water had seeped through the cracks in the ceiling and trickled down the walls leaving behind brown streaks. Adding to the radiance of the space were the missing bricks in the fireplace and warped floorboards.

"Quite a lot of work you still have here." She inspected our bedroom, washroom, and kitchen. "Where are the windows?"

"They've been ordered," I said. "They should be in next week."

She nodded. "It appears that your roof leaks."

"I know. I'm hoping some friends can help me fix it."

"Do you have running water?"

"We have a pump."

"What about bathroom accommodations?"

"We have an outhouse, though it's not functioning yet." Sweat dampened my palms.

She laid a hand on the kitchen table. It wobbled under her

touch. "Do you own other furnishings?"

"Not yet. When I lived in Manhattan, we rented a fully furnished apartment."

She exhaled a slow, steady breath. "June, I ask that you be frank with me. Do you have the necessary resources to complete such a project?"

My eyes averted to Alice. Worry colored her cheeks pink. I was certain that my face matched the same hue. Thelma had voiced the very question that looped through my head daily. Can I afford to fix this place and buy the necessary items to live in it? I folded my hands. "It will be difficult. I'll have to do it a piece at a time."

"Currently, you are renting a room at the hotel," said Thelma. "That payment takes away funds that can be spent here, correct?"

"Yes."

She scanned the room again. "You have gumption buying a house like this." Her lips curved into a smile. "I don't know a single woman who would ever purchase this kind of house without a husband to help her. But you're not like most women. You'll do well as a troop captain." She placed her hands on her hips. "Now, I've learned a thing or two about woodworking in my years of being a scout. This floor has suffered from a leaky roof and rot. But it can be fixed. We must remove the boards that are rotten and replace those with new ones. Before we can do that, we must evaluate the roof to locate the places where water is getting in." She studied the ceiling. "From the looks of it, I'd say you have four problem areas."

"My boss inspected it yesterday. He told me that I needed a whole new roof."

"Can you afford a new roof?"

"No."

"Very well, I will teach you how the Algonquian Indians roofed their wigwams with bark. Their roofs never leaked."

"Where are we getting the bark?"

"From the trees surrounding your home. We will need some proper tools. Do you have a hatchet?

"No."

"A saw?"

"No."

"Do you have a ladder?"

"No."

"How about a hammer and nails?"

"Yes!" I was happy to announce this much.

"That's a start."

"Where is your nearest hardware store?"

"Two stores down from the hotel."

"We'll go there first." Thelma looked from me to Alice. "Ladies, today your Girl Scout training begins."

CHAPTER FOURTEEN

Saturday, April 26
12:30 PM

The library was crowded.

We had replaced the study tables in the center of the room with thirty chairs. All of those were filled and the rest of the audience stood among the bookshelves.

I was pleased to see many young ladies in attendance with their parents. Among the faces, I recognized a few—Elex and Etta, Salvatore, Lloyd, Frieda (she wouldn't miss a chance for gossip), and Ishmael Davis and his family. Clyde Lockwood also showed up. Beside him was a hard-faced woman and a young lady, whom I presumed were his wife and daughter.

At precisely one, I started the meeting. "Welcome everyone. Thank you for coming. I'm June Flynn. I recently moved here to become a typist for The Saugerties Daily Journal. It's a pleasure to be a part of your fine city. Today, I have the privilege of introducing Thelma Parker. She is the Applications Director at the Girl Scouts of the United States. She is here to tell you about the program and how we're implementing it here in the city of Saugerties. Let's give a warm welcome to Thelma." I clapped my hands.

Rising from a chair beside Alice, Thelma joined me at the front of the room. "Thank you, June."

Thelma talked about how scouting began in England as a means of training young soldiers when they first enlisted to become handy, capable men. The training was so successful that the program opened up to include all young men. It became known as the Boy Scouts. It wasn't long until young ladies asked for a scouting program of their own. In response, Girl Guides was formed in England. Desiring to see Scoutcraft in America, Juliette Gordon Low established the Girl Scouts of the United States. Through the program, young ladies were able to learn about camping, observation, woodcraft, lifesaving, patriotism, and the necessary skills of home keeping and self-preservation. "When a young woman completes her years as a scout, she will be a mature, sufficient, and contributing member of society." Thelma lifted her chin with pride. "I'd like to open up our forum for questions."

A tall girl stood up in the front row. She had her brown hair pulled tightly into a ponytail. "Hello, I'm Myrtle Mellus. I want to thank you both for setting up a troop here. I've been hoping for this day for quite some time." Giving a brief nod, she sat back down.

So, this was the girl who put up the brochure in our hotel. I hoped I would do this troop justice.

"Thank you, Miss Mellus. I'm glad we're able to make this happen," said Thelma.

A woman near the back of the crowd rose to her feet. A distinct frown pulled at the corners of her mouth. "Who placed the advertisement in the paper?"

"That was me," I said, lifting my hand.

The woman's frown deepened. "My name is Beulah VanBuren. The ad said that all ladies are welcome between the ages of thirteen and eighteen, regardless of race, class, or disability. Does that mean you intend to have all the girls in the same group or will they be divided into smaller segments?"

I knew this question was coming. "I plan to have all the girls together. I think there is much that can be learned from being with girls of different backgrounds. When Juliette Gordon Low founded this organization in Georgia, her first troop had 18 young women that were culturally and ethnically diverse. Juliette wanted to ensure that all girls had a place to grow and develop their leadership skills, and so do I."

"You know, Ms. Flynn, this kind of integration of girls isn't right." Beulah placed a hand on her rotund hip. "You're sending the wrong message. Colored girls ought to be with colored girls, white girls with white girls, and the disabled with their own kind. That's how it has always been done. It's proper."

Several cheers and hear-hears sounded around the room.

Beulah's voice rose higher. "Since the war, things have already been stirred up, what with the negro soldiers coming back and forgetting their pre-war status." She cast a glance toward Ishmael. "Everyone has a designated role. We need to stick to those."

My hands clenched at my sides. I stared into her tiny eyes that seemed lost in her pudgy face. "Beulah." I kept my voice level. "In my troop, all ladies will be equal. So help me God, I'll see to it that they rise above simple-minded decorum and embrace the rights and freedoms that were purchased off the backs and with the blood of men like my late husband. If you don't like that, I suggest you leave now."

The room came alive with angry whispers and a stampede of people exiting.

My heartbeat pounded in my ears. I told myself to breathe.

Thelma leaned close to me. "Today, my dear, you drew a line in the sand."

I swallowed. "So be it."

Mrs. Lockwood hoisted her daughter by the arm, snapping at Clyde that they were leaving. They followed the majority out of the library door. Even Lloyd Ennis left. When the mayhem settled, only thirteen people remained in the room.

"Right." I clapped my hands. "Now, the real meeting begins. Do any of you have questions?"

A pale, petite girl lifted her hand.

"Yes, dear."

She rose to her feet, holding onto a cane. With the slope of her shoulders, it seemed the world rested on her back. "Hello. My name is Nellie Mott."

I had to strain to hear her whispered words.

"Your ad said that girls with disabilities could join your troop. Can someone who is blind join in?"

Nellie's mother held her hand, unable to meet my eyes. Her father looked at me without much hope.

I wanted to hug them all. "There will no doubt be some difficulties, Nellie, but if you're up for the challenge, so am I. I would love to have you in my troop."

At this, she stood a little taller. "I would like that."

"For those of you present," I said. "How many of you ladies would like to join?"

Four hands rose along with Alice's.

My heart soared. "That's wonderful!" Turning toward Thelma, I asked, "What happens now?"

"Each of you ladies need to fill out an enrollment card. Then, you will be added to June's troop. June will be your captain. You will respect and honor her as she teaches and trains you in the ways of the Girl Scouts. You must attend one month of meetings and complete your Tenderfoot Test before being officially sworn in. Now, each of you may come forward to complete your enrollment."

Once the cards were finished, I welcomed them into my troop. "Our first meeting will be held at my house on Tuesday at six o'clock."

Parents exchanged a few glances.

"Don't you live in the old Krall cabin?" asked Myrtle.

"Yes."

Her forehead creased. "Isn't that place haunted?"

Etta waved her hand in dismissal. "That all be a myth. I done been in it. The worst thing in that house do be the smell."

Elex put a hand over his face.

"Which we're also fixing." I hurried to clarify.

Alice piped up—"Girl Scouts get to wear snazzy uniforms!"

Giddy chatter echoed through the girls.

Bless my daughter. She knew just when to chime in.

"For Tuesday, please bring a yard of cord, notepad, and pencil to our meeting. If you have any other questions, feel free to ask. Otherwise, I'll see you all on Tuesday."

Myrtle bounded over, shaking my hand. "Thank you, Captain Flynn. I'm honored to be a part of your troop."

"It's a pleasure to have you join."

Giving me a nod, she walked away. As she departed, I noted that she had come alone.

Nellie's father approached me next. "Ms. Flynn, I want to thank you for accepting my daughter. Due to her blindness, schools and programs have excluded her, which is unfortunate because she's a bright girl. A real whiz with her at-home studies." He lowered his voice. "But if you ever find it too difficult to have her in the troop, we'll understand."

"I think it's going to be okay. This troop will be a team, and we're going to help each other."

Saying goodbye to the Motts, I found the Davis family waiting patiently in the back row of chairs. As I approached them, they rose to their feet.

Ishmael pulled off his hat, nodding to me. "Thank you for forming this troop Ms. Flynn. Cora is mighty excited about it."

"I'm excited too." I smiled at Cora. "I'm looking forward to getting to know you."

"Thank you." She met my eyes with a beaming smile. "I look forward to learning all those things you talked about."

"Can I let you in on a little secret?" I took a step closer, leaning in.

As Cora leaned closer to me, her mother flinched. "Sure, what is it?"

"Most things, I'll be learning too."

Her head tilted a bit. "You mean you don't know all the stuff you were talking about?"

"Not everything, but I'm happy to learn."

Cora laughed. "This should be interesting."

Her mother tapped her arm. "Cora."

"It's okay. She's right." I chuckled. "I'm not the most qualified, but I have a manual and Thelma to help me."

I outstretched my hand to Cora's mother. "It's nice to meet you, I'm June."

"I'm Sabina." She shook my hand for a brief moment, her gaze darting downward.

"I work at the paper with Ishmael." I turned to him. "Can I call you Ishmael?"

"Yes ma'am," he said. "How you liking it so far?"

"Feels like I entered a whirlwind, honestly. Can't quite get my bearings, and yet, I think I love it." I held up my hands with a shrug. "I'm used to a fast-paced life. We originally lived in Manhattan."

"I've visited there once," he said. "Sabina and Cora haven't seen the big city yet. Maybe someday."

"Sabina, your dress looks like the ones I would see in the storefronts. It's lovely. Where did you get it?"

"I sewed it myself. I'm a seamstress."

"My mom is the best seamstress around," said Cora with a proud jut of her chin. "Most women in this town hire her to sew their dresses."

"Really? That's marvelous. I never learned how to sew. Such a great skill to have. Actually, I believe sewing is a badge the scouts can earn. Do you think you'd be willing to do a lesson or two with our troop?"

Sabina glanced at Ishmael and then at Cora.

"Of course, there's no pressure." I hurried to clarify, hoping I didn't overstep.

"You will, won't you, Mama?" Cora looked at her with expectation.

Sabina folded her hands in front of her skirt. "I would be happy to."

"Thank you, Sabina. I need all the help I can get."

We said our goodbyes, and the Davis trio exited the library. I noticed Sal loitering by a shelf of books with a rather thick one in his hands. I strolled to him, wondering what he was reading.

He snapped the book shut and pushed it back into place on the shelf.

I glimpsed the title on the spine. *The Hound of the Baskervilles.* Strange title. "Doing some light reading?"

"Just browsing."

"What does that mean, The Hound of the Baskervilles?"

"Just a mystery about some dog." He shrugged. "Don't really know." He positioned himself in front of the books, pressing a hand to his front lapel. "Well done today."

I clasped my hands in front of my skirt. "I did what I set out to do."

"Five girls seems like a solid beginning. You think your house will be ready for Tuesday's meeting?"

"It has to be."

"If not, you can always meet in the newsroom."

"Thank you, Sal." I smiled. "For everything."

"Glad I can help." Exchanging goodbyes, he departed.

Looking back at the bookshelf, I plucked *The Hound of the Baskervilles* from its spot. The author was Conan Doyle. On the stamp card, I read over the listed names and laughed out loud. Salvatore Saviano had checked it out four times. Apparently, he enjoyed the dog story. I'd have to check it out sometime.

I found Thelma and Alice perusing the badges in the handbook.

Thelma looked up. "Well done, today."

I exhaled a heavy breath. "There were some hard moments in that meeting, huh?"

"I'll say," agreed Alice.

"You have made a virtuous statement, but many will oppose it." Thelma placed a hand on my shoulder. "Brace yourself, it's just the beginning."

I swallowed, knowing full well that she was right.

"It looks like our troop contains the outcasts of the town." Alice grinned.

The outcasts. A picture of my rundown home filled my mind. The majority of Saugerties residents considered my house to be unacceptable. Did the town see me and these young ladies the same way? Were we unsuitable? Unqualified? I thought of each girl who had enrolled today.

Cora had been denied opportunities because of the color of her skin.

Nellie had been denied education because of her disability.

Etta had been denied her childhood because of her mother's addiction.

Myrtle, I didn't know her story, but I deduced that she longed for purpose. Which is why she had called Thelma for the last nine months asking for a troop.

Then there was my daughter, denied friendship because her mother had bought a house.

"You might be right, Alice. Maybe we are the outcasts." I gazed out the front window, seeing the sunshine gloss the street. Light could brighten anything, even dingy pavement. "But that's okay. This town can judge us all they like. Because I know this—what is seen on the outside doesn't define what is found within. Someday, maybe they'll see that."

Alice crossed her arms. "I wouldn't get your hopes up."

CHAPTER FIFTEEN

Monday, April 28
3:00 PM

Today was the day. We were officially moving into *the house.*

As expected, I had help.

Lloyd arrived first. "Hey, you've gotten the smell out."

I smiled. "Yeah, it was a vinegar and lemon solution that Thelma Parker, the Girl Scouts director created."

"Hmmm." He casually walked through the house, seeing what improvements we've made. "Who helped you fix the floor?"

"Thlema cut out the rotted boards, and Elex installed the new ones." I was glad Elex had come over. It gave me a chance to apologize for implying that Etta's troubles were a result of him going to war. He brushed it off, but I saw that my words had meant something to him.

Lloyd turned up his nose at the mention of Elex. "Looks like you did some rustic work on the roof too. Did *Elex* do that as well?"

"Actually that was Thelma's handiwork." I perked up with pride. "She taught us the Algonquian method with bark shingling."

He snorted. "We'll see if that holds up."

My smile vanished. Did I ask for his opinion?

Alice entered the house carrying a box. "Mom, where should I put this? It's labeled LINENS."

"In our bedroom for now. I'll sort through it later." I dragged my eyes to Lloyd. "Are you here to help or snoop?"

He drummed up a grin, placed a hand behind his back and gave a slight bow. "Please, direct me."

His attempt at charm was futile. I still didn't like him. "We have boxes in the car that need to come in."

As he moved to exit, Sal showed up at the door. Lloyd pushed past him without so much as a hello.

"Nitwit," Sal muttered below his breath. He entered the house with a tall boy in tow. "Hey-ya, June. Hope it's okay that I brought my nephew, Matteo. Thought more hands would make lighter work."

Matteo popped off his hat, revealing shiny black hair. "Pleasure to meet you, Ms. Flynn. My uncle's told me all about you."

I didn't expect the low voice that came from his lips. How old was this boy? His baby-face made it hard to tell. "All good things, I hope."

"The very best." Matteo sent a grin at Sal.

A flutter danced in my stomach. "Well, good. Thank you for coming." I shook his hand.

Lickety-split, Alice was at my side ready to shake the tanned Italian boy's hand. "Hello, I'm Alice."

"I'm Matteo." He gifted her an impeccable smile.

Swell. My daughter looked like a star-gazed sap.

"Where would you like us to pitch in?" asked Sal.

Trying not to be bothered by the looks crossing between Alice and the handsome-I-need-to-know-his-age-Matteo, I cleared my throat. "My dresser, bed frame, and mattress were delivered on Saturday. Unfortunately, the delivery men never assembled the frame. They left as quickly as they came. I don't think they wanted to spend another second in my house."

"Don't worry 'bout it. Matteo is as handy as a pants pocket."

He placed a proud hand on the boy's shoulder. "He even brought his tools."

"I'll go fetch them," said Matteo.

"I'll give you a hand." Alice followed him out with a smile the width of New York.

My gaze walked out the door with them, wondering if I needed to chaperone.

"Want to show me your bed?" asked Sal.

My attention snapped to him. "Beg your pardon?"

"You need it assembled, right?"

"Right." His expression was the picture of innocence, but I caught the mischievous glimmer in his eye. Ushering him into my bedroom, God help me, I pushed down the feeling of indecence. "It seems simple enough. Just some nuts and bolts that need to be screwed together." As the words left my lips, I felt my cheeks redden.

Before I could kneel down, I heard Elex call out. "June, I be after bringin' yer windows."

I hurried out of the bedroom, glad for the escape. "They came early." I fully anticipated sleeping in a windowless house for days. I told myself it would be close to camping. Something I had never done in my life. Something I wasn't excited to try. But as a Girl Scout leader, I had to embrace nature. I kept telling myself that.

"Me men came to help with the install. Etta came too. She be outside with Alice."

"Wonderful." I looked past him to see Alice and Etta chatting it up with Matteo.

"Etta be mighty excited to join yer scoutin' group."

"It's going to be a real adventure." I chuckled. "I'll be learning right alongside the girls."

He smiled. "Yer a brave lass."

"I'm either brave or unwittingly hopeful."

"At either rate, yer doin' somethin' special for our town. Means a lot."

"Thank you."

He nodded, cleared his throat, and looked away. "Better help me men with those windows."

Noise erupted from around the house with old panes being cleared, hammers pounding, and Lloyd offering his unsolicited opinion as he meandered about, inspecting the work.

I set a box labeled HOUSEWARES on our rickety kitchen table and pulled off a strip of tape. Opening a flap, I found my dinner plates. I didn't have a cabinet yet, so I set them, one by one, on the top of the range. Without fire know-how, I wouldn't be cooking anytime soon.

The voices of Etta and Alice trickled in through the kitchen window. They must have been standing outside, near the water pump.

"That Matteo is an absolute finer," said Etta.

Alice chuckled. "He's got the kind of looks you see in movies."

"He done make me want to dip bread in oil and sing. But ya saw him first, so it only be right that ya get to stake yer claim."

"Who says he'll claim me back?" said Alice.

"What are ya on about? Yer pure class. I say ya give it a lash. From the looks of him, he probably has a crackin' bowl of spaghetti, if ya know what I mean."

"I'm not sure I do."

"Ya know, his tortellini and meatballs."

"Etta!" Alice's breath burst out with the utterance of her friend's name.

My hand flew to my mouth, covering my own gasp.

Etta laughed out loud. "Ya think me bad, ya oughta meet me cousin, Mattie O'Keefe. That one do be sufferin' from a double-dose of original sin."

Goodness, it sounded like Etta's family was a bit rough.

"Geez Louise, I think we've done it." Sal entered the kitchen along with Matteo. "Your frame is set up, and the mattress is on it."

I pulled my focus from the window. "Thank you once again. I don't know what I'd do without all you fellas pitching in."

"It's nuttin', doll." He waved his hand in dismissal. "Glad to help." He glanced at his pocket watch. "Hate to run, but we gotta head out. I'm expecting a shipment."

"Of course. I'll see you tomorrow."

"Seventy-thirty's my favorite time of day. It always starts with the sun." Sal winked at me.

A nervous chuckle left my lips. This man was an unabashed flirt.

He tipped his hat. "Until tomorrow."

I shook my head as they left. In my bedroom, I observed my new frame. It looked stable. I ran a hand over the cotton mattress. Lying backward on it, I studied the dingy ceiling. We hadn't painted the ceiling white, only the walls. Paint cost money. Everything cost money. Being on my own, I realized that now more than ever. There were so many things we still needed. Sofa. Chairs. Cabinet. Rugs. The list went on. We had come so far, but we had so far to go. The weight of that reality pressed down on me. While voices and sounds echoed from the living room and outside the house, I felt alone.

I curled on my side, closing my eyes. I saw Niall's face painted on my thoughts. Before he left for war, he said, 'No matter what Junie-girl, ye'll be okay.' Tears escaped and trickled down my nose. I didn't feel okay.

A thud came from behind me. I turned to see Elex through the new glass pane.

He looked as surprised to see me as I was to see him. He quickly disappeared from sight. I wiped my tears away, sucking in a shaky breath.

A female voice called from the living room. "Hello? Captain Flynn?"

I found Myrtle Mellus standing in the doorway, holding a loaf of bread wrapped in plastic. "Myrtle, how nice to see you. Come on in."

"I stopped by to bring you this." She held out the loaf. "I made it today. By myself."

"That is very kind. Thank you."

"Yeah, well. See you Tuesday." She spun around to leave.

"You don't have to rush off. You can stay awhile if you want."

"I have chores to do at home." With that, she jogged to her bicycle and peddled away.

Huh. Myrtle was an unusual girl. I looked at the loaf of bread in my hands. It was still warm. One sniff confirmed that it was heavenly. None of my loaves of bread ever looked or smelled this good.

By eight o'clock, everyone had departed, leaving Alice and me alone in the house. We ate some of the bread, then crawled into bed. Alice seemed to doze off in a minute. Though I was tired, I couldn't sleep. To make matters worse, the howling wind made the house creak and groan. Then I heard an even stranger sound. Like nails clawing against brick. My heart sped up. What was that? Was that the tree branches hitting the house? It didn't sound like branches. My hands fisted at my sides.

"What's that sound?" whispered Alice.

Well wouldn't you know it, she wasn't asleep after all. "Probably the wind."

"That's not the wind. It's in the house."

"Let's stay here, and maybe it'll go away."

More sounds of scratching and creaking came from the living room.

Alice scooted closer to me. "What if it's Albin or Irena?"

I had the same thought. "Of course not. That's all a myth."

"Could it be rats?"

I sighed. "I'd better check or neither of us will be able to rest." Slipping out of bed, I lit the oil lamp on the dresser. I hated the fact that my legs were trembling. Bending over, I grabbed one of my boots.

Alice bolted out of the bed, staying beside me. "What are you going to do with that?"

"I don't know. Whack something."

"You can't whack a ghost. It'll go right through them."

"It's not a ghost." Creeping into the living room with her on my heels, I saw a shadow dart past me. Goosebumps surfaced on my arms. Oh sweet heavens, was that a dark spirit? I stepped back. A board below my foot creaked. (We missed a lose one.)

A shrill cry sounded, followed by a swarm of shadows dashing out from the fireplace.

Alice and I screamed at the top of our lungs. I swung my boot, yelling, "Die Irena!"

Flutters of something hit our faces and tugged our hair.

I connected with an object, and it fell to the floor. Feeling elated, I cheered, "I got her! I got her!" I lowered the oil lamp to shine it on my victory. Laying motionless on the floor was a small black bat. Heart pounding, I tried to regain my composure. My voice came out more breathless than I wanted. "See, I told you it wasn't a ghost."

Alice crossed her arms. "You were yelling, 'Die Irena!'"

"You heard that wrong. I yelled, 'Die…I'll get rid of ya.'"

"I heard you, Mother! You were just as scared as me."

I flung a hand in the air. "Okay! You're right. I was scared. But look, it was only one little bat. No harm."

We stared at the tiny thing.

"I think I knocked it unconscious. I should probably put it in a box or something and get it out of here."

Alice tapped her chin. "You know, it seemed like there were more shadows than one?"

"It did seem that way."

Like a magic force pulling our heads upward, we turned our eyes to the ceiling. Hanging on the beams, we saw a small army of little black demons.

Screaming, we ran out of the house.

CHAPTER SIXTEEN

Tuesday, April 29
7:40 AM

I peeked into Sal's office. "Have you ever dealt with bats?"

"Bats? You got bats in your house?"

I nodded.

"Creepy little bandits." He shuddered.

"Tell me about it. Alice and I had to sleep in our car last night."

"I still can't believe that you bought that house." He shook his head, grinning. "Bats are tricky. You'll need someone who knows how to get rid of them. I'll ask around for you."

"Thanks." As I walked to the door, Sal went back to reading the paper on his desk. I paused under the doorframe, considering whether to broach the second question in my head.

"Something wrong, June?"

I spun around. "Well…" The voice in my head told me to mind my own business, since I've only worked here for a week. Trouble was that my heart usually won these battles. "I have a small question." I used my fingers to show him it was about the size of a pinch.

"Go on."

"In one of our recent articles, our paper ventured whether the disappearances of Henry Brickmore and Stuart Ellsworth were a product of actual abduction or due to the ghost of Irena Krall. Wouldn't you consider this kind of speculation to be more propaganda than real news?" The words tumbled out so fast. Once they had left my lips, I mentally kicked myself for being too frank.

He leaned back in his chair, folding his hands on his desk. He studied me with a stoic expression.

Fiddlesticks. My body temperature went from cool to toasty.

He gestured to a chair in front of his desk. "Please sit."

I felt like a child about to be scolded.

"Have you worked in the news industry before coming here?"

"This is my first time."

"Are you a reader of the news?"

"Yes. When my husband was in France, I read the same four papers every day. I didn't want to miss anything. Since then, I've grown attached to the news. It makes me feel more connected with the world around me."

"There's lots of newspapers in Manhattan, and lots of readers too. But Saugerties is small, and we're up against The Telegraph. Have you heard of it?"

"No."

He leaned forward, placing his elbows on the desktop. "The Telegraph has been in business for close to a century. It's a cornerstone in this city. When my grandfather started The Saugerties Daily Journal, he was lucky to sell ten copies a day. By his second year, he sold about fifty copies a day. That was it. Most men would have given up. My Nonna told him to quit. But my grandfather had an idea. In a small town, people wanted to know what was happening among the town folks. They would pay a cent to know what seeds other farmers were planting and tips on how to make a bag of flour stretch. His paper was practical and personal. It set itself apart from The Telegraph, and its popularity grew. This however, upset The

Telegraph. As our readers grew, theirs diminished. Ever since, it's been a rival between our papers. Who can put out the best stories? Who has the best tips? Who can release the breaking news first?" He paused, letting his words sink in. "Do you know much about Irena Krall?"

"I know that I bought her house." I offered a sheepish grin.

He did not smile. "Do you know her story?"

"Parts of it. From what I've gathered, it's not a happy tale."

"It's not. Irena was the daughter of a farmer in New Paltz. Albin Krall was a German immigrant who was looking for work. He took a job in the fields of Irena's father, Daniel Jansen, but that didn't last, since Albin was a lazy worker. When Mr. Jansen fired Albin, Irena ran away with him. He had won her over with his musical charms and big dreams. But money ran out quickly, and they ended up in Saugerties working for Charles Whitaker. Because they were immigrants, Charles didn't allow them to live in the mansion's servant's quarters. Instead, he put them in the cabin you now own. From what I've heard, Irena had it hard with Albin and the Whitakers, but she stayed."

"How do you know this?"

"Clyde's been digging."

I thought about the letter I'd found. I could show it to him, but to what end? For him to print it in the paper? Something about that felt wrong. "I understand that Irena's story didn't have a happy ending. However, I don't believe that her ghost is seeking revenge on the Whitaker bloodline. Do you?"

"In truth, no I don't. But the person behind these abductions wants us to believe it. If the real perpetrator thinks we believe that it's Irena, they might get sloppy. Then, we'll catch them."

"Are you saying that you're baiting the villain?"

"If it works."

I studied his face. "Is your aim to find the rich captives or sell papers?"

"That's a weighty question, June. A very weighty question." He exhaled. "I don't like either of the men that vanished. They paraded themselves around our city like they were untouchable. Looking down their noses at everyone out of their social sphere." He crossed his arms. "Regardless if a man has worked hard and earned a level of status, those men rejected anyone who wasn't born rich. I wish I could say that I worried for their well-being, but I don't." His brow furrowed as he looked down at his desk. "It seems that the abductor is targeting only those of Whitaker descent. However, I worry for the safety of our city. No one wants a lunatic on the loose."

His words were heavy. I didn't expect such an honest answer. "I don't either."

"Then, let's do something about it."

"Like what?"

"Find the truth."

I leaned forward. "Are you saying you want my help?"

"I think you've decided that on your own." A smile softened his features. "No one has ever come into my office after a week of employment and dared critique the stories we're printing. Until you showed up."

"I'm sorry, I know I—"

"It's okay. I like your tenacity. I think you should help solve this mystery since you're the one who bought Irena's house. From now on, feel free to dig up whatever you can. You have my permission to read any old newspapers in the morgue. Especially since you're already doing it." He smirked at me.

My eyes widened at this acknowledgment. Clyde must have tattled. I thanked him for this opportunity and left his office. For the rest of the day, I wondered how we'd solve this case. What was the truth? A strange excitement welled inside my stomach. I wondered if all reporters on a mission felt like this. Of course, I wasn't exactly a reporter, more like a helper, but I felt exhilarated just the same.

"Hello, June." Clyde tapped the top of my table.

I realized I had been staring at my typewriter, lost in thought. "Yes?"

"My daughter, Geraldine, has decided that she would like to join your girls' group."

I blinked. "You mean the Girl Scouts?"

"Yeah, that."

"If I recall correctly, your wife all-but dragged your daughter from the library at our meeting. How then is she being allowed to join?"

"I felt the opportunity could benefit her. In order for her to learn new skills, my wife and I are willing to concede on the *mixed* company."

A holy struggle of words battled in my head, words I so badly wanted to shout in this oaf's face. "How old is she?"

"Fourteen."

"She will have to fill out an enrollment card at our first meeting. It's tonight at my house."

"The Krall house?"

"It's my house now."

"Is it sanitary?"

My jaw clenched. "I wouldn't have young ladies come if it weren't. The meeting starts at six."

He huffed. "Very well. I'll have her there."

Why on earth did Clyde want his daughter to join a troop for educating girls, when he seemed against female empowerment? Unless…I drummed my fingers on the table. I bet that bald-headed bastard wanted to spy on me, and worse, he wanted to use his daughter to do it. My hands clenched into fists. Well, he wouldn't get the best of me.

Once I finished my stack of typing for the day, I walked to the library. I had a few minutes to spare before picking Alice up from school. I was relieved to find *The Hound of the Baskervilles* on the shelf. I was curious to see what kind of book could be so fascinating that Salvatore Saviano read it four times.

—

Alice dropped into the car. From the expression on her face, she was either ready to cry or yell.

"Another bad day at school?"

"When were you going to tell me?" Her words came out low.

I inclined my head. "Tell you what?"

"You work at a newspaper. You hear everything before it goes to print. Yet, you somehow failed to tell me that two men have vanished behind our house. And worse, the town blames us." She trained a hurt pair of eyes on my face. "They blame *us*."

I blinked, unable to format a response. I should have told her. I should have known she'd hear the news at school.

"At first, I thought people didn't like me because I'm new," Alice continued. "They'd whisper strange things as they passed me in the hall. But the comments started getting more direct. More personal. Today, a girl cornered me and said, 'It's your fault. You're the reason Irena's back. You're the reason my brother is gone.' I didn't know what she was talking about, so I asked George. He told me about the missing Whitaker men. He told me that they disappeared in Esopus Creek. The townspeople believe that when we entered the house, we awakened the wrath of Irena. The girl who cornered me was Gladys Ellsworth. Her brother is the second man to vanish." Her voice trembled. "Why didn't you tell me?"

I opened my hands, pleading. "I'm sorry. I should have told you. I thought that if I didn't say anything, that somehow, I could shield you from the whole thing. Which was idiotic, I know. This town talks." I swallowed. "It's a scary thing, and I know you don't like the house, and I thought this would make you dislike living there even more."

"No kidding. It's terrifying. George said they haven't found the bodies. It's like these men went into the creek and then—poof!—vanished into the air!"

"I know it's bad. Very bad. I don't know what I was thinking when I bought that house."

"Neither do I." She sighed loudly.

We both sat in silence, staring out the windshield of the car at nothing in particular.

In a soft voice, I said, "I will try to sell it."

She huffed. "We both know it won't sell. Especially now that men are disappearing behind it."

I rubbed a hand against my forehead. "I know."

"You said that Dad didn't leave us much money. So, I'm thinking we're stuck." She slumped in the seat.

Every fiber of my being wanted to cry. I wanted to weep because I had to bear this burden alone. I had to care for a daughter, provide for us, and do it all alone because Niall thought he *had* to enlist. It was more important to help a country that wasn't his own, instead of a family that was. The dull ache in my chest grew tighter. It was that painful reminder that I wasn't enough. I wasn't enough to make him stay. He chose an impossible war instead of me. He chose to die, rather than live with me. I always had a hunch throughout our marriage that I loved him more, but the day he left, I knew for sure.

"Mom, do you believe that the ghost of Irena is luring men to the creek?"

Her question drew me back to the reality that I had to face. I shook my head. "No, I think that's nonsense."

"Then who is luring them?"

"That's what I'm trying to figure out."

"What do you mean?"

"I've been digging into Irena's past, trying to learn more. I think someone wants to use her ghost as a scapegoat, but I don't know why. I've heard that Irena and her husband, Albin, were servants to Charles Whitaker and weren't treated well. Shortly after Irena drowned, Charles, his wife, and youngest sons all died. Rumor spread that her ghost was taking revenge on them. The eldest son, Felix sold the house and fled for fear of his life. After that, there was peace."

"Until we came."

"Exactly."

Alice drummed her fingers on the car door. "So someone is blaming us and Irena in order to enact their revenge?"

"It would seem so."

She nodded, looking contemplative. "Do you think our lives are in danger?"

This was the question that looped through my mind. "It seems like the culprit is only targeting men related to the Whitakers. We aren't men or Whitakers. My hope is that we are safe, but I don't really know." I took her hands into mine. "Tell me how you feel. Are you afraid? Are you wanting to leave?"

"Well yeah, I'm afraid. But I'm angry too." Her forehead creased. "We've been working hard, spending our money and time to improve the *Krall* house. That's why this whole thing is unfair. We haven't done anything wrong. Yet, we're getting blamed by townspeople who are either too scared or too gullible to discover the truth." Alice made a derisive sniff. "It's ridiculous."

"You're right. It is ridiculous. Which is why I'm going to find out the truth. I'm not going to let Irena or us get blamed. I'm going to prove this town wrong. Somehow, I will find out what's really going on and see justice served." I slapped my hand against my thigh. "Then they'll all owe us an apology!"

Alice's eyes lit up. "Yes! We will prove them wrong. Then, we'll rub their noses in it and point and laugh!"

I chuckled. "Hold on there. Just because they're being nasty to us doesn't mean we're going to stoop to their level. Justice will be the salt in the wound and show them the errors of their thinking."

"Well shoot, that kind of justice isn't much fun."

I chuckled again. "However, when truth is served, it might be sent in the form of an anonymous letter to Gladys Ellsworth saying, "You were wrong, you little shrew."

She threw her arms around me. "Thanks, Mom." Leaning

back, she folded her hands like she meant business. "How do we start finding clues?"

"What's this *we* talk?"

"Mother, like it or not, we're in this together."

"This could get dangerous. I will be the one digging into it."

"Two heads are better than one. We need to put our brains together to solve this." Her jaw jutted forward with a firm resolve.

My goodness, when did she become so much like me? "Fine, keep your ear to the ground, but be careful. We don't know what we're dealing with."

CHAPTER SEVENTEEN

Tuesday, April 29
5:45 PM

I laid out seven pillows in a circle on the living room floor.

Alice watched me. "We're sitting on the floor?"

"No, we're using pillows because we don't have enough chairs."

At ten minutes to six, Myrtle arrived.

"Good evening, Myrtle. Come on in and have a seat on a pillow."

"What an adventurous idea," she said.

I whispered to Alice, "See, it's adventurous, not cheap."

Nellie arrived with her parents. The Davises followed after them, looking around as if mystified to be standing in the *haunted* Krall house.

"Hey, it don't smell anymore," said Etta as she walked inside.

Elex swatted her.

"What?" She gave him an indignant look. "That be a compliment."

"It's a work in progress," I said. "But we're making strides."

"Aye, ya are." Elex nodded.

"Thank you again for leading this troop," said Mr. Mott. "Nellie's been counting down the days."

"Yes, Cora too," agreed Ishmael.

Exchanging pleasantries, the Motts and Elex departed. Ishmael guided Sabina toward the door. She paused, looking back at Cora. Her brows pinched together.

I crossed over to them and said quietly, "I'll take good care of her, I promise."

Sabina exhaled. "Thank you."

With the parents gone, I sat on a pillow facing the girls. "All right." I clapped my hands together. "Welcome to our first troop meeting. I am grateful to have you here and to be your captain. We will begin every meeting with our salute and quoting our promise. The salute is made with the right hand. The palm faces out, while the thumb holds down the little finger. Then you bring up your fingertips next to your forehead, level with your eyebrow, like this." I showed them all how to do it. "Now you try."

Nellie, while she couldn't see my instruction, nailed it on the first attempt.

"As we salute, we will recite the Girl Scout promise. Repeat after me, 'On my honor, I will try to do my duty to God and my country, to help other people at all times, and to obey scout laws.'"

The girls repeated the salute.

A knock sounded on the door before it swung open. There stood Clyde and his daughter, Geraldine. He paraded into my house, openly scrutinizing it. "The outside of this place hasn't changed, but you've made some moderate improvements inside. The painted walls help."

"You're late, Clyde." I stood up.

"You can't afford chairs, I see." He gestured to the young ladies seated on pillows. "Almost like you're hosting a pow-wow."

I envisioned myself plucking off his bottle-shaped glasses and stomping them to bits. I inhaled a breath, willing myself to remain calm. "Please have a seat, Geraldine. We've already begun the meeting." I gestured to the door. "Pick up is at eight."

Clyde crossed his arms. "It better be done on time, I don't want to have to wait."

"Tell you what, you don't waste my time, and I won't waste yours."

He exited with a stiff stride.

Geraldine lowered her plump frame primly onto a pillow. It squashed below her weight like a pancake. I saw some disappointed expressions on other troop members. Her reputation must have proceeded her. If she was anything like her father, well, God help us all.

"Let's go around in the circle and say your name, age, and why you joined our troop. We'll start to my left." I gestured to Cora to begin.

Surprise crossed her eyes for a moment, then she smiled. "I'm Cora Davis. I'm fifteen years old. I joined this troop because I love being in nature, and I want to learn new skills."

Myrtle, who sat on her pillow with magnificent posture, spoke up next. "My name is Myrtle Mellus. I'm fifteen. When I first heard about the Girl Scouts, I knew that it was meant for me. While I waited for a troop to be formed in our city, I learned all I could on my own about scouting and the outdoors. I know that being a scout will make me a better person."

I paused, wondering how to process that last sentence. "Thank you for sharing, Myrtle, and thank you for hanging up the brochure in the hotel's restaurant. Had I not seen that, I never would have known about this wonderful program."

She gave a quick nod.

"Next, we have Nellie," I said. "Tell us about yourself."

"I'm Nellie Mott," she said in a timid voice. "I'm sixteen years old. I joined this troop because I wanted to be with girls' my own age."

Sweet Nellie. "Glad you're here."

Etta combed her fingers through her wild red hair. "Me name's Etta O'Keefe. I be fifteen years. I thought to meself that this scout thing sounded mighty fun. Then, when ya said we'd be gettin' spiffy uniforms, that sealed it right there, so it did."

Etta's candor made me smile. She definitely didn't lack personality. "Thank you, Etta." My gaze moved onto my daughter.

"My name's Alice. I'm sixteen. You probably know that Captain Flynn is my mom. We moved here from New York City over a week ago. Leaving everything behind has been pretty hard." There was a faint catch in her voice as she made the admission. She rubbed a hand over her skirt flattening a crease. "Since we're new and we live here," she gave a flip of her wrist, "it's not easy meeting people. This troop gives me a chance to do that and learn new skills."

Her vulnerable honesty touched my heart. I was proud of her. Before I could acknowledge her bravery, Geraldine piped up.

"I'm Geraldine Lockwood. I'm fourteen years of age. I've joined the Girl Scouts because my father feels it will be good for me."

There it was. I doubted that Geraldine even wanted to be here. "Okay. Thank you all for sharing. As you know, my name is June Flynn. I chose to start a troop in Saugerties as a way to get connected and to grow along with each of you. Today, you will be receiving your very own copy of the Girl Scouts Handbook." I grabbed a box off the kitchen table. "Thelma Parker has generously provided one for each of you to keep." One-by-one, I handed them out. As I placed a book in Nellie's hands, I said, "I apologize that we don't have a copy in braille."

"Don't worry, Captain Flynn. My mother will read it to me."

I patted her shoulder. "This manual contains the various skills that we will learn in this club. With each skill that you master, you will receive a badge. We'll be covering skills like path-finding, sewing, pioneering, and the list goes on! Goodness, isn't this exciting?"

The girls echoed their agreement. Everyone except for Geraldine.

"As I said before, we must begin with the Tenderfoot Test. It encompasses a foundation for a scout. Upon passing the test, you will each get a Tenderfoot Pin, which is a gold medal."

Geraldine perked up at the mention of gold.

I flipped to the back of the handbook. "In here, you will find several other pictures of badges that you can earn."

The girls leaned in with curiosity.

"This evening, we will begin by warming up our bodies with some light physical fitness. The motto of the Girl Scouts is *BE PREPARED*. If we are to be prepared for anything, we need to be in a good state of health. Which is why we need to exercise our muscles."

Myrtle lifted her hand.

"Yes, Myrtle?"

"I greatly enjoy fitness, Captain Flynn. I bicycle everyday."

I wasn't surprised. "Well done, Myrtle. Before engaging in physical activity, it is important to loosen up. This is called stretching." I proceeded to demonstrate a series of warm-ups, describing each move aloud for Nellie. The girls followed my example, bending and stretching their arms and legs. I noticed that Geraldine was decidedly stiff.

Next, I showed them how to do sit-ups and push-ups. It wasn't an all-star performance, but they understood the general concept. I divided the girls into pairs to practice these techniques—Myrtle and Nellie, Alice and Cora, and Etta with Geraldine.

Etta laid on her back. "Geraldine, hold me shoes."

"But they're dirty." Geraldine's face scrunched up in disgust.

Etta looked at the faded mud on the sides of her boots. "Are ya scared of a bit of dust? Come on now or Captain Flynn will tell yer daddy that ya aren't participatin'."

Sighing, Geraldine held onto Etta's shoes, while she practiced her sit-ups.

Myrtle propped a hand behind Nellie's back. "You will bend forward as if your chin is reaching for your knees. Yes, like that. Good job, Nellie."

I watched Alice attempting push-ups and tried not to laugh. "With push-ups, the goal is to keep your posterior level with your back like you're balancing a board."

"Cora, is my backside in the air?" whispered Alice.

"A little," replied Cora.

"How's this?" Alice lowered her rear.

"Better."

Etta heaved a sigh. "Geraldine, it be called a sit-up. Yer back has to leave the ground."

"It won't budge." She groaned. "This is too hard."

Etta rolled her eyes. "For cripes' sake, squeeze yer stomach and rock up."

Geraldine's whole face reddened with effort.

"That's it. Just a wee bit more."

"Ughhhh…" Geraldine peeled her shoulders off the floor, and her back came up half an inch. At that moment, a loud blast burst forth from her undercarriage. Her eyes widened with horror.

All the girls stopped moving.

"What was that?" asked Nellie.

Geraldine's face brightened to a hue of scarlet. She stared at Etta, knowing she could expose her right then and there.

"Ducks," said Etta. She flicked her hand toward the ceiling. "Must be flyin' overhead."

I buttoned my lips, nodding.

"Ducks are lovely creatures, aren't they?" said Nellie in her small voice. "With their cheerful squawks."

The girls murmured agreement as they returned to their practice.

"How about we work on some push-ups instead?" asked Etta.

"Okay." A soft smile crept to Geraldine's mouth. In a hushed voice, she said, "Thanks."

Etta winked. "Ducks like to fly over me house too. Pesky little rascals."

I rotated around, watching each pair assist one another. Alice talked to Cora as she held her shoes. Myrtle guided Nellie through a push-up. Etta said something in Geraldine's ear and made her giggle. The scene before me was beautiful.

We closed down our meeting with practice on tying the reef, bowline, and clove-hitch knots as found in the handbook. Try as I might, I struggled to get my knots to look like the pictures. Luckily for us all, Myrtle knew how.

"Next weekend, Thelma Parker will be taking our troop on a camping adventure."

The girls gave a collective gasp—the tune of which sounded joyful—except for one.

"Thelma says that a scout needs to know and understand the great outdoors. Therefore, we will spend one night at a campsite. We will leave Saturday morning and return Sunday. Your parents will need to give me approval for you to attend this trip. Please wear wool knickers and a wool middy. Skirts will not be suitable clothing for the outdoors. On your feet, please wear wool socks and leather boots." I applauded myself for sounding so skilled. As I gave them a brief packing list, I heard a tap on the door. Hopping off my pillow, I added, "Don't forget to ask your parents and start reading your handbooks."

Behind the door stood Clyde. "It's eight."

I pulled out my pocket watch. "It's 7:58 to be exact. Next Tuesday, the meeting will begin directly at 6:00 PM. I'm sure that *you'd* hate for Geraldine to be excused from the group due to tardiness."

As Clyde hurried his daughter out the door, I wondered how long this charade would last. What was he after?

Before Myrtle left, she saluted me. "Thank you for a most educational night, Captain Flynn." Once again, she left on her bicycle.

When Sabina stepped inside, Cora rushed to her mother

with a bounce in her step. "I learned how to tie knots and do proper push-ups."

A laugh escaped Sabina's lips. "Sounds like a good time."

Cora nodded. "I'll show you when we get home."

As they moved to leave, Sabina caught my eye and smiled.

I smiled back.

With the troop gone, Alice and I sat down to eat sandwiches for dinner. "How do you think tonight went?"

"It was fun."

"Seemed like you were getting to know Cora a bit."

"We talked some." Alice took a bite of her sandwich. "She said my shirt had fine stitching and that her mother is a dressmaker."

"Yes, I actually asked Sabina to teach you girls how to sew. Then you can earn a badge for it."

"Where do we get the badges?"

"Thelma." I took a bite of my sandwich. "The badges get sewn on the sleeves of your uniform."

"When do we get our uniforms?"

"I'm not sure."

Alice took a drink of water. "Mom, can I ask you a question?"

"Of course."

"Tonight, when we heard that loud noise. Was that really a duck or did Geraldine break wind?"

My hand flew to my mouth, covering my grin. "Put it this way, if that had been a real duck, it sounded awfully sick."

Alice burst into laughter. "I knew it!"

With smiles on our faces, we finished our meal and prepared to go to bed. Luckily, the bats were gone now, thanks to Sal.

"Will you go to the outhouse with me?" I asked Alice. "It's creepy in the woods at night."

"You're telling me."

Side by side, we squeezed together in the outhouse. Neither of us wanted to be left in the dark. Outside, I heard faint hollering. "What's that?"

The yelling grew louder.

Exiting the outhouse, I shined the lamp around. "It's coming from the creek." I walked toward the sound.

Alice stayed close, clutching my arm. "Why are we going toward the yelling?"

I whacked away branches and brush, increasing my speed. "What if it's another victim being lured to the creek?"

"If it is, why are we intervening? We don't have a weapon."

The shouting grew clearer as we got closer to the creek's edge. It was men's voices. Over the creek, the moonlight glowed. Though we had to be more than a hundred feet away, I could make out the shadows of three human figures getting into a boat and pushing off from shore.

Alice breathed heavily next to me. "Who are those people?"

"I don't know. I can't make out their faces."

"Should we get the police?"

"We don't know if a crime has been committed."

"They're definitely trespassing. That's a crime."

"This isn't our land. It belongs to the owner of the main estate. He'd have to report trespassing, not us."

"Who is the owner?"

That was a good question. "The signature on the seller's documentation for our cabin wasn't even a full name. Just initials—I.L.J."

"I.L.J?" repeated Alice. "That's cryptic."

I nodded, thinking about those three letters. Something stirred in my stomach like I had seen those letters before. Then it hit me. "Irena Louise Jansen."

"What?"

"Those initials. Could it stand for Irena Louise Jansen?"

"Irena's last name was Krall."

"Her maiden name was Jansen."

"Why would the person who purchased the Whitaker house use Irena's old initials?"

"Maybe it's someone who is connected to her."

"If they're connected to her, why would they buy the old Whitaker house? I doubt any past relation or friend would want to own anything from Charles Whitaker, considering he might be the reason she's dead."

"I guess so, but who really knows? The story is 18 years old. It's hard to know what is true. But I have a hunch that the current owner knew Irena." I looked around the trees. "We should head back inside. This is giving me the creeps."

CHAPTER EIGHTEEN

Wednesday, April 30
7:30 AM

The newsroom buzzed with life. Every department was in full swing—reporters barked into the phones, editors haggled over words, composers collected documents, Frieda typed, and Sal circulated the room, giving orders.

I set down my handbag on the tabletop. "Good morning, Frieda."

She exhaled a heavy breath. "Where have you been?"

"It's 7:30 AM. I'm on time."

"Sal called everyone to come in early. We have breaking news."

I furrowed my brow. "I don't have a phone at my house. How would I have known?"

Frieda flicked her wrist in dismissal. "It's fine. You're here now." She handed me a stack of notes. "Type these."

It looked like James' handwriting. I read a few lines. It was about a recent golf tournament. Surely this wasn't the breaking news. "What's going on?"

She exhaled again. "Another abduction."

"What?" My mouth gaped. "Who?"

"Rhett Mills."

"Is he related to the Whitakers?"

"No one knows for sure. There isn't a clear connection."

This was the third abduction in three weeks.

Frieda paused from her typing. "You might not believe in Irena's ghost, but she is somehow connected to all of this."

"How do you know that?"

"The police found evidence on the bank of the creek. It was a framed picture of Irena."

A chill swept through my body. A framed picture. Could it be the one I had seen in the cellar? "Was it near Stony Point?"

"Yes."

My heart pounded in my chest like a train speeding up. Last night, Alice and I heard yelling near the creek. We saw shadows getting in a boat and rowing away. We had witnessed Rhett's abduction. I trembled.

"The police found a trail of boot prints that led from the woods onto the bank," said Frieda. "Near the water, a picture had been left along with Rhett's boots. He must have entered the creek barefoot. Patrol has searched the creek, no body has been found."

"Why would Irena's picture and Rhett's boots be left on the bank?"

"To let everyone know who lured him there."

I shook my head. Someone was working very hard to pin this on Irena. The police thought Rhett had entered the water alone, but I had seen three figures on the creek's edge. Sure, it had been a distance, but I knew what I saw. If the police only found one set of prints, someone must have returned to wash away the others. The thought of someone lurking that close to my house sent tremors up my spine. How were Alice and I safe?

Sal clapped his hands. "Hurry up, team. I want this edition out by 11!"

Each department rose up to meet the task and by 10:40, circulation had the papers bundled and out the door. When today's issue hit the stands bearing the main headline, *Another*

Tragedy Befalls The Town of Saugerties, the copies flew off the shelves. Every copy was sold by 12:30 pm. An all-time record for The Saugerties Daily Journal.

To celebrate, Sal brought in lunch for the whole team. Team members patted Clyde on the back, congratulating him on another great story.

I nibbled on my sandwich, troubled by the celebratory mood in the room. Yes, the booming sales were a victory for our paper. I grasped that. But was it okay to celebrate a triumph that came at the expense of a man's life? Did civility take a backseat to sales? Was this the genuine nature of this company?

What troubled me more was *who* continued to uncover these stories. Every time, it had been Clyde Lockwood. No one else. How did Clyde manage to learn of each abduction before word reached the other newspapers? Was he that good of a reporter or did he have an inside source?

Something told me it was the latter.

If he did have an inside partner, who could it be? I looked around the newsroom. Each abduction had benefited our paper. Each abduction had increased our readership, giving us an edge against our biggest competitor—The Telegraph. This is what Sal wanted. This is what he had been telling me earlier. His grandfather had a vision. Sal and his father were carrying it out.

My mind sparked with a thought. Sal's father. Carmine. Sal told me that his father was away on business. Like a typewriter in my head, my thoughts keyed in the words—*Or is he?* What if Carmine was the one abducting these men? What if all of these stories were a twisted scheme to drive up business? Heat surged through my veins. I felt dizzy.

A hand touched my shoulder. "June, are you okay?" asked Frieda.

"I…I…don't know."

"Hey Sal," Frieda called. "June's not looking so good!"

Faces turned in my direction.

Sal hastened to my side. "Is something wrong?"

I placed a hand to my throat. "I think I need to go home."

"Of course," he said. "I'll drive you."

"I can drive myself. It's not far."

"Please, June. If you're not feeling well, I should drive you."

"I'll be fine." Inhaling a breath, I plucked my handbag off the table, proceeding to the door.

He trailed after me. "I really think you oughta let me drive you."

I managed a tight smile. "Don't worry about me. I've survived for nearly a year without a man caring for me, I think I can handle a five-minute drive home."

His eyes widened at the bite in my words.

Closing my car door behind me, I drove away, leaving Sal in my wake. As I pulled up the gravel driveway, I stopped near the Whitaker house. Jogging over to the cellar doors, I yanked them open. With a deep breath, I descended the steps, then stopped in my tracks. The picture of Irena was gone.

I knew it. The one the police had found was the same one that Alice and I had discovered here. Whoever had placed Irena's picture at the creek had taken it from this cellar. Was it possible that Clyde, Carmine, or Sal had taken the portrait and planted it as another trick to sell their ghost story? If they were abducting these men—where were they keeping them?

Placing a plate with a sandwich before Alice, I sank into my chair. "Did you hear anything new at school today?" I emphasized the word new.

Her brow arched. "Did something happen?"

I looked down at the table. "Last night, there was another abduction. It was a man named Rhett Mills."

She gasped. "So last night…"

I gave a slow nod. "I think so."

"I told you we should have gone to the police."

"It was too dark. We couldn't see much."

Her eyes were big and round. "We saw three shadows that looked like men."

"Perhaps, but we don't know that for sure. We were too far away."

"We witnessed it, Mom. We witnessed that abduction."

I rubbed a hand over my neck. "It seems like it."

"What do we do? Do we tell the police?"

"I'm not sure they'd believe us. We don't exactly have hard evidence."

A knock on the front door interrupted us.

"I'll see who that is." Getting up from the kitchen table, I opened the door to find Myrtle Mellus holding a container.

"Hello, Captain Flynn. I heard that you left work early today due to sickness. I made you chicken noodle soup." She extended the container.

"Oh, thank you." I took it from her, wondering who had spread the gossip on me. I had my money on Frieda. "That's thoughtful of you."

"Hope you feel better soon." She spun around, heading for her bicycle.

"Myrtle, wait a minute, dear."

She came back to me. "Yes, Captain?"

"When you say you made this soup yourself, does that mean your mother helped you or did you do it *all* by yourself?"

"I did it by myself because my mother is gone. I do the cooking for my father and me." She showed no emotion in this statement.

"Your mother is gone?" I inclined my head. "Does that mean she passed away?"

"No. She left." The words dropped from her mouth deadpan.

I could hardly believe my ears. "Your mother left you and your father?"

She nodded.

"How long ago?"

"Ten years."

That meant Myrtle would have been five when her mother left. How could a mother leave her five-year-old daughter? Trying to remain positive, I said, "I bet that means you and your father are very close."

She tipped her head to the side, considering this. "I love him because he is my father. I think he feels the same."

Her words pricked my heart. Poor Myrtle. She's had no choice but to grow up and be tough. She'd been fending for herself for the last ten years without the nurture of a mother, and likely a father too.

"It will be getting dark soon," said Myrtle. "I'd better go. Hope you like the soup." With a salute, she peddled away on her bike.

I watched her go, wishing I had hugged her.

CHAPTER NINETEEN

Thursday, May 1
6:50 AM

An incessant tapping on my shoulder pulled me out of my sleep.

"Mom, it's 6:50 AM. I'm supposed to be at school in 25 minutes. Unless, you want me to skip. I'm okay with that." Alice's face lit up.

I pried my head off the kitchen table, where I'd fallen asleep reading. "What? How's that possible?"

She dangled my watch in front of my face. "Aren't you supposed to work today?"

I pushed myself into a seated position. "I stayed up too late reading *The Hound of Baskervilles.*"

"Isn't that a Sherlock Holmes mystery?"

"Yes, I couldn't put it down. I finished the book at two this morning. Then my mind did circles for hours until I fell asleep."

She sat down opposite of me and patted my head. "Sounds like we should stay home. It's a great day to relax."

"No. I have to go to work." I ambled into the bedroom, opening a dresser drawer. "I need to talk to Salvatore Saviano. He has some real explaining to do."

Her eyebrows rose. "I'd like to be there for that."

I threaded my arms into a blue blouse. "You're going to school."

At 7:30 AM, I breezed into Sal's office. Closing the door behind me, I slapped the book on his desk.

He jolted in surprise. "You feeling better, June?"

"Not really. I hardly slept a wink last night, but I did manage to read this entire novel." I jabbed a finger at the book. "Of course, you know this book well, don't you? You've checked it out seven times!"

He studied my face. "It's a masterful work of mystery."

"Indeed it is. As the story goes—Dr. James Mortimer asks Sherlock Holmes to help him solve a crime pertaining to his friend, Sir Charles Baskerville, who was found dead in the park surrounding his manor. The death was labeled as a heart attack, but according to Mortimer, Sir Charles's face held an expression of terror, and not far from his body were footprints of a gigantic hound." I placed my fingertips on his desk. "Here's where the story gets interesting. According to an old legend, a curse runs in the Baskerville family. The curse started when Sir Hugo Baskerville abducted and murdered a woman in the mires of Dartmoor, only to be killed in turn by a huge ghostly hound." I paused. "Did you catch that? We now have a legend and a ghost."

He nodded. "I caught it, yes."

Striking a finger in the air, I continued on. "Supposedly, the same creature continued to haunt the place, causing the deaths of many Baskerville heirs. Mortimer fears that Sir Henry Baskerville, the next kin in line, is also in danger. Sherlock goes on to discover that the hound is in fact real and belongs to the neighbor, Mr. Stapleton. Stapleton exploits the old legend as a cover for his plot. He killed Sir Charles, and he plans to kill Sir Henry because he is the next heir to the Baskerville estate!" I propped a proud hand on my hip, looking intently at his face.

Sal folded his hands on his desk. His demeanor remained calm, completely unfazed. "Well done. A concise recap."

Frustration at his cavalier response spurred me onward. "I find it interesting that this legend is about a ghostly hound targeting only the family line of Baskervilles. It sounds awfully parallel to the legend in Saugerties. Irena's ghost is targeting the family line of the Whitakers. Coincidence?" I leaned closer, narrowing my eyes. "I think not."

He blinked several times. "We don't know if Rhett is connected to the Whitaker family line."

"I am certain that he is."

His forehead creased. He looked down at his hands, shaking his head. When he looked up, his eyes were wide with amazement. "This is incredible." He stood up, walking around his desk. "Incredible." He scooped the book off his desk, turning it in his hands. "I've read this book seven times, and it never dawned on me. How did I miss that? I can't believe I missed this! You're absolutely right. The legend. The ghost. The family line. It's all there." He paced back and forth in his office, mumbling to himself as he flipped through several pages.

I watched him, trying to figure out what was happening.

He halted. "You read this whole book in one night?"

"A day and night."

"Incredible." He shook his head. "June, you're such a bright gal. Glad my father hired you. I can't believe how quickly you made all those connections."

Aha! Hear we go. "So, you admit it?"

"Admit what?"

"Admit that you're behind this whole thing. You're exploiting Irena's story by abducting the Whitaker relatives in order to sell newspapers!"

His expression morphed from amazement to complete and utter shock. "What?"

"Admit it." I crossed my arms. "You're behind it. You must be."

His shoulders drooped as he sank on the edge of his desk.

"You think I'm abducting these men?"

"It may not be you specifically. It could be Clyde for all I know, but yes, you're behind the orders to take these men. Goodness, please tell me they are all okay?"

His face blanched with a look of supreme hurt.

I shifted in my heels. Sweet merciful heavens, I was right, wasn't I? He had to be behind this. Didn't he?

"You honestly think that I'm having these men captured in order to sell newspapers?"

I tried not to allow the pain on his face weaken my resolve. "It stands to reason." I gestured to the book sitting beside him. "You had the perfect plot to follow. You yourself said that this company means everything to you. That you would do anything for this business, just like your grandfather. You also alluded to the fact that you don't like Henry Brickmore or Stuart Ellsworth. So, why wouldn't you do this?"

His expression grew serious. "Because I'm not a monster. I love this company, yes, but never at the expense of a human life."

"Well you certainly threw a celebration at the expense of Rhett Mills' misfortune, didn't you? His abduction sold all our copies, and you threw a party. How is that not exploiting the life of a man for your benefit?"

He looked down at his shoes in silence.

Tension hung between us for wordless seconds.

"I see what you mean." His five words pierced the stillness.

My ears perked up at this acknowledgement.

He released a slow exhale, then met my gaze. "I did celebrate at Rhett's expense. That was wrong. I shouldn't have done that. This business ain't easy, June. I wanna make my grandfather and my father proud. I wanna make a name for us. But I'd never do it at the cost of another person's life. I don't know who is behind these abductions, but it ain't me." He laid a hand over his heart. "I promise you."

Darn it. He seemed genuine. But things weren't adding up.

"If you aren't connected to this, then how does Clyde get the leads before anyone else?"

Sal sighed, looking uncomfortable. "Clyde's been getting anonymous tips. It started when a letter showed up in his mailbox. It was a single sheet of paper in a plain envelope. The paper had cut-out letters spelling Henry Brickmore. He didn't know what that meant, until he looked into it and discovered that Henry was missing. Then, he found another note the morning after Stuart Ellsworth vanished."

"Have you shown these notes to the police?"

"Absolutely, but without a way to know who delivered them, they aren't helpful. They always come after the abduction." Sal lifted a finger. "That's why Clyde and I decided after Stuart's disappearance to take turns staking out Esopus Creek in the evenings. Yesterday was my shift. I saw two men with scarves covering their faces, dragging Rhett Mills to a boat docked on the creek's edge. Rhett's mouth and hands were bound. I jumped out of the trees and ran toward them yelling for them to stop. The men threw Rhett into the boat. I tried to save him. Even got in a punch." He looked proud of this fact. "But a stocky fella socked me in the stomach. As the boat paddled away, I saw a light coming through the trees. I hid because I didn't know if it was the police, and I didn't want to be linked to the abduction."

Last night replayed in my head. "It was my lamp that you saw last night."

His eyebrows rose. "You came out to the creek?"

"Alice and I."

He gawked at me, dumbfounded. "Why would you do that? That's madness. Why would you go toward potential danger?"

"In order to protect my daughter."

He rubbed a hand against his forehead. "That don't make any sense. If you wanna be safe, you avoid harm. You don't seek it out."

"I live there. Stony Point isn't far from my outhouse. How

safe am I? I have to find the abductor so they can be put behind bars. Then, my daughter and I can rest at ease."

He expelled a heavy sigh. "While you make a valid point, I don't like you being near that kind of danger. I'd hate to see anything happen to you or Alice."

"I'm not sure what else to do. It's my house."

He stroked a hand through his hair, mumbling, "I wish it wasn't."

"We'll be okay since we're not Whitakers." I said it like it was fact, but inside my stomach twisted. "That night, did you see the framed picture of Irena on the shore?"

"No, did you?"

I shook my head.

"That means someone must've returned later with the picture."

"Why would someone go back to plant it?"

Sal tapped his hand on the book. "Remember how the Baskerville portrait contained a clue? Sherlock noticed that Stapleton bore a resemblance to Sir Hugo. This led him to realize that Stapleton was a potential heir to the Baskerville fortune and that he was concealing his identity in order to throw suspicion off himself."

"You're right! Do you think the portrait of Irena looks like someone we know?"

"I've looked at the photo several times. Gives me the willies." He shuddered. "Not sure who it would resemble."

"I think the abductor either wants to be caught or wants to flaunt his genius. Otherwise, he wouldn't send Clyde clues and place the picture at the crime scene."

"Unless, there is a third reason."

I tipped my head. "What would that be?"

Sal shrugged. "I have no idea. At any rate, I believe we're missing something."

I considered this. What was I missing? Then the thought came…who was missing? Carmine. Sal's father was nowhere to be seen. Maybe Sal was innocent. Maybe he didn't have any knowledge of these abductions. But Carmine might. He could be the one sending Clyde the clues. "Sal, where is your father?"

His eyebrows jumped at the mention of Carmine.

"You said he's away on business. Do *you* know what kind of business he's up to?"

For the first time in the conversation, his expression grew angry. "What're you trying to say, June?"

I swallowed. I was entering deep water. I knew it, but I couldn't stop now. "I just wondered if you knew."

Picking himself off of the front of his desk, he stepped closer to me. We stood parallel like two soldiers in a standoff. "All right. You caught me. My father is not away on business." The muscle in his jaw twitched. "He's at Memorial Hospital in Manhattan. He's been diagnosed with cancer. He's undergoing experimental treatments."

I blinked in rapid succession. Cancer? The word hit me hard. I stared at him, speechless.

"Now you got nothing to say?" He shook his head. Walking behind his desk, he sank into the chair and picked up a pack of cigarettes. He lit one between his lips, dragging in a breath. The dashing façade of Sal slipped away. In its place was a worn and tired man. "He didn't want anyone to know because it might show weakness in the company."

My tenacious excitement faded into embarrassment. I shrank into the chair facing him. I thought back to my interview with Carmine over a month ago. I recalled the purple circles under his eyes and the strain in his voice. At the time, it didn't strike me as anything major, probably a lack of rest. But cancer? With what I knew of this disease, it usually meant a death sentence. "Do the doctors believe he will recover?"

"Hard to say." His brow pinched with emotion. "I wish I could be there with him, but he insisted that I run the paper. Since he's a research patient, he has a room at the hospital. I'll give you the address and room number if you wanna check it out." He uncapped a pen and scrawled down the letters and numbers on a notepad." Ripping the page off the pad, he extended it to me. "Look into it. Then, you'll know I'm not lying."

As I stared at his handwriting, guilt and frustration clawed at my nerves. How did I get this all wrong? It seemed so clear. So straightforward. "Sal, I…" my throat tightened.

He blew out a stream of smoke. "Yeah?"

"I'm sorry. I was certain, what with the novel and that conversation I overheard, but I see now that I was wrong."

"What conversation?"

"You were in the basement with Clyde."

He propped his elbows on his desk. "You been spying on me?"

I should have left that part out. "It was a mere happenstance. I went to the powder room and heard voices coming from below. I recognized them as yours and Clyde's. The tone in which you were conversing led me to venture a bit closer. That's when I heard you say to Clyde—" I lifted my pointer finger for emphasis—"'Are you certain no one saw you there?' To which Clyde replied, 'Positive. I was careful.'" I arched an eyebrow.

"I don't think typing accurately suits your skill set, June Flynn." He inhaled another drag. "Clyde and his wife went to the Whitaker house on Sunday to search for clues about Irena—like old files or forms. I was against him taking Mrs. Lockwood, but he said that she could find a needle in a haystack, so I agreed to it. They entered the house through a cellar. When they entered, they saw a framed picture of Irena. It terrified Mrs. Lockwood, and she screamed. Afraid the neighbors had heard the scream and would alert the police, they made a quick dash through the house. In the study, they found a ledger and a cluster of letters, all addressed to Irena from her mother, Mrs. Jansen. That was all they found."

As he told me this last shred of information, guilt stirred my stomach. Sal was innocent. The scream that Alice and I heard on Sunday was Mrs. Lockwood. "Did the letters contain any information that could be helpful?"

"Nothing much. Mrs. Jansen told her details of the farm and asked her to return."

"I see." I stared at my shoes. A mixture of nervousness and shame caused my palms to sweat. I had gotten it wrong. My actions were not only insubordinate, they were cruel. Sal had every reason to fire me. "I am terribly sorry."

There was a long pause.

I waited for him to tell me to collect my belongings and leave.

"I accept your apology."

My chin rose with surprise. "You do?"

He tapped his cigarette in the ashtray. "I know you mean well. You wanna find the truth. I respect that. You have the makings of a reporter. 'Course I wish I wasn't on the receiving end of your scrutiny, but I see how you connected the dots."

"Does that mean you won't fire me?"

"I should," a small grin curved his mouth, "but no, I think I'll keep you around."

Relief washed over me. I thanked him and hurried out of his office before he changed his mind.

CHAPTER TWENTY

Friday, May 2
4:00 PM

It had been five days since Alice and I moved into the old Krall house. While we no longer had rats, bats, or a roof that leaked, the house still creaked and groaned every time the wind blew. Without indoor plumbing, we had to hike to the outhouse whenever nature called and haul in a bucket of water to take a cold sponge bath. Since we didn't know how to build a fire in the stove, our survival had been built upon the consumption of sandwiches. Without a pantry or cabinet, we stored our food staples in a box on the kitchen table. Now that the box was empty, it was time to replenish our supply.

Entering the Grand Union Market Place, I grabbed a shopping basket. Alice spotted a rack of magazines, and I knew instantly this would be a solo mission.

"Do you mind if I have a quick look?" she asked.

"Go ahead."

She skipped away as I collected a bag of apples and oranges, dropping them into my basket.

Other women glanced in my direction as they placed items into their baskets. When I nodded to them, they turned their faces. Ever since I'd started the troop, the townspeople had gone from whispering to snubbing. In the small space of the store, I felt their rejection acutely.

In the middle of the canned goods aisle, I spotted Geraldine and her mother. Word had spread within days of her enrolling into our troop. It didn't matter that her father had forced her to join; her school friends wouldn't abide by it. Finding herself on the outskirts, Geraldine resorted to eating lunch with Alice and George. While I found Geraldine's predicament unfair, I knew that Alice would be a better friend than any of those fickle schoolgirls. "Geraldine!" I waved as I approached.

Mrs. Lockwood pretended not to see me as she bent at the waist, perusing a lineup of jellies.

"Hello, Captain Flynn," said Geraldine.

"Hello, dear." I collected a jar of strawberry jam. "Hello, Mrs. Lockwood."

She plucked a marmalade off the shelf, placing it in her basket. "Afternoon." Her words came out bland.

I remained upbeat. "Did Geraldine tell you about our camping trip for next weekend?"

"She did."

"Will she be able to join us?"

"We haven't decided yet. She's only fourteen. I'm not sure that I'm comfortable with her staying overnight outdoors without proper supervision."

"The girls won't be alone. I'll be there and so will Thelma Parker."

She didn't blink. "I know that."

Three words. How could three small words cut so deep? From behind me a female voice called out. "Florence Lockwood?" I turned to find Beulah approaching.

"Florence, did I hear correctly that your daughter has joined this woman's troop?" Beulah gestured to me with a dull flip of her wrist.

Mrs. Lockwood's face twitched. She was uncomfortable being caught in the can aisle with me. Cupping Geraldine's elbow, she ushered her past Beulah without a word.

Beulah gave me a weary eye before moving along.

My shoulders dipped, and I sighed. I told myself that I didn't care what the other women thought of me. I told myself that kindness would conquer all. When those words didn't suffice—I told myself that those ladies were homely.

Sneaky tears surfaced in my eyes. My heart hurt. I came to Saugerties broken with grief. And now, my broken heart was being trampled by hypocritical high heels.

"Hello, June."

I wiped a quick hand under my eyes and turned around. "Sabina! Hello." I pasted on a smile.

She studied me. "Are you all right?"

The concern on her face made my emotions rise up. In a hushed voice, I said. "They don't like me here."

She tipped her head to the side. "Beulah and Florence are only two people. They don't speak for everyone."

"I think the majority supports their opinion."

"Then maybe you don't need their opinion." She said in a soft voice. "What you're doing matters."

My lower lip quivered. "You think so?"

She nodded. "Cora came home from your first meeting with a smile that wouldn't quit. You'd have thought she'd been given a puppy." She shook her head and chuckled.

"Cora is a quick study. She's going to do well in the troop."

"Thank you." Pride shone in her eyes. "Cora's got a real gift for learnin'. Always has."

"I can tell."

Sabina looked down at her basket. "Don't lose heart, June. This town needs you. Even if they don't know it yet."

Just like that, the tears came streaming. "Thank you. I needed to hear that."

Her eyebrows lifted at my onslaught of emotion. She reached out an unsure hand to pat my arm. "There now."

I wiped at my face, but the tears continued to fall. "Sabina, I'd really like us to be friends. Will you be my friend?"

Her eyebrows shot higher. "You wanna be friends? With me?"

I nodded. "I'd really like that."

She mumbled under her breath. "This woman must be desperate." Then she smiled. "All right, June. We can be friends."

—

A car rumbled up to our house. I peeked out the window to see Elex's pickup. Etta sat in the front seat with him. They exited the car and hefted a cabinet out of the truck's bed.

I hurried outside with Alice on my tail. "Hello."

They set the cabinet on the grass.

"Hi-ya," beamed Etta. "We come bearin' a belated house-warmin' gift."

"Oh my goodness." My hands went to my mouth as I looked at the beautiful wooden cabinet. "This is too much."

Elex waved his hand in dismissal. "I done get a store discount. It be nothin'. Why don't we get it inside fer ya."

Helping him with one end of the cabinet, we hefted it into the kitchen. Amazing how an extra amenity helped my house feel more like a home.

"Mom, Etta brought her rope," said Alice. "Can they stay awhile so we can practice tying our knots?"

"It's fine with me, if Elex doesn't mind."

He shrugged. "We don't be in a rush as it were."

"Very well, go ahead ladies."

The girls settled on the floor pillows.

"Would you care for a Coca-Cola?" I asked him.

"That'd be grand." He took the outstretched bootle, popped off the top, and took a swig. "Nice night. How'd ya like to take a sit outside?"

"All right." We carted the kitchen chairs outside the door. Thanks to Lloyd (and Elex), the grass around the house was fairly short. Sitting down, I shifted my knees toward him. "Do you have any family in town other than Etta and her mother?"

"Not anymore. Me parents died a year ago due to the influenza."

"I'm sorry to hear that."

"Terrible loss it was. Do ya have any family back in Manhattan?"

"My parents both passed away years ago. I have an aunt, but we're not close. My husband's relatives are all in Ireland."

"Etta and I still have relatives back in the home country. What was yer husband's name?"

"Niall Flynn."

He looked up at the sky, turning the name over in his head. "I knew a couple of Flynns. Wished I could have met yer Niall. Sure he was a good man."

I inhaled a soft breath. "He was."

"Have ya been," he paused, "nervous livin' here by yerselves?"

"Honestly, I don't sleep well."

"I wondered about that." He sighed. "The paper printed that it might be the ghost of Irena. Ya think there be any truth to it?"

I scoffed. "Not a bit. It's all a stunt. Someone's trying to use Irena's story as a scapegoat."

"How can ya be sure?"

I searched his face, feeling that I could trust him. "Because I witnessed the last abduction."

His eyebrows shot up. "Janey Mac! Are ya certain?"

"I heard yelling Tuesday night. I went to the creek with my lamp and saw three figures get into a boat."

"Fer the love of Mary, why didn't ya stay in yer house? Ya could've been hurt."

"They didn't see me."

"Yer lucky fer that." He heaved an exhale and set his bottle on the ground. "From now on, stay in yer house. Stay where it's safe."

"How am I safe when there's a crazy person abducting people in my backyard?"

He shifted closer to me. "If ya don't go lookin' fer trouble, ya won't find it."

"So, I should ignore what I hear?"

"That be the long and short of it."

I huffed. "I refuse to do that. There is more to this story, and I'm getting to the bottom of it."

"Do ya hear yerself?" His voice rose an octave. "Do ya hear the actual words comin' from yer mouth? How are ya gonna solve this case? Yer not a police officer. Yer not a detective. No good will come of it. Ya need to stop. Please, June. I don't want to see anythin' happen to ya. Yer a special lass and…" he looked down.

I saw his Adams' apple bob with the force of a swallow. When he lifted his face, there was an intensity I hadn't seen in his hazel eyes before.

"It don't be me place to tell ya what to do. But it do be hard fer me to stand by, knowin' ya are puttin' yerself in harm's way."

"I know that since I'm Etta's captain, you probably feel—"

"It don't be that." He picked up my hand.

The gesture was surprising, but I didn't pull back.

"I care about ya. Ever since ya showed up that day in the hardware store, I can't stop thinkin' about ya."

Warmth filtered through my body.

He shifted to the edge of his chair, leaned forward, and pressed his lips against mine. When I didn't pull away, he pushed deeper into the kiss. I curved into him as he wound an arm around my waist.

It felt good. I wanted to stay here and kiss him. I wanted to fall into this moment, but I couldn't escape the nagging guilt that Niall might be upset. It was too soon. I wasn't allowed to move on. I didn't deserve this. I pulled away and stood up. "I–I'd better see how the girls are doing."

CHAPTER TWENTY-ONE

Monday, May 5
7:20 AM

Dropping Alice off at school, I popped in at the local diner for a cup of coffee. I desperately needed it this morning.

The whole weekend, I had pondered…the kiss. It had left me flustered. Alice had noticed my faraway looks into the great unknown and asked if anything was wrong. I brushed off her concern, but internally I couldn't sweep it aside. Elex had feelings for me, and I couldn't deny my own attraction.

At first, I thought I was drawn to him because it felt familiar. He was Irish like Niall. And he had dark hair and kind eyes. But it was the differences that held my attention. Niall had always avoided conflict, but Elex wasn't afraid to disagree. Niall had restrained his emotions, while Elex showed his feelings. Niall couldn't fix anything, but Elex was handy. Niall had moved slowly with his affections, but Elex was bold.

I'd only known him for a few weeks, and he'd kissed me! Did part of me like the kiss? Yes. Did his lips feel smooth? Yes. Did part of me regret not kissing him longer? Yes.

But that didn't make it okay. It hadn't even been a year since Niall's passing. And here I was kissing another man. I should be ashamed of myself. I *was* ashamed of myself. Which was why I would never enter Martin's Hardware again.

Coffee in hand, I walked into the newsroom. People sat with heads bowed talking in quiet voices. Reporters on the telephones didn't speak with the usual bluster and enthusiasm. Even the tone of the typewriter's keys sounded sluggish and heavy. Something had happened. Something bad.

Frieda's shoulders hunched as she plunked on the keys.

"Good morning," I said.

She didn't look up. "Morning."

"The newsroom is awfully quiet this morning. Is something wrong?"

Her fingers paused. "A body was found."

I sank into my chair. "Who?"

Frieda lifted her chin, meeting my gaze. Her eyes were red like she had been crying. "It was Henry Brickmore. A fisherman discovered him at 5:00 AM this morning. It was on the bank of Esopus Creek near the end of Partition Street."

I placed a hand to my mouth. "That poor man."

"I never liked Henry much. I hate to admit that now, but I didn't. Thing is," her lower lip trembled, "no one deserves to die like that. It's not right."

"What do you mean?"

"The police found his body with bruises, cuts, and puncture wounds. The theory is that Henry was tortured and then drowned."

I gasped.

Tears surfaced in Frieda's eyes. She grabbed a handkerchief from her purse. "It's horrible. I can't believe this is happening in our town."

I rubbed a hand on her back.

"You were right about Irena, after all. She's not to blame." She rubbed below her eyes. "Whoever is taking these men is very much alive."

Chills rolled through my body. Irena wasn't to blame. I knew that all along. But whoever was behind these vanishings had crossed the line into new territory. Henry Brickmore was no longer missing. He had been found—dead. What did this mean for the other two men? What did this mean for anyone else connected to the Whitakers? What did this mean for Alice and myself, living alone, so close to the creek?

I laid my palms on the table, struggling to keep my breath even. Here's what I knew—Alice and I weren't Whitakers, and we weren't men. While that gave me a sliver of reassurance, I wouldn't rest easy, knowing that these attacks were transpiring behind my house.

What would Sherlock Holmes do if he were in my place?

An angry confidence roiled in the pit of my stomach. He'd continue the hunt.

CHAPTER TWENTY-TWO

Tuesday, May 6
5:45 PM

Tonight was our second troop meeting, and Sabina was going to teach us the art of sewing. As Sabina set out her sewing supplies on the kitchen table, I heard more voices outside the front door. Etta was beside a light-haired woman, trying to guide her back into her car. "Ya don't have to come in. Just remind Uncle Elex to get me. Ya won't forget, will ya?"

"Etta?" I walked outside. "Is this your mother?"

She looked down at her shoes. "That she be."

The woman rotated to me. "Ahh, ya must be the lass Etta's been bangin' on about. Captain Tin?"

Her words were slurred, and she seemed unsteady. I noted the embarrassment on Etta's face. "Captain Flynn, actually. But you can call me June." I extended my hand.

She gave it a weak shake. "Me name's Imogen."

"Uncle Elex be workin' late, so Ma drove me." Etta said in a low voice.

"I'm glad she did." I gave her a reassuring smile. "I've been wanting to meet your mother."

"Grand so, but we best get on, meetins' gonna start soon." Etta ushered her mother to the car and gave her mother a light kiss on the cheek. "Be careful."

As Imogen drove away, she nearly clipped the side of Clyde's car.

Clyde parked, leaping out of his car in a fury. "Did you see that?" He said to me, pointing in the roadster's direction.

"See what?" I feigned ignorance.

"That wild woman almost hit me!"

"She did?"

He huffed. "Imogen O'Keefe has no business being behind the wheel. She's a menace in this town!"

I glanced back at Etta. Her cheeks had flushed crimson. "Settle down, Clyde. No harm was done."

"Maybe not this time, but she's caused problems before. She's a drain on society."

"Enough," I snapped.

He pulled back at the anger in my voice.

I looked between Etta and Geraldine. "Ladies, please head into the house." They nodded, hustling toward the house.

Narrowing my eyes, I said, "This is my property. You talk like that again, and you won't be welcomed back here."

He squared his shoulders. "Then I might have to pull my daughter out of your troop."

"Do as you must."

His lips clenched in a tight line.

I knew he wanted to drag his daughter away, but he wouldn't. I'd found his weakness. Clyde was proud. Maintaining his superior image was important to him, though it wasn't the most important. Securing his next story held ultimate importance. He'd do anything to find a story, even if it meant taking grief from a woman who lived in a shack.

"I am still your superior," he sneered. "Remember that." He stormed back to his car.

Walking into the living room, I knew one thing for certain—Clyde was watching me. But I didn't care. Let him watch. Let them all watch.

We began our meeting with the salute and then I introduced

Sabina. "This is Cora's mother, Mrs. Davis. She is a professional dressmaker. She'll be teaching us how to sew. The Girl Scout slogan is 'Do a good turn daily.' This means that each day, we should look for ways to show kindness to others. Community service is a way to do a good turn. That is why we have decided to make a blanket for each returning soldier. Mrs. Davis has graciously donated pieces of fabric for us to use. Let's give her our best attention as she explains this project."

Sabina launched into a demonstration, showing how to thread a needle and the stitch we'd be doing for the blankets. Then, she handed out fabric squares, thread and needles to each girl. One-by-one, they threaded their needles and practiced sewing squares together. Sabina knelt beside Nellie, guiding her fingers stitch by stitch.

Nellie smiled. "This is fun."

"I think so too," said Sabina. "My mother taught me how to sew when I was four-years-old."

"Ouch!" cried Geraldine. She held her finger closer for inspection. A little blood bubbled up.

"My fingers had lots of pin pokes when I started," said Sabina. "Don't worry, you'll get the hang of it."

"Captain Flynn," said Geraldine, "Do you have a bandage for my finger?"

"Stick it in yer mouth," said Etta. "Saliva be nature's cure."

Geraldine's nose scrunched in disgust. "I'm not sticking my finger in my mouth after I've been using Mrs. Davis' needles."

My mouth dropped open. The whole room fell silent.

"I always wash my hands," Sabina said quietly.

Cora glared at Geraldine. "My mother isn't dirty."

"I…I didn't mean that." Geraldine fidgeted with the fabric in her hands.

Cora tilted her head to the side. "Then what did you mean?"

Sabina placed a hand on her daughter's shoulder. "Let it go."

"We aren't going to let it go," I spoke up. "Here, we are

equals. We will treat each other with respect. There is a lot of judgment in our world. Judgment that gets passed down." I glanced at Geraldine. "We are all different. We look different, talk different, and think differently. But in this troop, our differences will be celebrated. I hope we can all learn from tonight and select our words with more care in the future. Now, let's get back to sewing."

As the girls returned to the project, silence permeated the room, leaving a somber tone. At the conclusion of our meeting, I reminded the troop that this Saturday was our camping trip. We would meet at my house at 9:00 AM. The scouts thanked Sabina for her lesson as they departed.

Before Geraldine left, she approached Sabina with a shy stance. "Mrs. Davis, I want to apologize for what I said earlier."

Sabina swallowed, then nodded. "I accept your apology."

Tonight, I hoped that my troop had learned more than sewing.

Mr. Mott opened the passenger door, as I led Nellie out to him. "Thank you again for having Nellie. It means so much to us."

"It's a pleasure. Good work tonight with your sewing, Nellie. How did you like it?"

"It's tricky," she admitted. "But I liked the challenge."

"It is tricky. I can only imagine how much harder it must be when you can't see the needle."

"My fingers got pricked a lot, but that doesn't hurt as bad as walking into a wall."

I saw a cheeky grin appear on her mouth. Was quiet little Nellie making a joke?

Mr. Mott laughed. "Walls and chairs."

"Chairs are the worst. My shins' bruises have bruises." A giggle escaped her lips.

It was a tiny magical sound.

I marveled at how they could make light of a hard and probably frustrating life. Walking into walls and chairs, this was

Nellie's normal. And yet, she laughed.

Mr. Mott helped his daughter into the car and closed the door. "Are you sure it'll be all right for her to attend the camping trip?"

"Thelma and I will take good care of her. Besides, I think Nellie is going to really enjoy it."

"I believe that she will. Thanks again." He tipped his hat.

When I returned to the living room, I found Sabina tucking her supplies back into her bag. "Thank you for teaching the girls tonight."

"I was happy to do it."

I handed her a spool of thread. "I'm sorry for what Geraldine said."

She held up her hand. "It's done."

"It still bothers me. It wasn't right."

She exhaled slowly. "The fact that you have opened up your home and this troop to Cora has spoken good things to our hearts. Being a Girl Scout is an opportunity she wouldn't normally get."

"She shouldn't be denied opportunities. That in itself isn't okay."

Sabina paused in her clean-up and looked at me. She opened her mouth like she was going to say something, but then she closed it and stuffed the last thread away. She offered me a weak smile. "We'll see you next Tuesday." With that, she and Cora left.

My heart felt heavy. It wasn't fair. The Davises should have the same rights as everyone else.

A throat cleared behind me.

I spun around.

Elex gave me a nod. "Hello, June. Mind if I speak with ya fer a moment?"

"Uh, yes okay."

"Perhaps we can step outside?"

"Of course." As I followed him out, my nervousness rose.

Did he want to talk about the kiss? Oh sweet heavens, please don't ask about the kiss.

"So, I do wonder…was it wrong of me to kiss ya the other night?"

Fiddlesticks. I swallowed past the forming knot in my throat. "Well, I…I just don't think I was ready for it."

"Right. Fine enough so."

The way his brown eyes searched mine made my stomach flip. Goodness, he was handsome. "See, I haven't kissed anyone since my husband." Elex sure had broad shoulders. "And it surprised me." I could see the outline of his muscles through the sleeves of his shirt.

His gaze flicked to my lips and back up. "I won't kiss ya again, if it's too soon."

My heart pounded quicker. I found myself lingering on his mouth. "I think…"

He waited, watching me.

"I think…" Mercy, who was I kidding? I stepped up, grabbed his face in my hands and kissed him. I couldn't stand it. I needed to feel his lips. I wanted to feel his arms around me.

With as much hunger, he wrapped an arm around my waist and pulled me against his chest. His other hand ran up my side and cupped the back of my neck.

It was probably wrong, but it felt good. I needed to be kissed. Deeply. And Elex, good heavens, he knew how to kiss.

But…but what if Alice came out? What if she saw us? I pulled back, our faces still only inches apart. I could feel his breath.

"June?" he whispered.

"Elex, I…" I stepped out of his arms.

His forehead creased.

"I think we should call it a night."

He reached for my hand.

I held it away. "It's late."

He looked hurt. "June, what kind of game are ya playin' here?"

I swallowed. "I shouldn't have kissed you."

"Then why did ya?"

"I don't know." I looked down.

"I think that be a load of shite. Why can't ya let yerself feel this?" He gestured between us. "Ya have feelings fer me. I know ya do."

"It's too soon."

"Fer who?"

I didn't answer.

"I think yer scared. Scared to let yerself love again. Scared of what Alice might think. But, livin' scared is no way to live."

My hands trembled at my sides. "You don't know what I feel."

"How could I? The moment we get close, ya pull away."

"I can't do this right now."

He shook his head. "Have it yer way." Collecting Etta, he left without another look in my direction.

CHAPTER TWENTY-THREE

Wednesday, May 7
9:00 AM

Sal stopped in front of my table. "Today I'm gonna follow up on the story of Rhett Mills. I have an interview with his sister, Dorothy Hollis. Since she is of the female persuasion, I thought it would be wise to bring another woman along to ensure her comfort."

Frieda's gaze flicked over to me while she typed.

I nodded. "I'd be honored to accompany you."

"Excellent." He clapped a hand on the tabletop. "She lives in East Kingston. It's about a thirty-minute drive. Bring a notepad and pen. We leave in fifteen minutes." He strode back into his office.

Frieda whistled. "It's not everyday a typist gets to join a reporter."

I inclined my head. "Is Sal considered a reporter?"

"Absolutely. When his father was present, Sal was our lead man, hunting down stories."

Sal hadn't mentioned this before.

"Quite a special thing to be chosen." Frieda smirked. "Especially since you've only been on staff for a couple of weeks."

I waved my hand in dismissal. "I'm sure he would have chosen you if Martha wasn't gone."

"Something tells me he still would have picked you."

Fifteen minutes later, I sat beside Sal in his fancy Stutz, watching the awnings of Main Street fade behind us. In this close proximity, I could smell the husky sweetness of his cologne.

As we rounded the corner, he glanced in my direction. "How're you adjusting here?"

"Still acclimating, I guess."

"How's Alice?"

"All right. The Girl Scouts have been a good thing for her."

"How's she handling the events that have been transpiring around your property?"

"With more strength than should be expected." I sighed softly. "If I had known what we were moving into…" my voice trailed off.

"You wouldn't have taken the job?"

"I don't know."

He patted my arm. "It'll get better. As soon as this case is solved, it'll all be over."

"How are we going to solve it if the police can't?" I shook my head. "I lie awake at night worried that something will happen to Alice."

His brow lifted a fraction. "You worry for her, but not yourself?"

"Her safety is my priority."

He cleared his throat. "I think it would be best if I pay for yous gals to stay at The Exchange until this situation is resolved."

Shifting my body, I faced him. "You would do that?"

His gaze flickered over me. "Of course."

I looked down at my clasped hands. "It's a tempting offer. To be honest, Henry's death has me shaken. I haven't even told Alice about it."

"There's bound to be talk at school."

My shoulders drooped. "I know."

"Tell you what, I'm gonna to put you up at the hotel. You'll feel safer, and I'll feel better knowing you're safe."

His offer was enticing. I wanted him to rescue me. I wanted someone to worry for me as much as I worried for Alice. But the fact remained—I wasn't Sal's to care for. "I can't run away from my problems. I bought the house, now I have to live in it."

He shook his head. "You're brave, June. Too brave, I think."

"I'm more stubborn than anything."

"I like your stubbornness." He grinned at me. "If you change your mind, the offer stands."

Again, Sal's flirtation caught me off-guard. I changed the subject. "Have you discovered any new clues?"

"Not yet. We didn't get a tip about Henry's death either. With any hope, today's meeting will provide some new leads."

Around ten o'clock, we arrived at a two-story Colonial stone house nestled among some flowering crabapple trees. A maid ushered us into a spacious parlor with velvet drapes and plush carpets. We sat on a stiff settee, waiting for Rhett's sister, Dorothy, to enter.

A tall gentleman appeared in the doorway, his arm linked with a petite brunette.

"Good morning," said Sal, extending his hand. "You must be Mr. and Mrs. Hollis?"

The man shook Sal's hand. "I am Chester Hollis and this is my wife, Dorothy."

"It's a pleasure to meet you. I'm Salvatore Saviano, reporter with The Saugerties Daily Journal, and this is my colleague, Ms. June Flynn."

I extended my hand to Dorothy. "Thank you for allowing us to come."

She gave my hand a weak shake. "Anything to help my dear brother, Rhett." Her voice had a small, shy sound. She lowered into a chair opposite the settee. Her husband took a seat next to her.

Sal and I returned to the unyielding sofa.

"Have you heard any news about him?" asked Dorothy.

"No ma'am," said Sal with a solemn tone. "That's why we're here, to see if there's anything you might be able to share about the day he went missing. I was told that he visited with you that morning."

Dorothy touched a light hand to her throat. "Yes, Rhett had come by for coffee."

"So far, there's been a pattern to the abductions," said Sal. "It's been men who are related to the Whitakers. Dorothy, is your mother or father's family related to the Whitakers?"

"No, sir. They are not."

I noticed Dorothy's eyes flick toward the ground as she answered.

Sal folded his hands. "How many siblings do you have?"

"Three of us total. Rhett is the oldest." Dorothy shifted on her seat. "And we have a sister who is younger than me."

"How much older is Rhett than you?" asked Sal.

"He is four years older than me."

"How many years are between you and your sister?"

"A year and a half."

"Were you closer to your sister than Rhett?"

"I was close to both of my siblings." Her hands fidgeted with a button on her dress.

"Since you were so close, did you confide in one another about personal matters?" asked Sal.

She tucked her shoes closer to the chair. "There weren't many things to confide."

I spoke up about this. "Did Rhett tell you things he wouldn't tell your sister?"

"I don't know what these questions have to do with finding my brother?" Her shaky voice raised an octave. "After what happened to Henry Brickmore, I'm terribly worried."

Mr. Hollis reached out a steady hand to Dorothy. "My wife is very upset over this news. I fear this kind of questioning is only disturbing her more."

"I apologize," said Sal. "We don't mean to upset you."

Dorothy collected a handkerchief from her husband to dab away invisible tears. "I don't have the strength for this today."

"I think it's best to end our dialogue," said Mr. Hollis, standing. "If you have any further questions, you should call and speak with me personally. My wife is in a delicate place right now."

"Of course, Mr. Hollis." Sal rose to his feet.

I looked straight at Dorothy. "Perhaps, one more question."

Dorothy sniffed. "I don't think I—"

"Did you know that your brother was born of a different father?" I asked, cutting her off.

Her eyes sprang wide with surprise.

"How dare you!" blustered her husband.

"Why are you saying that?" Her body trembled. "Who told you that?"

"No one told me. I put it together."

Sal's mouth gaped enough to slide in a strawberry.

"Ms. Flynn, that's quite enough." Mr. Hollis gestured toward the exit. "It's time for you to leave."

I ignored him, my gaze intent on Dorothy. "Rhett told you, didn't he? He told you that he was scared because his father was Charles Whitaker. Am I right?"

This time, real tears came to her eyes. "Please. Please no one can know about this," she pleaded. "My brother's life is at stake."

I withdrew from the settee, kneeling beside her. I took her hands in mine. "Listen to me, Dorothy, whoever took your brother learned of his past. Do you know how anyone would have discovered this information?"

"No." She shook her head emphatically. "No one knows about it. Rhett didn't know until I told him the morning he came for coffee. I discovered the truth several years ago in my mother's diary. Before she passed away, she gave it to me. She wanted me to know her story. I should have told Rhett a long time ago, but I couldn't bring myself to do it. Then Whitaker men began disappearing. I knew I had to warn Rhett. When I invited him to coffee, I told him what our mother's diary had said and that he needed to go away for a while." Dorothy wiped at her falling tears. "He didn't believe me."

Sal stepped closer to her. "We are going to find Rhett, and we are going to find whoever is behind these abductions. We will not rest until we bring this person to justice."

"That is why we need your help," I said. "Is there anything, anything at all, that you haven't told us?"

She wiped her nose. "Charles Whitaker wasn't Rhett's father."

I blinked. "Then who?"

"It was the oldest son, Felix. He wasn't a good person. He did bad things. He hurt a lot of women."

Sal and I exchanged a look.

I rose to my feet. "How was he allowed to get away with this?"

"Money can buy silence." Sal said through tight lips. "Charles Whitaker had a lot of money."

"Not all people with money are bad," said Dorothy, lifting her chin. "My father was a good man. He married my mother and loved her. He raised Rhett as his own. I think that is why Rhett didn't believe me when I told him."

"He is fortunate to have a loving family." I smiled. "And with hope, he'll be returned to you all very soon."

She nodded.

We said our goodbyes and were ushered from the parlor by the maid. Inside the car, Sal turned to me. "How did you know that Rhett was illegitimate?"

"First, I noticed that Dorothy was fidgety. I ventured that she knew something that she wasn't telling us. Second, I surmised that the gap of years between Rhett and his sisters could have been a result of an unplanned pregnancy. Third, since the abductor has been targeting the Whitaker bloodline,

I presumed that Rhett's actual father must have been Charles."

"Though, it was actually the son, Felix."

"Right, but a Whitaker nevertheless."

Sal tipped his head with appreciation. "You got smarts, June Flynn. Well done."

"Thank you."

As we drove back to Saugerties, he pulled his watch from his pocket. "It's close to noon. How about lunch. On me?"

I knew I should decline to avoid town gossip, but then again, they'd talk no matter what. "I *am* hungry."

"Excellent. I know the perfect place."

We arrived at a little whitewashed building off of Washington Avenue. The sign outside said *Café Clementine.* A waiter ushered us to a table draped in white linen. Quite a swanky place for lunch. I couldn't help but wonder how Sal could afford his luxurious lifestyle.

Our waiter handed us each a menu. "While you peruse the selections, can I get either of you a beverage?"

"I'll have water and a cup of coffee, please," I said.

Sal ordered a Coca-Cola.

Our waiter nodded, then excused himself.

Opening the menu, the meal prices jumped off the page. "Goodness, this is quite a ritzy lunch venue."

He looked up. "Is that all right?"

"I suppose it's fine since you're paying."

He chuckled. "You earned it after grilling that young woman with questions."

"What? I didn't grill her."

"You brought her to tears."

"That wasn't because of my questions." I held my head high. "It was from the burden of keeping her brother's true identity a secret."

He smirked. "Whatever you need to tell yourself."

I gaped at him.

He broke into laughter. It had an infectious ring.

I found myself laughing too. "Well, someone had to do it."

"Truth be told, I thought you were great. You didn't stop until you had the truth. I believe Conan Doyle's novel has inspired you."

"Maybe a little." I shrugged.

Leaning forward, he rested an elbow on the tablecloth. "So, if you're Sherlock, what does that make me?"

The waiter interrupted with the return of beverages and took our order.

I sipped my coffee from a dainty porcelain cup. The warm liquid washed down my throat.

Sal studied me from across the table. "You hear about the gala happening in a couple weeks at the Maxwell Hotel? It's a fancy event. The whole town is invited."

"I didn't hear."

"Ah, well, you're lucky I'm here then. It'd be a crying shame for you to miss it."

"I suppose Alice and I could make an appearance."

"Actually it's an adults-only occasion." He straightened his silverware. "Most of the newsroom are attending."

"Ah, I guess I should go then."

He cleared his throat. "I could pick you up."

Realization dawned on me. He wanted *me* to attend with *him.* "I have a car."

"Right, well," he played with the silverware again. "Thing is, I thought maybe if we go together, I could introduce you to people. You know, help you get more acquainted."

I folded my hands on the table. It was clear that Sal's offer to help me 'get acquainted' was a thinly veiled gesture of courtship. But maybe I needed the distraction from the tangled emotions I felt toward Elex. Or maybe, I just wanted to have some fun. "I would like to meet more people."

He perked up. "Absolutely, it's important."

I stifled a smirk. "Right well, *as friends*, I see no reason we can't attend together."

His smile faltered. "Right, as friends, of course."

As our lunch plates arrived, we chatted easily about the newspaper and life in Saugerties. Sal told me stories that made me laugh. It felt good to laugh. When our plates were empty, the waiter asked if we'd like dessert. I loved pie, but I was full and this meal was already costing a pretty penny.

"You sure?" asked Sal. "They have the best apple pie in the city."

Apple pie. My greatest weakness. "Maybe a slice to go?"

He snapped his fingers. "You got it."

With pie in hand, we left the cafe. Driving down Main Street, I noticed a group of young adults standing outside the Orpheum Theatre. One of the faces caught my attention. "That's Alice!"

"Huh?"

"At the theater. She's supposed to be in class! Please stop."

He pulled to the curb. "I'm sure there's a reasonable explanation."

"There had better be." I hurried out of the car with Sal on my heels. Heat surged through my veins as I saw Alice, Etta, Matteo and some kid I didn't recognize outside the theater holding a bag of popcorn. Alice's face flushed ten shades as she saw me march up. "Just what do you think you're doing, young lady?"

"N-nothing. Just having a little fun."

My eyes narrowed. "To me, it looks like you skipped school to see a movie. Is that right?"

She looked down.

"Whatta you thinking?" Sal swatted Matteo upside the head. "You know Alice is supposed to be in school. You know better than this. Wait 'til your mother hears about this."

"Ah, come on Uncle Sal," Matteo opened his hands, pleaing. "Don't tell Mamma."

"Oh yes." Sal struck his finger in the air. "She will hear about this."

Matteo put a hand to his head, mumbling something in Italian.

I grabbed Alice's arm, steering her toward Sal's car. "You're going back to school."

"Now? But it's almost done."

"I don't care." Pausing, I looked back at Etta. "You're a smart gal. You should consider using your time to further your education and not your knowledge of movie actors."

Sal drove us to Saugerties High and waited in his car, I paraded Alice into the principal's office. After apologizing, I exited the school. Opening the passenger door, I sank onto the seat, feeling my energy fade.

"What did the principal say?" he asked.

"He'll forgive her behavior, but tomorrow she must submit an essay on good versus bad choices." I heaved a heavy sigh. "She was so close to getting away with it. Had we not been at Café Clementine, I wouldn't have caught her."

"Children do dumb things. That's part of growing up. I gave my parents plenty of grief."

"Ugh." I placed my face in my hands. "It was hard being a parent when I had a husband to help. Now, it's even harder."

He placed a hand on my shoulder. "From what I can see, you can handle just about anything."

"I must have you fooled." I mumbled.

"Nah, I'm a good judge of character. Right now, you're tired. You been fixing a house, running a troop, and raising a young adult. Heck, I'd be tired if I was you. Most people wouldn't commit to so much. Seems you can't help yourself."

"Why do you think that is?"

"Because you have a big heart."

I looked into his eyes. "I wish I didn't."

He brushed a stray hair off my cheek. "At least you have that piece of pie. That should ease the stress a little."

Despite the turn of the day, I smiled. Sal had a way of lifting my spirits. "You're right, Dr. Watson. I do have the pie."

He snapped his fingers. "I knew it!"

CHAPTER TWENTY-FOUR

Wednesday, May 7
6:00 PM

Alice scowled at the sheet of paper below her pencil.

"How's the essay coming?"

"Fine."

I offered to make her a sandwich. She said she wasn't hungry. I sank into the chair across from her. "Why did you skip?"

"I thought it'd be fun."

"You're a bright girl, Alice. Too smart for games like that."

"Most girls my age don't attend school. It's not a big deal."

"School is a privilege. It's there for you to learn, grow, and give you opportunities. You need to take advantage of it. I didn't get the chance to go as far as you in school. You should be glad."

She set her pencil down. "Well, I'm not. Just because you couldn't do something, doesn't mean that I have to. I don't want to be a teacher. I don't want some fancy job. I want to be a wife and a mother."

"You don't need to go rushing into marriage."

She frowned. "I'm sixteen and a half. You married Dad when you were seventeen."

"Times are changing. The National Woman's Party is

working hard to raise the status of all women, so that girls like you can receive a good education and good jobs. Soon, women in every state will have the right to vote! Don't you see how big that is?"

She blinked at me, her face unmoving.

Okay, new angle. "I married young because that's what was expected. But you don't have to. You can take advantage of your freedoms. I want you to have opportunities to achieve more than I could. That's another reason that I'm leading the Girl Scouts. With the skills listed in the handbook, there's no telling what you could do. Dream big, sweetheart. Dream as big as you can." I beamed at her, thinking this speech should be printed and passed out.

She leaned forward with a challenge in her eyes. "What if my dream is to be a wife and mother? Is that dream not big enough for you?"

My smile faded. Standing, I walked to the cabinet and pulled out my box of pie. (Sugar had a way of solving problems. Or at least making them easier to swallow.) Meeting her gaze, I said in a matter-of-fact voice, "No, it's not." Then I grabbed a fork and took a huge bite.

She gawked at me. "Well, I don't care what you think."

"You should. I've experienced a whole lot more life than you." I said with a mouthful of spiced apples. "Everything I do is to protect you and give you better opportunities. You should be grateful."

"Grateful?" She gave a derisive laugh. "Oh yes, I'm super grateful that you moved us from Manhattan. I'm grateful that I go to a school I hate. I'm grateful that my father is dead. I'm grateful that my mother gets to make all the decisions, and I'm left to deal with the aftermath!"

"Hey!" A piece of pie flew out of my mouth. "I didn't know about the stuff happening around here when I bought the place."

Alice sprang to her feet. "You do now!"

"You said you were okay with it!"

"I'm trying to make you happy!"

"I'm a grown woman. You don't need to take care of me."

"Well I'm a grown woman too, and I'm done sitting down for it all. I have a life of my own to lead. The war has taken so much from me, but I refuse to let it take away my chance for happiness. I'm going to seize the moments I have and let the chips fall where they may!" Alice grabbed the oil lamp off the table and stormed toward the front door.

"Where are you going?"

"To the outhouse."

"Why?"

"Because I have to pee!"

CHAPTER TWENTY-FIVE

Thursday, May 8
8:00 AM

I thumped on the typewriter keys, feeling glum. I hated arguing with Alice. We hadn't spoken a word to each other since last night. But she was in the wrong, and I wasn't ready to break the silence. Plucking out my typed page, I organized it into a neat stack with the other pages.

Frieda plopped down in her seat beside me. "Did you hear about Sabina Davis?"

The mention of Sabina made me sit straighter. "No. What happened?"

"Apparently, Beulah is making a fuss. She heard that Sabina taught sewing at your last troop meeting. There was mention of needles being shared with the white girls. She says this is going too far. She says that the ladies of the town should protest by refusing to purchase Sabina's services."

My mood swiftly turned to anger. "That wench! How dare Beulah do this!"

Frieda crossed her arms. "Probably wasn't the best idea to have Sabina do the lesson."

I narrowed my eyes. "Why, Frieda? Why shouldn't the person who actually knows how to sew teach the girls?"

"Because she's black."

She said it so matter-of-fact that I rocked back in shock. "And that means she shouldn't be allowed to teach white girls?"

"Goodness, June. You act as though my words are foreign. You know how it is."

"It's wrong." My hands clenched into fists. I saw my father's prejudice against my husband because he was a poor Irishman. Niall was denied jobs and given lower pay because he wasn't native-born. I knew how much that hurt him. Being punished for a thing you can't change was not only ludicrous, it was detestable.

Her forehead scrunched. "Are you one of those fighting-for-rights kind of gals?"

I held my head high. "Yes. I am."

"Well, in Manhattan that might be fine, but in Saugerties, it won't fly."

Snapping up the stack of papers, I stood up from my chair. "Small minds can only think small thoughts." As I walked away, I heard her huff.

My heart pounded so hard, I heard it in my ears. I had to do something. What could I do? All day, I could barely focus. At 2 PM, I popped into Sal's office and told him about Sabina. I asked if I could leave work early and make up the minutes tomorrow.

He leaned back in his chair. "I told you there would be opposition when you started this troop."

"I know, and I'm willing to bear the brunt of my decision, but now it's affecting others."

"Our choices usually do."

"Please, Sal," I opened my hands, "I have to at least apologize."

"Fine. But you need to make up the time." He gave me directions to the Davises house. "I doubt she'll want to talk. She's a private person. Same as Ishmael."

Crossing over a bridge, I drove to an outside part of

Saugerties, on the other side of Esopus Creek. The Davis' house was a tiny stone cottage with a little stable beside it and a fenced pasture. Knocking on the door, I hoped Sabina would be home.

"Who's there?" called a voice from inside.

"It's June Flynn."

The door swung open. Sabina looked surprised to see me. "Hello, June. What brings you by?"

"I heard about Beulah." I exhaled. "I'm sorry."

"It's all right," she gave me a weak smile. "I knew giving that lesson could stir things up, but I chose to do it anyway."

"But your business," I shook my head, my face reddening with frustration. "Beulah can't be allowed to get away with this. I won't let her get away with this."

"June, let it go." Her tone remained calm.

I was anything but calm. "But Sabina, it's wrong."

"It will blow over. There ain't no other seamstresses in our town. Soon as they need an alteration or dress made, these women will forget their grievance."

I stared at her, mouth agape. "Doesn't it make you mad?"

A pinch formed between her brows. "I'm a black woman, June. I don't get to be mad."

"But Sabina, it's an injustice. We have to stand up to women like Beulah or they'll continue to dominate and bully."

Sabina looked down, releasing a slow breath. When she looked up, there was pain in her eyes. "It's not that simple. The problem isn't Beulah. She's a byproduct of the problem."

I tilted my head to the side. "What do you mean?"

Her gaze drifted past me. "Why do you care about this?" Her words were so soft, I barely heard them.

"Because you're my friend."

"You barely know me."

"That's true." I sighed. "But I want to know you."

Her face twitched as she continued to look forward. "Did you know my Ishmael fought in the war?"

"No, I didn't."

"He returned only a few months ago. I was so scared when he left." Her voice caught in her throat. "Your husband fought too, is that right?"

"Yes, and I wish he never did."

Sabina turned to me. "I'm sorry he didn't return."

"Me too." The old familiar ache formed in my chest. "Did Ishmael choose to fight? Or was he drafted?"

"He enlisted almost immediately. President Wilson asked men to fight so that we could make the world safe for democracy. Ishmael believed that this war would make a difference for us and our democratic rights too." She ran a hand over her sleeve. "If only."

"Seems to me if men fight as equals on the battlefield, they should be given equal rights when they return home."

"One might think so, but that hasn't been the story. Our black veterans have returned and nothing has changed for them. Their service hasn't awarded them any honor. When Ishmael returned, he couldn't get his old job back and other employers wouldn't hire a black man." Her lip quivered. "My husband should be able to walk proudly on the street with his head held high. Men should shake his hand and thank him for his service, but they won't because of the color of his skin." Tears surfaced in her eyes. She wiped them away with a quick hand.

I didn't know what to say. My pride was injured because the town snubbed me, but that didn't come close to the isolation the Davises lived through day after day. "I'm sorry." I reached a hesitant hand out and took hers into mine. "I'm sorry that our world is like this."

She looked down at my hand, but didn't pull hers away. "I am too, June."

I knew I couldn't solve Sabina's problem. It was bigger than me. Bigger than her. But I could stand beside her and be her friend.

We said our goodbyes, and I walked toward my car. Then a thought occurred to me. I turned back. "Sabina, do you know if Beulah is any good at sewing?"

A small smirk crept to her face. "No, she's terrible."

I nodded. "Perfect."

CHAPTER TWENTY-SIX

Friday, May 9
6:00 AM

Was revenge wrong? Maybe. Should I turn the other cheek? Maybe.

But I wouldn't.

Salvatore allowed me to place an ad in today's paper. It took some convincing, but he had a penchant for seeing justice served too. Or maybe he just had a penchant for me. I wasn't certain.

The issue came hot off the press with this short blurb…

Looking for a new seamstress? Look no further.
I, Beulah VanBuren, am proud to offer my sewing expertise.
I am now accepting clients.
Please make an appointment by calling ULSter 5141.

Holding the paper in my hands, I laughed out loud. I wished I could see Beulah's face when people started asking for her services. Would she deny that she was an expert? Not a chance. She was too proud. She'd definitely take the clients. I could only imagine what those poor people would do when they received their finished products.

CHAPTER TWENTY-SEVEN

Saturday, May 10
9:00 AM

It was time for the camping trip. Thelma gave instructions as we loaded our supplies into her Packard Touring. All six girls were present, including Geraldine. I knew Clyde would send her. He wouldn't want to miss a chance to spy.

In the front seat, Nellie sat between Thelma and me. Cora and Myrtle took the middle jump seats, while Etta, Alice, and Geraldine crammed into the back seat. I figured that Etta and Alice would choose the spots farthest from me. Alice and I hadn't spoken much since Wednesday.

"Where exactly are we camping?" Geraldine piped up from the back of the car.

Thelma lifted a finger in the air. "We're going to Devil's Tombstone."

The girls gasped.

"What's that?" asked Geraldine.

"It's a campground in the Catskill Forest Preserve beside Notch Lake," said Thelma.

"Why is it called Devil's Tombstone?" asked Cora.

"The campground is located in an old mountain pass called Stony Clove. The Clove is a deep pass, slicing through two Catskill peaks—Plateau and Hunter Mountain. It is rumored that Stony Clove was a favorite haunt of the Devil during the early settlement days of the Catskills. In the middle of the campground lies one object that marks his past presence." Thelma paused, glancing back at the wide-eyed scouts. "A tombstone."

More gasps.

"You can't be serious?" Geraldine's voice held a slight tremble.

Thelma smiled. "There is a large boulder in the center of the park. It looks like an enormous gravestone, but it was likely part of a rock face that was carried down the mountain many centuries ago by a landslide or glacier."

"Oh." She waved her hand. "I figured that."

"Did ya now?" muttered Etta.

Reaching the campground, we climbed out of the car and looked around. There wasn't a single building to speak of. All I could see were trees, a lake, and some flat spaces where former tents had been set. Goodness, this was a primitive place. "Thelma, is there an outhouse?"

"Of course not. This is the wilderness. We will have to dig a pit in the woods and hang a screen around it."

"Ah. Right. That will work." I wondered what I'd gotten myself into. My outhouse wasn't luxury, but at least it had walls.

"Would ya look at that? There be the tombstone!" Etta jogged over to a huge boulder. She clapped a hand to her cheek in surprise. "My word and willywigs, Geraldine, c'mere and look at this. There *do be* an inscription."

"Are you serious?" said Geraldine.

"Aye, so I am." Etta waved her over. "It says it right here—'This be the place that Satan once graced." Her eyebrows rose in shock. "Why, Geraldine, ya suppose he be watchin' us now?"

Looking terrified, Geraldine hurried to the boulder to see for herself. Her forehead scrunched. "I don't see any inscription."

Etta threw her head back, laughing.

"I knew you were lying." Geraldine crossed her arms.

"Go way outta that, I saw the look on yer face."

"Now, ladies," said Thelma. "Jokes can be fun, as long as they are not at the expense of another."

Etta's grin faded. "Fair enough, Captain Parker."

"I knew you were making it up the whole time," Geraldine hissed when Thelma turned her back.

"Relax yer cacks, Gerald," smirked Etta before jogging away.

Thelma launched into camp mode by teaching us how to set up the tents. The girls fumbled with the tarps and guylines. I made a mess of the knots, and Geraldine tripped over her own feet. Thank goodness we had Thelma. By completion, the tents looked tip-top.

Since each tent only slept four, the girls were divided between Thelma and myself. Alice, Etta, and Cora joined Thelma in her tent, and I took Myrtle, Nellie, and Geraldine. Spreading tarps on the ground inside the tents, we set up bedrolls. I assisted Nellie with laying out her belongings.

"I'm glad to be here, Captain Flynn," said Nellie. "I've never done anything like this before."

"Want to know a secret?" I leaned close to her ear. "Neither have I."

"Really? You're brave, leading all of us into the wilderness."

"I'm only brave because Thelma's here."

Nellie shook her head. "I think you're brave regardless."

"Thank you." I squeezed her hand. "You're very brave, too."

"I like it here with the smell of pine trees and the lake. Thank you for allowing me to come. I know that bringing me makes more work for everyone." Her head lowered at the admission.

"No, Nellie. You are not work. You are an essential part of this troop."

"You think so?"

I laid a hand on her back. "Of course. Like every girl here, you are going to grow and learn the skills that will impact our community for good. Disabled doesn't equal unabled. I believe in you, Nellie Mott."

Her face brightened. "Thank you, Captain Flynn."

"Are you ready for an adventure?"

"I'm ready!"

We exited the tent to the high squeal of Thelma's whistle.

"Scouts, fill your canteens with water and place them in your knapsacks with notepads, pencils, and compasses," said Thelma. "We are heading out for our first hike." Before we headed out, she told each girl to find a partner. As a procedure of caution, she said to always form pairs when entering the wild in order to look out for one another.

To my surprise, Alice turned to Nellie. "Would you like to be my partner, Nellie?"

"Oh yes, I would like that," nodded Nellie. "My cane is helpful, but being out here, I don't know my surroundings. Perhaps you could help guide me?"

Alice slipped her hand into Nellie's and together they walked on, side-by-side.

"Will you tell me when there is a bump or divot in the path?" asked Nellie. "I trip on those sometimes."

"Of course," said Alice.

We followed Thelma into the forest. The trees towered over us with their crooked branches.

"As we climb the mountain, we must keep all five senses alert to detect any *signs*," said Thelma. "Signs are little details that would usually go undetected if not for a well-trained eye or keen senses. In nature, signs could be paw prints, broken twigs, a feather, trampled grass, or scratches on trees. But signs are not always seen. The frightened cry of a bird could be a warning of danger. The smell of smoke could be an indication of a nearby fire. Signs give us clues. Imagine that you are a detective at a crime scene. You must look for anything that could be a clue like a button, a match, or fingerprint that is almost invisible to the naked eye. With practice in observation, you can tell pretty accurately who has come or gone before you. You can even tell the character of a person by tracking the signs." She motioned to the path. "Step lightly now, the trail is ascending."

My mind tossed around Thelma's spiel. The night that I witnessed the abduction, I hadn't looked for clues. If only I had gone to the creek's edge. Maybe I would have found something.

As we climbed higher up the trail, Thelma pointed out animals tracks, birds, and types of plants.

We'd been hiking for around fifteen minutes when Myrtle cleared her throat. "Ah, Captain Parker, my partner seems to be in distress."

Thelma turned to see Geraldine bent at the waist with her hands on her knees, sucking in shallow breaths.

"Exercise is the key to optimal health. Take deep breaths, dear. The lookout is just up ahead." Thelma patted Geraldine on the back. "On we go."

Faithfully, Myrtle stuck beside Geraldine, half dragging her up the rest of the way.

As the trail leveled off, we gazed out across the expanse of forest below.

"Tell me what you see, Alice," said Nellie.

"Well..." Alice looked out at the landscape below. "Imagine that you are a tree, and your arms are the branches. They are reaching up as high as they can."

Nellie set her cane down beside her feet, then lifted her arms overhead. "Like this?"

"Exactly. In the forest, there are many other trees too, with long branches." She waved over the other girls. The scouts crowded around Nellie, lifting their arms.

I had to manually lift Geraldine's arms. She had lost all will to live.

"The trees grow close enough that the branches even overlap at times," said Alice crossing an arm overtop of Nellie's. "At the ends of the branches are clusters of leaves, and they look up to face the sun."

Nellie lifted her chin, allowing the sun to radiate upon her face. "I can see it in my mind. It's beautiful."

I gazed upon each girl with her arms extended toward the heavens and whispered, "It is."

Geraldine sagged against me. "Can I sit now?"

"Yes, you can take a break."

She sagged onto the ground, unscrewing her canteen of water.

"Hey, look at those prints," said Cora, pointing to a distinct set of tracks near Geraldine's bottom.

Thelma inspected them. "Those are coyote tracks. I can tell by the four oval shaped toes. Why don't you all take some time to write about our sightings in your notepads."

By the time we hiked back to our campsite, all of our faces were coated in sweat. Thelma suggested we take a dip in the lake. Stripped down to their shifts and bloomers, the scouts plunged into the brisk water, releasing squeals and shrieks. Thelma laughed as we joined them. "It's invigorating, isn't it, June?"

Invigorating wasn't the description I had in mind.

—

The moment of truth had come. Thelma announced it was time to make a fire. Lord knew, I needed to learn this.

After Thelma dug a small hole in the ground, she instructed me on how to make a fire. We took it step-by-step, arranging the tinder and kindling in the form of a teepee, setting that aflame, and adding twigs. As that burned brighter, I added bigger branches. Soon we had a lovely little inferno. If I had let myself, I might have cried. Since Niall had passed, I had learned that I could do more than I ever thought possible. Staring at the flames, I felt peace wash over me. I hadn't felt that in a long time.

"Okay it's time to make the campfire stew," said Thelma. She doled out assignments to each girl. As we peeled potatoes, diced carrots, and cubed the meat, she congratulated us on our climb today. She said that hard work is the key to achieving bigger things. "Locked inside each of you is limitless potential," said Thelma. "The question is, what will you do with that potential?"

Cora frowned at the peeled potato in her hands. "It's hard to believe that anything is possible, when the world says otherwise."

"There are societal hindrances. I can't deny that," Thelma said sadly. "And I don't know what it will take for that to change."

Geraldine hacked at a carrot that she was supposed to be dicing. "It doesn't matter if any of us have potential anyways. As girls, we don't get options."

"What do you mean by that?" asked Thelma.

"My future is already decided. I'm betrothed to Bram Pruitt. We'll marry in 3 years."

All of us stared at her.

"How well do you know this lad?" asked Etta.

Geraldine shrugged. "Not well. He lives two states away. I met him about eight years ago. Haven't seen him since."

"Cripes, what if he's got a face that can sour milk?" asked Etta. "What then?"

Geraldine looked dumbfounded. "I don't know."

Etta shook her head. "I do be sorry fer ya lass. I'd hate to have me fate decided."

"It's just how it is." She shrugged, continuing to hack at the carrot.

Sure, Geraldine wasn't my favorite girl, but hearing this made my heart ache. Every decision of her life was being decided for her. It explained so much. I wondered if it even occurred to her to have a personal opinion. I would never want to do such a thing to Alice. Then it occurred to me, *but am I*?

"It's not easy being a woman," said Thelma. "There are many expectations placed on us from childhood. We cannot always control our future, but we can control today. That is why you all need to take advantage of each opportunity you have."

After we finished the stew, we sat around the fire telling stories. I tried to focus on what the girls were saying but my thoughts looped back to Alice. In the span of the last two years, we'd both changed. Trials had made us tougher, taught us what we could do, and showed us what we truly wanted. Alice wanted to settle down. I wanted adventure. She wanted to be a housewife. I wanted something more. The idea of being a reporter intrigued me.

As we went to our tents to retire for the night, I laid a hand on Alice's arm. "Will you go with me to the latrine? I'm used to having an outhouse companion."

She sighed. "Truth-be-told, I'm scared a bear might catch me with my pants down."

Walking toward the makeshift outhouse, I said to my daughter, "I want to apologize."

She stopped walking. "No, mom, I need to apologize to you."

"Me first." I scooped up her hand. "I love you. I would never want to be the kind of parent who stifles your dreams. I want the best for you."

"I know that. I shouldn't have skipped school. That was a dumb thing to do."

"It hurt me that you snuck behind my back, but I realized that I wasn't listening to you. If I was, you wouldn't have done it. If you want this to be your last year of school, I understand. You're growing up, and if marriage is what you want, then I will support you." I swallowed. "Are you and Matteo courting?"

"We're only friends. He's a fine enough fella, but we don't have much in common." She grinned. "Besides, I've taken a liking to George."

"Is he the boy you eat lunch with?"

"Yes."

"Isn't he younger than you?"

"Only a year." She waved her hand. "He's very responsible and smart. He'll take over his parents' business someday."

"What business?"

"Martin's Hardware Store."

My eyebrows lifted. "I didn't think you liked Saugerties?"

"It's growing on me." She grinned.

"Has this George-fella asked to court you?"

"Not yet. I think he's working up the courage. But when he does, will that be okay?"

I knew this day would come. I just never thought I'd be facing it alone. "Well, a boy normally asks the father for permission. Since your father has passed away, I would appreciate it if George would speak with me first."

"Will you say yes?"

"It's highly probable." I winked.

"What about you, Mom? Is there a man you'd like to court?"

Sal, Elex, even Lloyd seemed interested in me. But did I have feelings for them? I thought about Elex and our secret kisses. I thought about Sal, and the fact that we were attending the gala together. I thought about Lloyd, and the fact that he didn't have a snowball's chance in hell. "I don't know. I find myself in a strange place. I loved your father. With every beat of my heart, I loved him. Trouble was that I needed him more than he needed me." My throat tightened. "Niall loved me, I know that he did, but he never knew how to fully let me in. He rarely spoke of his childhood or shared his burdens. I can count on one hand the times he said, 'I love you.'" Tears welled in my eyes. "I think the reason I miss him so much is because I never had much of him to begin with."

Alice's chin quivered. "He wasn't good at showing emotion, but I know that he loved you. And me too." Tears trickled down her cheeks. "But sometimes, I just wanted him to hug me."

I wrapped my arms around her, and she nestled close. There, next to the latrine, we cried. Grief had a tricky way of sneaking up when you least expected it.

CHAPTER TWENTY-EIGHT

Sunday, May 11
7:00 AM

The blast of a whistle shattered my sweet sleep.

"Rise and shine, scouts!" called Thelma.

Wiping my eyes, I saw Geraldine and Nellie still in their bedrolls. Myrtle was gone. She probably woke up as early as Thelma. "All right, scouts. Let's get ready for breakfast."

I emerged with Nellie to discover a campfire burning with a kettle and pot cooking over it. Myrtle sat crossed legged on the ground, stirring the pot. "The oatmeal is almost ready."

"Where is Geraldine?" asked Thelma.

"She's still asleep. I'll fetch her." Peering inside the tent, I found Geraldine squeezed deep into her bedroll with her head tucked inside. I bent over, tapping her. "Geraldine, you need to wake up."

She moaned.

"It's morning. We're having breakfast."

"Go on without me," she mumbled.

"No, we are a troop. We eat together. You need to dress and come out now."

"But it's so early."

"This is part of being a scout."

She moaned again.

Thelma entered behind me and blew her whistle.

Geraldine jolted upright. Her hair looked like a squirrel had been nesting in it overnight.

"Oh good, you're awake." Thelma smiled. "It's morning, dear. Do get dressed." She gestured to Geraldine's head. "I hope you brought a brush."

With that, I exited the tent behind Thelma. She glanced at me, and we both grinned.

After breakfast, we discussed our discoveries from yesterday's hike, cleaned up camp and returned to Saugerties. We arrived at my house a little past noon to find Mr. Mott, Sabina, Clyde and Elex clustered around the front of my house. My mouth dropped open as I noted what they were inspecting. A tree branch had fallen and broken through my window. "Oh no!" I hurried out of the car.

Elex turned to me. "Not sure how that branch gave way. There weren't a storm to speak of while yous were away."

"Was it windy?"

"Not much." He rubbed a hand on the back of his neck. "I do think critters got inside."

Peering into the window, my heart plummeted. Strewn across the floor was the white stuffing of my torn pillows. I rushed inside to see my kitchen chairs overturned, and the cabinet doors swung open. Dented cans lay on the ground, along with opened cereal cartons.

Alice gasped.

The scouts and their parents filed into the living room, observing the destruction.

I walked into my bedroom to find our blankets on the ground and scratches in the mattress. What type of animal could do this?

Alice voiced my thoughts aloud. "Do you think it was raccoons?"

"Maybe." I sighed.

Clyde peeked into the bedroom, scrawling words in his notepad.

"What are you writing?" I reached for his notepad, but he snapped it shut.

"This might be a potential story," he said.

"No," I pointed my finger at him. "I won't be your story. There is nothing to report here."

He pushed his glasses up the bridge of his nose. "No reason to get defensive, June."

"I don't want my misfortune printed for the public."

"When you bought this house, everyone knew it would only be a matter of time before misfortune came calling."

I gasped.

Elex stepped toe to toe with Clyde. "Ya better go before I do somethin' to yer face."

Clyde noticeably swallowed. He looked around the room, while the families watched. "Come along, Geraldine. I have work to do." He walked past his daughter out the door.

Nellie frowned. "Mr. Lockwood isn't a nice person. I don't like how he talks to you, Captain Flynn."

I sighed. "I'm okay, Nellie. Don't worry."

Mr. Mott wrapped an arm around Nellie's shoulders. "Can we help you clean up?"

Myrtle straightened. "I'd be glad to help."

Thelma lifted a finger. "Wait. No one move." Her gaze traveled from the window to the floor, then to the door. She drew closer to the window, and squatted down, careful not to let her knees touch the shattered glass. "That branch didn't fall on its own."

"How do you know?" I lowered next to her.

"Someone sawed the branch off that tree, there." She pointed to a tall oak that loomed close to the house. "Someone cut it and chucked it through your window. Then, they walked into your house."

A shiver rolled through my body. "Are you sure?"

"We all tracked in fresh shoe prints but," Thelma rose, pointing out a distinct pair of prints. "These are older, based on the dryness of the dirt."

"You think someone did this to June's house on purpose?" asked Sabina.

"I do." Thelma picked up a pillow, studying the scratches. "Animal claws wouldn't make perfect cuts. A knife did this." She passed the pillow to me.

I ran a finger along the tear. It was straight.

"Who would do this to us?" asked Alice. Fear laced her words.

"It could be a disgruntled townsperson," said Sabina with a frown.

"You might be right." I nodded.

"You need to report this to the police," said Mr. Mott.

"They might be hard pressed," said Elex. "Being tied up with the death of Henry Brickmore."

Alice's forehead pinched. "Henry Brickmore is dead?"

"His body was found seven days ago," said Myrtle.

"What?" Alice's voice shot to a higher pitch.

Heavens to Betsy! I hadn't told her yet. I touched her arm. "I didn't want to frighten you, so I was waiting to mention it."

She pulled away from me. "Is this a better time?"

Goodness, of all the occasions for this conversation to transpire, it would have to be in front of my troop, their parents, and Thelma Parker. Luckily, Clyde wasn't present. I cleared my throat. "If you all don't mind, I think we need some time to process this situation."

"Of course," said Mr. Mott. "I still think you should notify the authorities."

"I will consider it, thank you."

Sabina looked over a pillow. "I think I can fix these pillows for you."

"I would appreciate that."

"I'll come back sometime." With a sympathetic look, Sabina exited with Cora.

Myrtle scanned the room. "Are you going to be okay?"

"We're going to be fine." I said in my most reassuring voice.

"You don't need to worry. Go on and have a good day. I'll see you Tuesday."

She walked toward the door, glanced back for a moment, and left without another word.

Elex shoved his hands in his pockets. "Can I check in on ya tonight?"

I'd rebuffed him twice now, and yet, he still offered to look out for me. He really was a good man. "That would be nice."

After the troop had departed, Alice threw me a frustrated glare. "Now men aren't just vanishing, huh? They're dying."

"Only one has died."

"You should have told me."

"I know."

"You said we were going to figure this out together," she huffed. "But you're keeping secrets again."

I flung a hand in the air. "I know, Alice! But I'm scared, and I'm not sure what to do. I want to shelter you."

"Look around," she shot back. "Our house has been vandalized. You can't shelter me."

Thelma looked between us. "Would you like me to step out?"

"No, I need your advice. I have a theory about who ransacked my house." I caught her up on the history of the Whitaker family, the men who vanished, and the one who turned up dead.

"What are the police doing to solve this case?" asked Thelma.

"From what I can see, not much. Which is why Sal and I are trying to locate the abductor ourselves."

Thelma's forehead creased. "Who is Sal?"

"He's my boss at the newspaper. We've been working to find clues."

Thelma scanned the room. "Do you think someone did this damage in order to send you a message? Sort of like a threat to stop searching for clues?"

"I think so." My shoulders sagged.

"If that's true, are we safe here?" asked Alice. "Maybe we should check into a hotel."

"I will make arrangements for you to stay with Nellie or Cora until this is sorted. Then I know you'll be safe."

"I'm not leaving you alone in this house," she protested. "We should both go."

"If I leave, then whoever sent the message will think that they've won." I crossed my arms. "I can't allow that. If they're trying to scare me, then I must be getting closer to the truth. Which means I can't stop now."

Alice inhaled a sharp breath. "I don't want them to win, but how are we going to protect ourselves? We're only women."

Thelma lifted her finger. "You are women, but you're not powerless. I have learned several maneuvers for self-defense. You can learn these too. Do you each own an umbrella?"

"We do." I pointed toward the bedroom.

"Good. Get them."

"You are going to teach us self-defense with an *umbrella*?" Alice arched an eyebrow.

"Precisely."

"What if we don't have our umbrella with us?"

"Start carrying them. At all times."

—

Later that evening, Elex stopped by as he promised. We stood outside my front door under a clear evening sky.

He observed my attempt to *fix* the broken window. "Grand work ya done there."

I looked at the bed sheet I had nailed across the open space. "It keeps out the bugs and hopefully slows down intruders."

His eyes crossed over my face. "Would it be alright if I parked outside yer house at night fer awhile, to make sure yer safe?"

My first thought was to say no. It was too personal, but I

had to think of Alice. I couldn't afford a hotel, so having Elex watch over us was the next best thing. "Actually, I'd appreciate that, if it's not too much trouble."

"It be no trouble. I want to know yer okay."

Overcome by gratitude, I threw my arms around him. "Thank you, Elex."

He hugged me back. "Happy to do it."

When I released him, we stared at each other, not quite sure what to do next.

"Right so, guess I'll be in me car."

"All right. Good night."

"Goodnight, June."

That night as Alice and I lay in bed, I thought about Elex parked outside. Knowing he was there gave me peace. I finally slept soundly.

CHAPTER TWENTY-NINE

Monday, May 12
7:30 AM

That morning, I entered Sal's office holding an umbrella.

He set down his mug of coffee. "Is it raining outside?"

"No, but you never know when it'll pour." I told him about the broken window and damage to my house. To which he responded with fury and insisted that I stay in a hotel. I told him no. (I didn't tell him Elex was parking outside my front door at night.) Instead, I told Sal that I wouldn't run because that would be playing into the abductor's hand. If he was trying to force me to retreat, it meant that I was getting closer. I could feel it in my bones. The truth was in reach, some shred of evidence, something I had overlooked. "I need to reread the papers we printed in 1901. Maybe there's something we overlooked. Some clue."

Sal frowned. "I've read those papers a hundred times. There's nothing there."

"Still, can I have twenty minutes before I start typing? I won't be able to focus unless I check."

"Fine. Twenty minutes."

Thanking him, I hurried to the basement, descending the stairs into the Morgue. Opening drawers, I pulled out the papers, combing through each word.

A throat cleared behind me. Jolting, I spun around to find James.

He twisted an unlit cigarette between his fingers. "I overheard you tell Sal that your house was ransacked."

"You eavesdropped on us?"

He shrugged. "I knew you weren't going to let this Irena-thing go. I saw it in your eyes the day you interrupted my smoke break. You have the same spark that I had when I was your age." He shook his head. "I couldn't let enough be enough. Seems you can't either."

I crossed my arms. "It's wrong to sit idle while innocent men are being hurt."

"Yeah." He released a heavy sigh. "I figure that's true, which is why I'm going to tell you this. When Irena died, a woman named Amara came to me. She was a seamstress for the Whitakers. She saw things in that home. Saw the way the Whitakers treated their staff. She believed that Irena's death wasn't of her own volition. Since Amara died of influenza, you're not able to talk to her, but her apprentice is still alive."

I stepped closer. "Who is it?"

He looked over his shoulder and lowered his voice. "It's her daughter, Sabina Davis."

My brows shot up. "Sabina?"

"I warn you," he lifted a finger, "if you dig deeper, you might not like where you end up."

I inclined my head. "Where will I end up, James?"

"I don't know. Just be careful." Turning, he ascended the staircase, leaving me alone in the morgue.

The dim lights flickered on the paper in my hands. Sabina Davis knew Irena.

—

I ducked out of work early with a sub-par excuse. Once again, I drove to Sabina's house. Knocking on the door, I heard muffled voices inside.

"Who's there?" called Cora.

"It's June Flynn."

The door swung open.

"Captain Flynn, what are you doing here?" asked Cora.

"I came to speak with your mother."

"Come on in." Sabina waved me inside.

We walked through a living room decorated with colorful rugs and wall tapestries. In the kitchen, Sabina had big green plants overflowing their terracotta pots. Everywhere I looked was color. "My goodness, your house is lovely."

"Thank you." She smiled. "I've always liked bright colors."

"I wish I had your talents. My home is very plain."

"All in good time." She gestured for me to sit at the kitchen table. "Would you like a glass of lemonade?"

"Yes, please."

"I saw an ad in the paper recently." She poured us each a glass and joined me at the table. "So Beulah is offering her seamstress services, huh?"

A mischievous grin curved my lips. "I guess so."

"Uh huh." She studied me. "Have you heard if anyone has answered the ad?"

"Not yet. But we'll know if we see a fella with short trousers."

"Or a gal with crooked seams." A laugh slipped out. She clapped a hand over her mouth, trying to stifle it, but I saw her shoulders bob.

I laughed out loud. "I think your services will be back in demand shortly."

"They just might." A smile caused creases to show up at the corners of her eyes. "Thank you."

"For what?" I winked at her and took a sip of lemonade. "Sorry to show up unannounced today."

She waved her hand. "Like you said, we're friends."

"Yes, we are." I smiled. "Which is why I hoped I could talk to you about something important that came up today." I paused, waiting for her approval.

"Go on."

"See, I've been looking into the disappearances in our city. I think that whoever is behind the abductions might have vandalized my house as a warning."

Sabina's forehead scrunched in confusion. "You've been working with the police?"

"No, I've been working with Salvatore, at the paper. We've been digging into this case in order to find out who's behind it. We think that whoever is taking these men are doing it under the guise of Irena Krall."

"Hmmm." She looked down at her glass. "I'm not sure Sal should be asking you to do this kind of work. Especially if it's bringing harm to your property."

"He didn't ask me to do it. I chose to. If I'm going to ensure Alice's safety, then I need to make sure that this criminal is put in jail."

She sighed. "May I be frank with you?"

"Please do."

"All right. Are you ensuring her safety, if it means placing yourselves in danger in the process?"

I sank back in my chair. "I know it sounds bad. But if the perpetrator is trying to scare me, then I must be getting close."

She rubbed a hand to her chin. "My mother always told me that if you play with fire, you're gonna get burnt."

"But you have to light a match in order to see in the dark."

"Light usually doesn't reach the corners. The shadows can conceal a lot."

"That's why I'm searching the shadows."

Sabina shook her head. "You're a stubborn one, aren't you?"

"I can't deny it." I grinned. "Here's the thing, I have a lead, and I think you can help me. I was told that your mother worked as a seamstress for the Whitakers. Is that true?"

She shifted in her seat. "Did James tell you that?"

I nodded. "What your mother witnessed might be the key

to discovering who is behind these attacks."

"I don't want trouble, June. I've stayed out of all this for a reason."

I looked down at my glass. "I'm sorry to ask this of you. If there were any other clues, I'd hunt them down, but there's nothing else." I lifted my gaze to hers. "You're my only hope right now."

She looked away.

I waited as she thought it over.

"I care about you and Alice," she finally said. "Which is why I'll tell you what I know." She swallowed. "My mother, Amara, was the seamstress for the Whitakers, but I was her apprentice, which meant I went to most of the fittings. I never liked the way Charles and Harriet Whitaker talked down to my mother. She worked her fingers to the bone making their fancy clothes, and they paid her pennies. I told her we should refuse them service. She said if we did that, no one in town would hire us. So, we bore their sharp words. We weren't the only ones mistreated either. They treated Irena and Albin just as bad."

"You knew Irena?"

"Yes, I did."

"What was she like?"

"Quiet. Hard working. Had a kind disposition. She was a maid. When we'd come to the mansion, I noticed things."

"What kind of things?"

Sabina sipped at her lemonade. "The eldest son, Felix, seemed to take a shine to Irena. He'd touch her and whisper into her ear when he thought no one was around. But I saw." She shook her head. "Irena told me how she longed to have children. Albin and she tried to conceive. She thought she was cursed. Then after three years of working for the Whitakers, she became pregnant. She was thrilled. I told her that she must not have been cursed after all. She laughed, and then said something peculiar. I still wonder if I heard her correctly."

"What did she say?"

Sabina looked toward the ceiling in thought. "She said, 'It must have been Albin.'"

I leaned forward. "What do you think she meant by that?"

"I think she meant that Albin was the reason they couldn't bear."

"That would mean the child was fathered by someone else."

She nodded.

I thought about Rhett Mills. "Do you think Felix Whitaker was the father?"

She folded her hands. "Yes, I do."

"Do you think Irena drowned herself?"

A heavy sigh caused Sabina's shoulders to sag. "No."

"How can you be sure?"

She swallowed. "Because my mother saw Charles Whitaker pull Irena into the creek. He drowned her in order to save his family from scandal."

My eyes sprang open wide. "And she told this to the police?"

"Yes, but Charles denied it, and the police believed him. Trouble was that Charles had deep pockets. For the right price, anything can be bought."

My hands fisted on my lap. "What happened to Felix?"

"After his family members started dying, Felix grew terrified that Irena's ghost was plaguing them. He sold the property and moved away with his sister."

"Do you know where they went?"

"Never heard." Sabina rested her elbows on the table. "There's something else you should know. James came to my mother because he was told to talk to her."

"James said that Amara came to him."

"I figured he would tell you that. James knows things. He knows more than he's letting on. Be careful, June. I don't like any of this."

"I will tread with caution, I promise."

Elex arrived in his car before dusk.

I walked outside and opened the passenger door. "Want some company for a little while?"

"Won't turn that down."

For the next several hours, we talked. We talked about his life in Ireland prior to moving to the States. We talked about my life before I met Niall (and the boring Arthur Meade). We laughed about childhood blunders and recounted childhood dreams. We talked about missed opportunities, and the ones we took. Then we listened to the crickets chirp in the dark sky and said goodnight.

When I walked into the cabin, I found Alice seated at the table, reading beside the glow of the oil lamp.

"You stayed out there a long time." She smirked.

"We got caught up talking."

"Anything interesting?"

"Just life."

Her right eyebrow arched. "Did he kiss you?"

"No. Of course not." Mentally I added, *this time.*

She eyeballed me like she thought I was keeping secrets.

"It's late." I motioned toward our bedroom. "We'd better go to sleep."

We changed into our nightshirts, and I blew out the lamp.

CHAPTER THIRTY

Tuesday, May 13
7:30 AM

I searched the newsroom, bristling with questions for James. He wasn't in the main room, making his usual gossip lap. Walking down the hall, I checked in printing. No James. I scanned the morgue, still no James. Where was he? Clyde waved a hand in my direction, holding out a stack of notes. I breezed past him and knocked on Sal's door.

"Come in."

As I entered his office, I glanced back at Clyde.

He scowled at me.

Smirking, I shut the door.

Sal looked up from the newspaper in his hands. "June, to what do I owe the pleasure?"

"Do you know where James is?"

He grinned. "Good morning. Yes, I'm well. Thank you for asking."

I waved my hand. "Yes, morning. I need to speak with James. It's important."

He folded his hands on the desk. "James phoned in sick today."

"Sick? He told you that he's sick?"

"He said he's not feeling well and needed to stay home."

I crossed my arms. "I think he's lying."

"Why would James lie to me?"

"Because he knows things." I jabbed a finger on Sal's desk. "Things he's been keeping a secret."

"How do you know that?"

"Because James knows the truth about what happened to Irena."

"The truth? What do you mean?"

"There was a witness the day Irena died."

His brows shot up. "Who?"

"I can't say. But Irena didn't kill herself. She was drowned in Esopus Creek by Charles Whitaker."

His eyes sprung wide open. "That is a big accusation."

"It's not an accusation. It's a fact. The witness even went to the police but her claim was squashed."

"Her? What's her name?"

I mentally kicked myself for the slip. "It's not for me to say, but James can tell you. He told me who to speak with yesterday, and today he's home sick. I find that odd. Perhaps he didn't want me to follow-up with him. I think he knows more."

"He gave you the tip. Doesn't sound like he's hiding anything."

"Based on what the source told me, I believe James withheld some details. I think you should pay James a visit. Something is off. I can feel it."

He shrugged. "Very well. I'll pay James a visit and ask him myself. Maybe then I can get some information I can work with." He gave me a pointed look.

I flung a hand in the air. "I gave you something huge! Irena was murdered! How much bigger can you get?"

"Without a verified source, I have nothing."

"Go to the police and have them pull the report. Then you'll have your proof."

"If what you say is true, Charles would have made that report disappear."

"Oh." I didn't think about that. "Well, James can give you a verified source. And while you're at his house, you can verify if he's actually sick."

Sal crossed his arms. "Fine."

"Thank you." Returning to my desk, I typed Clyde's notes, waiting for Sal to leave and check into James' story. I waited all day. He didn't leave until 3:00 PM, which meant I'd have to wait until tomorrow to hear an update. That really chafed me. I hated waiting. And wondering. At least tonight, we had another troop meeting to keep me busy.

Tonight was going to be extra special. Earlier, I had tied small ribbons on branches in the trees behind my house that led to a hidden blouse. The object of tonight's lesson was for the girl's to track the ribbons and find the blouse. This way they could practice searching for the signs, as we'd discussed on the camping trip. I had doused my shirt with perfume as another means of tracking. (A clever idea, if I do say so myself).

Cora, a natural leader, took charge. The others followed her. Etta, who was normally chatty, remained quiet. Even Myrtle wasn't her usual motivated self.

Nellie stopped. "Do you smell that?"

"Do you mean the outhouse?" asked Alice.

I internally cheered that Nellie picked up on the perfume.

"No, it's gasoline and smoke."

Gasoline? What was she talking about?

"It's coming from that direction." Nellie pointed toward the back of the Whitaker estate land. She walked ahead with Alice beside her. Pausing, she shifted her direction, drawing closer to the creek. "The smell is more distinct now. Do you see anything?"

"Over there." Cora pointed. "Looks like a burn pile." She jogged over. We followed.

Sure enough, there was an ashy pile of rubbish about ten

feet from the water's edge. Circling it, I bent over. "Looks like bits of burnt leather."

Cora nudged the ash and picked up a chunk. "This looks like it came from the sole of a boot."

"Why would someone burn their boots here?" asked Alice.

Myrtle leaned close to Cora, inspecting the sole. "It's very flat. Doesn't have any hobnails or patterns on the soles."

Cora pointed to the tracks around the burn pile. "These must be the tracks made by the boots. They have flat soles."

"If they wore the boots here, and then burned them, did they leave barefoot?" asked Alice.

"Maybe." Cora nodded. "But it's odd that we don't see any footprints. There aren't any prints besides the boots."

"That is strange." Myrtle glanced around her. "Someone must have erased their footprints as they left. Based on the width and length of the print, I'd dare say it was a male boot."

The seven of us hovered around the ash pile, inspecting the flat prints. An odd sensation welled in my stomach. This print looked familiar.

Myrtle rubbed her chin. "Is it just me or does this print match the one from your house, Captain Flynn?"

Sweet merciful heavens. She was right.

"Wait, are you saying the person who broke into our house burned his boots back here?" asked Alice.

Myrtle nodded. Her face grim. "I think that might be the case. Trying to erase evidence."

Alice let out a frustrated huff. "Well ain't that peachy. This deranged person went through our house and then burned the evidence."

"Not all of it. We have the sole and boot prints," said Myrtle.

"Fat lot of good that does us," muttered Alice.

Goodness, what was I thinking having the girls track in our woods? This was the worst idea. Clapping my hands, I said as chipper as possible, "Good tracking, ladies. Let's go back and practice our knots."

Walking back to the house, Myrtle said, "What were we supposed to be tracking, Captain Flynn?"

I sighed. "A perfumed shirt."

Myrtle looked down. "Oh."

The rest of the evening, the girls practiced their tying. But I could tell, none of us were thinking about the knots. At eight, they left one by one. All except Etta. She hung back, looking uncertain.

"Etta, is something wrong?"

She rubbed a hand against her arm. "Ever since I saw that print in yer house, it be botherin' me. I think I know that sole. It done match the soles of me uncle's combat boots. The ones he had in the war." She swallowed. "But he'd never do a thing like this. Never. He cares about ya, Captain Flynn. Ya know that, don't ya?"

Combat boots. Etta was right. Niall's combat boots had flat soles too. Why didn't I think of that before? "Of course, Etta. I know Elex wouldn't wreck my house." Why would any military man hurt the home of a military widow?

I walked Etta outside and found Myrtle standing beside her bicycle. Normally, she left at the stroke of eight, but tonight she'd stuck around. I crossed over to her. "Myrtle? Is something wrong with your bike?"

"No." She shifted her weight like she was uncomfortable. "Thing is, well, are you going to be safe here?" She didn't meet my eyes.

"Oh, sweetheart. Of course, we will. You don't have to worry."

Her voice came out quiet. "I'd hate to see anything happen to you."

I laid a hand on her shoulder. "Nothing is going to happen."

"How can you be sure?"

Well geez, of course I couldn't be sure. (But I couldn't tell her that). "The police are on the case. It's all going to work out."

She searched my face like she wanted to say something else, but instead, she nodded. "Okay, Captain Flynn." She left without another word.

I shook my head as she peddled down the gravel drive. For the life of me, I couldn't figure Myrtle out.

As I entered the living room, I found Alice standing with her arms crossed and forehead scrunched in thought. "Some night, huh?"

She spun to me. "Elex is coming again tonight, right?"

"Yes, I believe so."

"If he doesn't come, can we check into a hotel?"

"We'll go if we have to, but we do have our umbrellas, and we know how to use them."

"What if the other person is carrying a gun?"

I waved my hand in dismissal, but the truth was, I had already thought of that.

Before turning in for the night, I stepped outside to talk to Elex. I brought up the boots we discovered and watched his face for any sign of guilt. There was none. Only the look of concern. He assured me that he'd continue to come over as long as we needed. I wondered how long I could ask this of him. As much as I hated giving in, I wondered if we should return to the hotel.

That night, I didn't sleep well. From the way Alice tossed and turned, I knew she didn't either.

CHAPTER THIRTY-ONE

Wednesday, May 14
8:00AM

I wanted to breeze into Sal's office first thing that morning. Instead, I used restraint, typed two stories and then entered. "Well, was James home sick?"

A crease formed on Sal's brow. "He didn't answer his door."

I slapped the side of my leg. "I knew it. He is lying!"

"Not necessarily, he called again today. He says he's still unwell. I told him that I stopped by his house yesterday to deliver him soup. To which he replied that he was probably out back fetching wood for his stove and didn't hear me." He shrugged.

"When you had him on the phone, did you at least ask about the source?"

Sal shook his head. "That kind of thing is better done in person. But trust me, James has been a loyal employee for years. Heck, he's even served our country. If it seems like he's hiding something, I'm sure there's a good explanation."

All I heard in Sal's words was that James was former military. "He served our country?"

"He was in the army."

"How long ago would that have been?"

"Probably over thirty years."

I frowned. Would a man keep a pair of combat boots that long? It wasn't likely.

"June, I know you're trying to piece it all together. So am I. But, if we presume everyone is a suspect, we'll go mad."

"I'm not presuming that everyone is a suspect."

"No?" He arched a brow. "So far, you have accused me, my father, Clyde, and now James. I think it's safe to say that while you have good intentions, you might be getting ahead of yourself. I recommend that you take a step back and reevaluate your notes."

Take a step back? He couldn't be serious. Sure, my skills of deduction needed honing, but I wasn't about to step back. I was on the brink of solving this case. On the brink! The only thing I'd be reevaluating was the quality of Sal's thinking. "Perhaps some reconsideration is necessary." I managed a tight smile.

"Excellent." He tapped his desk. "Shall I pick you up Friday at your house for the gala?"

"I'll meet you there." With that, I strolled out of his office, not mentioning the burned boots by the creek.

CHAPTER THIRTY-TWO

Thursday, May 15
8:00 PM

Once again, I sat beside Elex in his car. Evening talks had become our new habit. Truth be told, I looked forward to them each day. Tonight we talked about our favorite movie stars. I listened to the soothing lilt of his voice as he talked about the first time he saw a silent film seven years ago. I could hear the smile in his words and see the peaceful outline of his posture in the moon's glow.

"Have you seen anything with Irene Castle?" I asked him.

"I saw her in a film not long ago."

"She's an extraordinary dancer and has great fashion sense. Someday, I wouldn't mind bobbing my hair like hers. Do you think I could pull off short hair?"

"I think ya could shave yer head and still be beautiful."

I laughed. "Oh go on."

"I do mean it." He rotated toward me. "Yer lovely."

I hoped he couldn't see my face blush. "Thank you."

He ran a finger along the side of my cheek. "Yer welcome."

Like magnets, our bodies drew together until our knees were touching, then thighs, then mouths. He pulled me onto his lap, and I leaned into him, wanting to be close, longing to be loved. To heck with my previous decorum. I needed this, and so did he.

Then the front door opened, and light from the oil lamp in Alice's hand spread toward us.

I dove off Elex's lap.

"Mom, are you coming in soon?" she called out.

I straightened my blouse and called back, "Yes, I'll be right in."

The light died away as Alice retreated into the cabin.

I cleared my throat. "I guess I better head inside."

Elex nodded. "Before ya go, I had a thought. Don't know if ya heard, but there be a gala happenin' tomorrow at the Maxwell Hotel. I never been one fer fancy parties but if ya'd like to go, I could take ya."

Oh no. The gala. I never dreamed that Elex would ask me. Of course, I never dreamed that I'd be engaging in these sensual moments either. So much had happened in the last five days. I swallowed. "Actually, I'm already attending."

"With someone?"

"Sort of. There's a group of people attending from The Saugerties Daily Journal."

"Would the group mind if I brought ya?"

Dear me. I swallowed again. "That won't be possible."

"Can I ask why?"

"Because…Sal is bringing me."

His body shifted back. "I see."

"Sal and I are only friends." I hurried to explain.

"Friends." He sniffed, looking away. "He mightn't be yer best choice."

"Why is that?"

"Sal and his family don't play by the rules. They be a bunch of swindlers." He exhaled. "Years back, I played cards from time to time. I be a good player, sometimes, got right lucky. A man at the table was losin' and accused me of cheatin'. That man be Sal's cousin. I told him I don't cheat, he just played bad. He threw a punch, and things got dicey. More dicey fer him cuz he fought like a wee lass. Then Sal jumped in. Next, the Sheriff be showin' up, and the blame was pinned on me. Made me spend a night in jail for disturbin' the peace. After that, the Savianos set out to make me life hard. They done spread rumors about me bein' a liar and a cheat. When the war needed men, I decided to leave town."

Elex's side of the story settled on me. "If you knew you were innocent, why didn't you walk away? Why did you fight?"

"I defended me honor. Amn't no one standin' up fer a man 'cept himself."

"I understand wanting to defend yourself, but is it possible that you went too far?"

He sighed. "It wasn't Sal's fight."

"Sal has a scar above his left eye. Did that happen during the brawl?"

"Ya want the truth?"

"Yes."

"Aye, I struck him in his pretty face and didn't feel a bit sorry. He shoulda minded his own."

"Seems like the fight wasn't fair. Maybe Sal had to intervene because you weren't stopping."

"But I didn't cheat."

"But you still weren't innocent."

"Well yer not the picture of innocence yerself."

"How's that?"

"Sweet and gentle Jaysus." He rubbed a hand against his forehead. "It be impossible to keep up with ya. One moment, yer pinnin' me against the car seat, and the next, yer goin' to a gala with another lad. It be entirely frustratin'."

"Well I'm trying to figure this all out, and it's hard."

"Guess that do be where we differ. Fer me it seems quite easy. Ya don't play with a person's heart."

My mouth gaped. "I'm not tryin' to hurt you."

"Grand so. Clears it all up." He gestured to the house. "Ya better go. Alice is waitin' fer ya."

"Fine." I exited his car and flung the door shut.

CHAPTER THIRTY-THREE

Friday, May 16
7:00 AM

Alice scooped a bite of oatmeal. "What sort of gala is it?"

"It's an annual party that the Maxwell Hotel puts on."

"Does that mean I can attend?"

"It's for ages eighteen and older. I've already asked Sabina if you can visit with Cora."

"Are you going to the gala alone?"

"Most of our staff is attending. I'm driving myself to the gala after I drop you off."

Alice narrowed her eyes. "Are you meeting someone there?"

I brushed a strand of hair behind my ear. "Does it matter?"

She dropped her spoon in the bowl. "You're going with Sal, aren't you?"

I huffed. "Why do you say that?"

"Because he likes you. Did he ask you to go with him?"

"Kind of."

"Did you say yes?"

"Sort of."

She lifted her chin. "You like him, don't you?"

"No, I…he's fun and all…but I…I don't know."

"Do you like him more than Elex or Lloyd?"

"Lloyd?" I laughed. "He never stood a chance."

"Does that mean Elex or Sal does?"

I sank into the chair across from her. "It's tough. I didn't come to Saugerties looking for a relationship. I thought my heart wouldn't be open to that again, and then these men fell into my life. I've tried to push them away, believe me, I have. But they keep coming back. They keep pursuing me. They're relentless. That's what they are. And I'm…I don't know…I guess I'm a little swept up in it." I sighed. "I know this isn't what you want to hear."

"You deserve to be happy, Mom. It's hard for me to think about you with someone else, but I think it might be good for you. I've watched you suffer. I know that Dad's death has been hard on you. It's been hard on both of us. Selfishly, I want to keep you to myself, but if I'm allowed to find happiness in companionship, then you should be allowed to as well."

"Really?"

She nodded.

"Oh, Alice." I squeezed her hand. "I needed to know that it was okay with you."

She smiled. "So, who do you like more?"

I chuckled. "I need more time with them."

"Who knows, maybe tonight will help your decision."

Parking behind the Maxwell Hotel, I proceeded to the front entrance. On the porch stood Sal. Heavens, he looked gorgeous. He wore a sleek black tuxedo, and his ebony hair was slicked to perfection. God must have spent a little extra time when designing Salvatore Saviano.

Seeing me, he jogged down the steps to my side. "My word, you look beautiful."

"Thank you. You look very nice yourself." Which was an understatement. I knew he outshone me.

For some reason, Sal stared at my appearance as if he was mesmerized.

I looked down at my simple black dress. Perhaps it was my hair? Alice had helped me roll my blonde hair into curls and fashioned them on top of my head.

"Excuse my staring," he said, "but you are exquisite."

Exquisite? I waved my hand. "Go on now."

He scooped up my gloved hand into his. "Thank you for joining me tonight."

Regaining my wits, I smiled. "Well, like you said, 'it's a chance to get more acquainted'…with the town of course."

He grinned. "Of course."

Together, we strolled up the stairs into the three-story hotel. I hadn't been inside before, but I had heard it was the most prestigious hotel in Saugerties. Upon entry, I knew the rumors had been correct. Shiny Italian tiles greeted our shoes while sparkling crystal chandeliers welcomed our eyes. Ivory stone columns outlined the perimeter of the lobby, along with upholstered armchairs.

"It's stunning," I breathed.

"That it is."

A crowd shuffled around the expansive room. I scanned faces, searching for any that were familiar. Spotting Clyde and Florence Lockwood, I promptly turned in a different direction. A quartet played a dreamy tune and a few couples danced.

"Would you like a glass of punch?" Sal asked.

"That would be nice."

He led me across the room to an attendant ladling out glasses of golden liquid.

I took a sip of the fruity sweetness. "Good punch."

"Only the best here." He waved at a man in a striped suit. "That man is Sammy Frasier. He's been a source for our paper for years. Recently, he's been harder to get a hold of. Would you mind terribly if I asked him a brief question?"

"Not at all." As he left my side, I moved closer to a wall with large windows overlooking the side street. To my left, I noticed a woman in a blue satin dress. Her hem was rippled and several seams were bunched.

"My what a lovely dress you have," I said, drawing closer to her. "Can I ask where you got it?"

"Beulah VanBuren sewed it for me." Her words sounded like a sigh.

I snapped my fingers. "Ah, yes. I saw her ad in the paper."

"It's all I had to wear." Frowning, she walked away with a hushed mutter, "Expertise, what a load of bunk."

"Hello, June." Someone said from behind.

Turning, I found Lloyd Ennis. "Hello, Lloyd."

"Make any new improvements on your house since I was there last?"

"No. But I'm finally using the stove."

"Learned to make a fire, did you?"

I lifted my chin. "I did."

He nodded, looking almost impressed. "Still can't believe you bought it. I never dreamed that it would sell. Everyone in town thought it was a joke when the advertisement was printed."

"The price was right."

"You drove a hard bargain." He ran a hand over his beard.

"There wasn't anyone else desperate enough to buy it. That served me well." I chuckled.

"True." He gave a half-hearted laugh.

"You know, I always found it odd that the owner of the property didn't attend the sale closing. I would have liked to meet them." I paused. "Do you know if the owner ever visits his property?"

"No, I don't." He shifted his stance. "I haven't had much contact with the client."

"But you *have* met the owner?"

"We've talked over the phone a couple times."

"How did you receive his signature for the documents?"

"He handled his papers at the bank without me present."

"Don't you think that's odd?"

"Not necessarily. The owner is a private person and probably doesn't wish to be attached to such a place."

"Then why buy it?"

"Like I said, I don't know. I just brokered the sale."

"I noticed that the mansion's property is groomed. Why would the owner pay money to have the grounds kept for a place he doesn't visit?"

He shrugged. "June, I don't know."

"Well maybe you know this, the initials on the sale said I.L.J. What do those stand for?"

Lloyd looked annoyed. "It's not my job to befriend the sellers, I just have to sell their houses."

"I get that, but here's a strange observation—the initials I.L.J. match that of my home's previous owner—Irena Louise Jansen."

He crossed his arms. "Irena has been dead for 18 years."

I heaved a sigh. "I know that. I'm saying I think someone is using her as a cover. And I think that person is probably connected to her. Maybe a relative?"

His gaze wandered away, uninterested. "Maybe."

"Look who it is," Sal returned, giving Lloyd a once-over. "How'ya doing?"

"Fine, thank you." Lloyd's words were kind but had an edge to them.

"How is business?" asked Sal.

"Can't complain."

"You manage to secure a partner for this occasion?" Sal's smile looked more like a smirk.

"No, I came alone."

"Ah," Sal touched his lapel. "That's too bad."

Lloyd frowned. "We're not all as lucky as you. Enjoy your evening."

As he strode away, Sal stepped closer to my side and said, "Might just be me, but I've never liked that fella."

I chuckled. "There is something strange about him."

He gestured to couples dancing in the middle of the lobby. "Would you care to dance?"

"Why not." Setting down our glasses, we joined the crowd. In a minute, I discovered that Sal was a good dancer. My shoulders relaxed as he spun me around the floor.

He smiled at me. "You're good on your feet."

"You're not so bad yourself."

"My mother taught me. As a child I protested, but now I'm glad that she did."

As the saxophone solo ended the song, Sal bowed to me. "Would you like to see the hotel's garden?"

"It's dark outside. How will we see the flowers?"

"It's lit with lanterns."

"Very well," I linked my arm with his. "Lead on."

Strolling through a hall, we exited a set of glass doors into a gated garden. Paper lanterns strung overhead sent a warm glow over the flowering bushes and cobble stone pathways. At the center of the garden was a white gazebo. Walking inside, Sal lowered on a bench and patted the spot beside him. I knew what kind of things could happen in private, but I sat anyway.

"You enjoying the party?" he asked.

"I am. Are you?"

He shifted to face me better. "It's been a night to remember."

"What will you remember about tonight?"

"That I had the pleasure of dancing with the loveliest woman in Saugerties."

"Thank you. That's very kind."

"No, thank you. You're something. You know that?"

I averted my eyes. "Goodness, I'm not sure–"

He lifted my chin ever so softly. "I mean it. I like you, June. I can't help it."

There it was. His confession.

"I'll wait," he continued. "If you're not ready to court me, I can wait."

I tried to pull oxygen to my brain. With him sitting this close and looking better than chocolate cake, I found it hard to breathe.

"Can you tell me if I've got a chance?"

"I think," I dragged in a ragged breath. "Mercy, you smell good."

A rumble of laughter vibrated in his throat. His head inclined closer to my neck. "So do you." Then his lips brushed my cheek.

It was a simple act, but it made me nervous. With him close, I wasn't thinking straight. "It's getting late, and I need to pick up Alice. I'd better go."

"But the night has only begun. We definitely need to dance more."

"One more dance. Then I have to go."

Five dances later, Sal walked me to my car. He placed a kiss on my gloved hand, and we said goodbye. It was a short drive to the Davis' residence. After offering my thanks, Alice and I headed home.

She studied me from her seat. "How'd it go?"

"It was nice. The Maxwell Hotel put on a ritzy party."

"Did you dance with Sal?"

"Yes."

"Was he a good dancer?"

"He was."

"Do you think you will go out again?"

"Maybe."

"Mother," Alice heaved a sigh. "I need more details. I want to hear all about it."

Laughing, I parked outside our house. "Okay. I'll give you the full story. Shall I put on a pot of coffee?"

"You bet." She looked around. "Where's Elex?"

"He must be running late tonight." I inwardly hoped that was the case, but I wondered if he wouldn't show at all. Last night didn't end well. "I'll fetch the water." Grabbing my electric flashlight and pail from the kitchen, I walked out to the pump. As I pushed the lever, I heard a twig crack behind me. Spinning around, I found a person standing only feet from me. "James?"

He lunged forward, grabbing me around my arms.

My flashlight dropped from my hand. I wriggled in panic, remembering I didn't have my umbrella. "Stop! Alice! Alice!" I drove a hard kick into his shin. He howled, loosening his hold. I broke free, sprinting for the house.

"Stop her!" yelled James.

Another set of arms wrapped around my waist, tackling me to the ground.

My breath knocked out of my lungs.

Hands grabbed my wrists, tying them behind my back. A burlap sack was thrust over my head, obscuring my vision. I dug in my heels as they dragged me away from the direction of my house. My shoes hit bushes and twigs. Twisting, I fought against them. I didn't know where I was until I felt the coolness of water fill my shoes. The creek! My body was lifted and tossed forward. My shoulder hit something wooden, what I assumed to be a boat's floor. Panic gripped my heart as I heard the faint sound of Alice yelling, "Mom."

ALICE

CHAPTER THIRTY-FOUR

Friday, May 16
10:00 PM

"Mom? Mom?" I ran out of the house holding an oil lamp and umbrella. When I reached the water pump, she wasn't there. I saw her flashlight lying in the weeds. Snatching it up, I shined the light in a circle. I saw a faint glow heading toward the creek. My mother's scream broke the silence.

I ran as fast as I could with my heart pounding loud in my ears. A stupid root caught my shoe, causing me to topple to the ground. I scrambled back to my feet, running again. Nearing the creek, I saw shadowed figures climbing into a boat. "Mom!"

Though it was soft, I heard my name called back.

My heartbeat increased from fast to frantic. My mother was being taken. When I reached the edge of the Esopus, the boat was too far away. In the moonlight, I could see two people rowing. They were in black. My mother must have been lying on the boat's floor. Running back to our house, I grabbed the ignition key to our Ford.

Mom had taught me how to drive, but this would be my first time starting the car without her assistance. I uttered a silent prayer.

Pulling out the choke, I cranked the lever three times to prime the carburetor. Jumping into the car, I turned the ignition key and adjusted the timing, throttle, and hand brake. Hopping back out of the car, I cranked the lever, again. The engine didn't start. Putting my full weight into it, I cranked it all the way around again. It still didn't fire. Slapping the hood, I yelled, "Dang you, car!" Inhaling a deep breath, I grabbed the fender with my right hand and gripped the crank with my left. Then I yanked the crank around with every fiber of my strength and released it. The engine backfired and then came to life.

With my veins pumping adrenaline through my limbs, I drove to the police station on Main and rushed up to an officer half asleep at his desk. Banging my hand on the tabletop, I said, "Sir, Sir, I need help!"

He jolted, blinking in surprised succession. "Calm down now, miss. What seems to be the problem?"

"I will not calm down. My mother has been taken!"

"Taken?" He tilted his head. "Are you sure?"

He sat there much too calm. I was about to lose my mind. "I'm positive! It happened behind my house."

"Did you see it happen?"

"I heard her screaming. It was dark, but I could see figures getting into a boat. They took her."

"Okay, young lady, please have a seat. I need to file a report on this." He reached into his desk drawer, rummaging around for the paperwork.

I gripped the armrests of the chair, to keep myself from springing forward and yanking out all the files.

"Ah, here it is." He laid a form on his desk. "Where do you live?"

"1 Esopus Drive." The words came out in a rush.

His pen hovered over the page. "Isn't that the address to the Whitaker house?"

"Yes, but we live in the small house on the property."

"The Krall house?"

"Yes, well it was, until we bought it."

He studied me, his attention more rapt. "You heard her scream?"

"Yes! She had gone outside to pump water. Then, I heard her scream. I ran out to see what was wrong. I couldn't find her, only her flashlight in the weeds."

"And you think someone took her?"

"I *KNOW* someone took her. I saw them. It was two people dressed in black. They shoved my mom into a boat. They rowed up the creek."

"Do you realize that we have had three people go missing near the back of your property?"

"Of course, I know! Everybody knows! This town doesn't stop talking. Fact is that my mother was digging into the disappearances. I think that's why they came after her."

"Goodness." He rubbed a slow hand over his mouth. "I need to call the Sheriff. He'll want to investigate the property as soon as the sun rises."

I sprang out of the chair. "Morning? My mother needs help now! The Sheriff has to come now!"

"Listen, dear, it's impossible to do a thorough search in the dark. We have no choice but to wait until daylight. I'm sorry. You can be assured we'll be there as soon as the sun rises. For now, I will take down a full report of everything you heard and saw."

Fuming, I ran out of the building. I couldn't wait until morning. I had to do something now. I needed to find Elex. He lived with Etta and her mom. I knew where their apartment was. As I drove, I repeatedly hit the curb but managed to make it. It took several knocks, before the apartment door opened. Etta's mother filled the doorway.

"Why ya knockin' at this hour?" Her words came out wobbly.

"I'm Alice from the Girl Scouts. I need to talk to Elex right away."

"He amn't here. Been gone all day."

I swore under my breath. Who would help me now?

Etta surfaced beside her mother. "Alice, what ya doin' here?"

I grabbed her arm. "My mother has been taken, and the Sheriff won't investigate until morning. I can't wait that long. My mother is in trouble. I have to find her."

"Cripes," Etta's eyes were wide. "What should we do?"

"I don't know. We need help. Maybe Salvatore Saviano. Do you know where he lives?"

"No, but Geraldine's dad will."

"Do you know where she lives?"

"That I do. Let me change outta me nightshirt." Etta hurried from the door, pulling her pajama over her head as she went.

Imogen plodded after her. "Ya can't go traipsin' around alone."

"Yer welcome to join, Ma."

Pulling her housecoat tighter around her shoulders, Imogen looked down. "I don't be in a right state fer that."

"Amn't that a shock. Yer never in a right state." Etta reappeared from her bedroom, yanking up a pair of trousers.

"Will ya be careful?" Imogen asked in a small voice.

"Of course, Ma." She placed a quick kiss on her mother's cheek, then hurried after me to my mother's car, which I had left running. "Ya know how to drive?"

"I know enough."

Lifting her rosary necklace from around her neck, Etta kissed the crucifix. "Dear Mary, full of grace…"

The car sputtered more than usual. I didn't have something right, but at least we were moving. We ended up on a road with big brick houses. At the end of the street was a long driveway which led to Geraldine's white house with a columned porch. We knocked, waiting for several minutes until light poured through a window in the door.

Clyde appeared in a velvety housecoat. "What on earth? What are you doing at my house at this hour?"

"I need your help," I implored. "My mother has been abducted!"

"Abducted?" He stepped back, waving us inside. "Come in,

come in." He led us into a room off of the foyer and turned on more lights. It illuminated a ritzy parlor. "Have a seat and tell me what happened."

Mrs. Lockwood burst into the room. "Why are these girls here?"

"Something has happened to June Flynn," said Clyde.

"She's been taken," I said.

Mrs. Lockwood's hand clapped to her chest. "Taken?"

"Who's been taken?" said Geraldine, appearing in the room, wearing a set of silk pajamas.

"Captain Flynn," said Etta.

"Oh no!" Geraldine hurried to my side. "Alice, I'm so sorry."

My shoulders slouched. "I heard her scream. She was dragged through the woods and taken away by boat."

Clyde slapped his leg. "That's how it's been happening. Have you contacted the police?"

"Yes, they said they'll investigate in the morning, but Mr. Lockwood, what if that's too late? One man is already dead."

"Now, now. I'm sure everything will be okay." He pulled out his notepad and ink pen. "You know, when she started putting her nose into this whole thing, I knew no good would come of it."

I didn't like his tone. "She's trying to protect me and this town. She has been putting herself on the line for the good of others. Can you say the same?"

"Young lady, I am a reporter. Your mother is a typist."

I narrowed my eyes. "My mother must be doing a better job or the abductor would have come for you."

His face reddened. "I will not be disrespected in my home. If you want my help, you will apologize."

"Quite right," said Mrs. Lockwood.

I huffed. "We both know that you don't want me to leave without telling you all the details. The only reason you've allowed Geraldine to be in our troop is to spy."

He blustered. "How dare you accuse me of such a thing? Geraldine, have you nothing to say to your so-called friends?"

"Ahhh." She looked between Etta, her father, and me.

"Don't just stand there looking foolish, Geraldine," scolded Mrs. Lockwood.

Geraldine's expression hardened. "I'm not the foolish one, Mother." She snapped her focus to Clyde. "Alice is right. You forced me to be in the troop. I did it because I wanted to please you. My whole life has been built upon getting your approval, and I'm tired of it." Her lip quivered. "You wanted me to be a spy and guess what, I've gotten pretty good at it. I've picked up the other phone during many of your "business" calls." Her eyes narrowed. "I heard the things you said to that woman."

Etta's eyes widened. "Fair play, Gerald."

"What woman?" Mrs. Lockwood's forehead scrunched.

"It's nothing," said Clyde, holding up a hand. "Geraldine, you don't know what you *think* you've heard. I'm a very busy man. I have to talk to many people to hunt down leads."

"Her name is Regina." Geraldine sniffed.

"Regina Wallace?" Mrs. Lockwood's normal staunch posture wavered. "Why are you talking to *that* woman?"

Clyde stroked a hand down his night coat. "I refuse to discuss this in the presence of these girls."

I stood to my feet. "Tell me where Sal lives, and we'll be on our way."

He looked between me and his wife. I knew he was torn between wanting to take down my story and smooth-over his current problem. He sighed heavily. "Sal lives at 60 Ulster Avenue. It's about a quarter of a mile from Main. It's a blue house with white shutters."

"Come on, Etta." I walked to the foyer.

"I'm coming with you," said Geraldine.

"We don't have time for you to change," I said.

"I'll wear my pajamas."

"You are not going with them," said Clyde.

"Mother please," she opened her hands in plea.

Mrs. Lockwood glanced at Clyde. He shook his head. She turned to us. "Be careful and good luck."

He blustered. "I'm the head of this household."

"My parents bought this house." Mrs. Lockwood's top lip curled back. "I'll decide who stays and goes."

As we left, I heard Clyde's voice reach a higher octave.

By the time we parked at Sal's, I was frustrated at how much time had been wasted. He answered the door, looking confused. "Alice?"

"My mother has been abducted!" I blurted out.

He rocked back a step.

"We need your help."

He waved us inside, turning on the lights. "Did you see it happen?"

"Yes, but I wasn't quick enough." I gave him the full account.

He shook his head. "I shouldn't have involved June. I knew it was too risky."

"It's too late for should-haves," I snapped. "My mother is gone. We have to sort this out now. We need to search the property for evidence."

"We can't go now. The officer was right. It's too dark. We won't be able to see anything."

"The longer we wait, the further away my mother could be taken. If something happens to her—" I put a hand to my mouth as tears pooled in my eyes—"I can't lose her too."

Etta wrapped an arm around me. "We're gonna find her."

"How?" I sniffed. "We're not doing anything."

Sal paced the floor. "The police will do their search, and then we'll be allowed to do ours. If we go now, we will be interfering. We have to stay off the premises."

"But I already walked the area."

"They will know your shoe prints from the others. But we can't add any more prints to the scene. Instead, let's take this time to process all we know." He grabbed a pad of paper from the coffee table.

"I'd like to have the whole troop here," I said. "They witnessed the damage to our house and the boots we found burnt."

"Plus the prints by the burn pile matched the tracks in your house," said Geraldine.

I faced her, surprised she'd even logged that in her brain.

"I didn't know about the boots." His expression grew more perplexed. "I think you're right. The more people we have trying to solve this, the better, but phone lines will be quiet at this time. We'll have to drive to their houses."

"I have the addresses on the enrollment cards."

"My car only seats three," said Sal.

"We can take my mother's car. Let's go."

CHAPTER THIRTY-FIVE

Saturday, May 17
6:00 AM

For the last six hours, Sal and our troop, plus Cora's and Nellie's dads (as usual, Myrtle's father was absent), considered all the facts we knew and hypothesized who could be behind my mother's abduction. Our list was short and unreliable.

When the sun rose, we all drove to my house. It didn't look as bad anymore. Mom believed she could make it a home. She saw the potential in it. Just like she saw the potential in her six scouts.

Several police officers milled around our property. One officer wearing a gold badge approached us. "Hello. Is one of you, Alice Flynn?"

I stepped forward. "That's me."

His expression wasn't optimistic. "I'm Sheriff Bretton. I'm sorry to tell you, but so far we haven't found any evidence. We have taken measurements of the prints, and we're sending a search team along the creek. When we know more, we'll contact you."

I managed a thank you while holding back tears.

Sidestepping me, he moved to Sal, Mr. Mott, and Mr. Davis, speaking in a lower tone.

Was there more to share? Was I too delicate because I was

a young woman? Instead he chose to talk with the men who accompanied me. "Sheriff Bretton, one more thing," I said loudly.

He turned to face me. "Yes, dear?"

"My troop and I would like to conduct our own search. Will that be okay?"

He glanced at my scout sisters. "That's nice that you've recruited some friends. Go ahead. We've already swept the area." He turned back to the men.

Clenching my fists, I faced my troop. "We're more than just a group of girls. We're a troop. We've been taught how to look for signs. It's time we put our skills to use."

Breaking into groups of two, we fanned out. Etta and I started at the water pump, eyeing the ground for prints and searching through the grass.

"There's a lot of broken brush in this area," Myrtle called out, "Probably the path they took from your house. Tips of the low hanging branches have been cracked."

I jogged over to her.

She pointed to the broken twigs. "My guess is that Captain Flynn was kicking her feet."

The thought made my chest tighten. My poor mother was fighting to free herself, and I wasn't there to help her.

"The tracks lead toward the creek," continued Myrtle. "We should walk alongside the path of prints so as not to disturb them." She pointed to the smaller shoe prints. "These are yours, correct?"

I nodded.

Ahead of us, Cora combed through the overgrowth. Geraldine floundered after her, trying to free her pajamas from briars. I knew those silk bloomers were good as gone.

Etta stood with her hands on her hips. "Should we stick to followin' the prints or should we be searchin' the whole woods?"

Myrtle rubbed her chin, studying the track of prints. "I think we should focus our attention on this route. And then go from there."

As we trailed the boot prints and bent branches, I prayed we'd find a clue. Something. Anything. Losing my father was hard enough. I couldn't lose my mom.

Cora called back to us. "Nellie, do you smell anything out of the ordinary?"

She shook her head. "Not today."

We caught up with Cora on the creek's edge. "The prints end here," she said. "Where they must have entered the boat."

I looked out at the water, remembering the boat as it drifted out of view. How far had they gone? How was I going to find my mom now? My lower lip trembled. I hugged my arms to my chest, willing myself to be strong. I felt someone reach an arm around me. I thought it would be Etta, instead I found Myrtle. She didn't meet my eyes. Instead she looked out at rippling water.

"I'm scared," I whispered.

"Me too."

I looked at her, seeing a few tears slip down her cheeks. Never had I seen Myrtle cry before.

"If something happens to Captain Flynn, I—" she trailed off.

Nellie piped up, "We're going to find her." She stood straight as she held her cane. Her face was the picture of determination.

"How do you know?" I asked.

"Because we won't give up until we do."

Etta patted Nellie on the back with a proud smile. "Aye, we won't."

Behind us, Geraldine groaned. She had given up on following Cora, and instead inspected the many runs on her nightshirt.

"Hey! I found something!" Cora yelled out.

Our troop ran to her, including Sal and the dads, who apparently had finished their debrief with Sheriff Bretton.

"It's a tie tack," said Cora, holding it out for us to see. It was a gold pin engraved with the letters I.L.J.

"My mother said that Irena's maiden name was Irena Lousie Jansen," I said, my hope growing. "This is her initials!"

"But Irena is a female," said Cora. "She wouldn't wear a tie."

"That's true." I frowned.

"Did she have any surviving relatives?" asked Myrtle.

Sal plucked the tie tack out of Cora's fingers, inspecting the engraving. "Her obituary mentioned relatives. Though I can't remember their names."

A relative. I recalled the note my mother and I had discovered in our fireplace. It was a letter from Irena's brother. I tried to picture the letter in my mind. What was the name written at the bottom? Did it begin with an I? I was certain it did. "My mother and I found a note from Irena's brother, I think his name started with an I."

Sal's face twitched. "You found a letter? Why didn't you mention that before?" He sounded frustrated.

"I don't know. I didn't think of it. But the note made it seem like Irena and her brother were close."

He waved his hand. "Where is the letter?"

"Same place we found it."

"And that is?"

"In the mortar of the fireplace."

"I need to see that letter." He spun around, running to the house.

I didn't like his tone, but stress had a way of bringing that out.

JUNE

CHAPTER THIRTY-SIX

Saturday, May 17
Midnight

Everything was dark, and my face itched from the burlap sack on my head.

My body lay in a crumpled heap on a cold hard floor. Ropes tied my wrists and ankles. Pain pulsated through my shoulder and down my arm.

"This wasn't part of the plan, June," a man whispered. "But you couldn't mind your own business."

"James? Is that you?" The only answer I received was the sound of a door shutting. I wriggled on the floor, trying to loosen my ropes.

"It's no use. You won't get them off," said a weary voice.

I stopped moving. "Who are you?"

"Rhett Mills."

My heart leapt into my throat. "Rhett? Oh my goodness, you're alive."

"For now."

A chill swept through my body. "Is Stuart Ellsworth alive?"

"Barely."

"Is he in this room with us?"

"I think so. But they keep the sacks on our heads most of the time." Rhett sighed. "Are you a Whitaker?"

"No, my name is June Flynn. I bought the old home of Irena Krall. Your abductions happened behind my house. Were you lured to the creek? Is that how they took you?"

"No, I was attacked in my home. Men stuffed me into a car, drove for a while, dragged me through the trees, and tossed me in a boat. We eventually ended up here."

I processed this information. The only reason James would take Rhett from his home, drag him through the woods, and then into the river was to once again connect the abduction to Irena. All of which didn't make sense. Didn't James want to vindicate Irena? Wasn't he the one who believed her death to be murder? "I work at The Saugerties Daily Journal. I've been digging into the disappearances of you and Stuart. I talked with your sister, Dorothy."

"Is she okay?"

I heard the sudden fear in his voice. "Yes, of course. She didn't have much to share, but she did help me link you to the Whitaker line." I sighed. "I'm sorry."

There was a pause. "You must have been getting close to the truth if they came for you."

"That's the odd thing. All of my theories have been wrong. I never imagined James was behind this."

"James isn't the one in charge."

Footsteps rushed past me and then there was a sharp smack.

What was that? My heart raced.

I heard the slow scrape of shoes on the floor, until they stopped beside my head. My skin prickled. Like a ghost, I felt its presence looming over me.

"Stop talking," a voice hissed.

Then the footsteps retreated, and a door closed.

I waited in silence.

Rhett didn't speak another word.

A draft from the floor seeped through my clothes. I shivered on the ground for hours, unable to sleep. No one came. I was left with my thoughts to haunt me.

—

My ears caught the soft sound of a door brushing the floor. There was a faint glow of light. Then the sack was pulled off my head. I blinked, trying to adjust my vision.

James knelt down before me. "Are you thirsty?" he whispered.

I noticed a glass in his hand and nodded.

He pulled me into a seated position. Placing the glass to my lips, he tipped it back, allowing me to drink. When I finished the water, he stood up.

"James, why are you doing this?"

"I don't have to explain anything to you."

"Sal trusted you. I trusted you. You lied to us. You gave me a tip so that I would talk to Sabina. Why? Why did you do that?"

He glanced toward the door where he'd entered, then knelt back down and whispered, "It wasn't supposed to go like this. I didn't want you to get hurt. I tried to warn you."

"How, by ransacking my house?"

"I didn't do that."

"Really? There were bootprints all through my house. Combat boots. We found the remains of those boots burned behind the Whitaker mansion. I think those boots belonged to you."

"My old boots have been missing. But I didn't do that."

My brow furrowed, trying to figure out if he was lying.

"What are you doing, James?" A voice spoke from behind.

James bolted to his feet. "Giving June a drink."

I craned my neck to see who was speaking, but they were too far in the shadows.

"Were you? It looks to me like you were having a private chat with our captive. Perhaps giving her more hints?"

James' expression betrayed a moment of surprise.

"You didn't think I knew what you were up to?" His tongue made a tsking sound. "I know about the branch through June's window and the portrait. I have methodically tracked all my steps…and yours. One doesn't plan all these years to let a louse mess up the finale."

James' Adam's apple bobbed in his throat. "I didn't do those things. And if anyone has loused things up, it's you. We made an agreement that women wouldn't be harmed."

"June gave me no choice."

"What about the other women? I know about Julianne Whitaker and her cousins."

"Fine. There have been a couple casualties of war."

"It wasn't a couple," said James. "You hunted them all down."

"I set out with a goal, and I'm finishing it." He gave a derisive sniff. "It's a shame you lost your way in the last hours."

"I haven't lost my way."

"Then why did you plant the portrait?"

"I didn't."

"I really hate liars, James."

I heard the slide of a bullet entering a gun's chamber. My heart sped up.

James drew back. "I'm telling you the truth. I've been with you the whole way. No one mattered more to me than Irena."

"When trust is lost, everything is lost. That is why my next question is very important. Did you take my tie tack?"

James stood rigidly straight. "No."

"I always keep that tie tack in my pocket. You know that. I don't go anywhere without it. And now, it's gone. Where is it?"

"I didn't take it. It could have fallen out of your pocket when you tackled her"—he pointed at me—"to the ground."

There was a stretch of silence. "You think it slipped out?"

"It must have."

"How about we ask our little detective friend for her opinion, shall we?"

The man stepped from the shadows into my line of sight, holding his oil lamp near his face. He was clean-shaven with dark eyes. The portrait of Irena filled my mind. Then I recognized *him*. I gasped, "It's you? All this time, it's been *you*?"

ALICE

CHAPTER THIRTY-SEVEN

Saturday, May 17
7:00 AM

Panting (the only time I ran in Manhattan was to escape the rain), I trudged into the living room to find Sal searching the fireplace mortar. Slightly annoyed, I stepped beside him and removed a loose brick. "It's right here." I held up the rolled note. His hand reached for the paper, but I drew it close, giving him a look that said 'don't you dare.'

The muscle in his jaw twitched.

The troop leaned close as I read the note out loud. Pointing to the last line, I said, "With fondest affection, Ivon."

"Ivon," Sal echoed. He looked at the tie tack that he'd taken from Cora. "Ivon L. Jansen. It's a match."

"I don't know anyone by that name in Saugerties," said Myrtle.

"He could be using a different name," said Cora.

Myrtle nodded. "That would make sense."

My eyes lit up. "The person who sold us the Krall house signed the documents, ILJ. If those are Ivon's initials, that would mean he owns the Whitaker estate." Like puzzle pieces falling into place, a picture formed in my head. The owl in the cellar. The portrait of Irena. The burnt boots. It all happened on the Whitaker property. What if that shriek hadn't been an owl after all? What if it had been one of the abducted men?

What if Ivon had been living there all along? What if my mother was there now? "Do you think Ivon could be living in the Whitaker house?"

Sal scoffed. "Nobody has lived there for years. Have you seen anyone come in or out of it?"

"No, but that doesn't mean he hasn't." Turning my back to him, I addressed my troop. "Think about it, with Ivon living there, he could easily keep watch of my mom and me. It's a perfect way to stay a step ahead of us."

Myrtle lifted a finger. "But you said your mother was taken away by a boat. Why would he travel the creek when his house is within walking distance?"

"Could be misdirection," said Cora. "A way to eliminate a trail to follow."

Cora's father, who had remained a quiet observer until this point, now spoke up. "Have the police searched the old Whitaker mansion?"

"The place is vacant," said Sal. "Clyde checked the place himself."

"That's private property," said Nellie's dad. "Are you saying Clyde broke in?"

Sal dismissed the comment with a wave of his hand. "It was hardly a break in. The house wasn't locked. But Clyde didn't find anything or anyone."

"I think we need to go in there ourselves," I said. "The initials on the tie tack are the same as the owner's initials. Ivon or whoever is behind these abductions has targeted the Whitaker family line. My mother was taken because she came too close to solving this case. Doesn't it seem like poetic justice to punish the Whitaker descendants in the mansion where Irena was mistreated?"

"Aye, I think yer right." Etta nodded in agreement.

Sal stroked a hand through his hair, looking perplexed. "Alice, I wanna find your mother as much as anyone, but there ain't anyone in there. The place is abandoned."

"What if Clyde missed something?" I shot back at him.

"I wouldn't doubt it," said Geraldine in a flat tone. "He's been awfully *busy* as of late."

Etta nodded.

"Sal, I think we should exhaust all options before we rule anything out," said Cora's dad.

At this, Sal conceded. "Okay, let's say this Ivon fella is there. If he left by a boat, then there'd be a boat on the shore. But Sheriff Bretton and his team didn't find a boat."

"If Ivon used a boat as a misdirection, then he would have returned by boat as well," said Myrtle. "Which means that the boat would be hidden somewhere on the Whitaker's land."

I snapped my fingers. "If we find the boat, then we know they're in the house!"

"We should start searching now," said Myrtle.

Sal held up a hand. "If the abductor is inside, then we need to be careful. We do not want to draw attention to our presence."

Cora's father agreed. "Luckily the woods will offer some cover, if we stay low, our bodies will be shielded by the overgrowth. We should check the shore first. See if there are any marks from a boat being dragged."

As we shuffled out of our cabin, I grabbed my brown umbrella. Mom had forgotten to take the umbrella with her to pump water last night. I didn't know who we'd encounter today, but I was going to be prepared.

We searched the shore from behind my house to the end of the Whitaker property line. Trouble was that the dirt had numerous sets of shoe prints from the police officers who had searched earlier. It looked like another dead-end.

Doubling back, Myrtle knelt down, looking at the ground and scanning the trees.

"Do you see something?" Cora knelt beside her.

"Not sure." She continued to look. "You see how the dirt looks like it's been raked beyond these shoeprints?"

Sal squatted down, eyeing the ground. "How can you tell?"

"The ground should have natural divots and texture from rain and wind. But around here, the ground looks like it's been raked," said Myrtle. "Nature doesn't do that. Humans do that. If someone has tampered with this dirt, it might have been to remove tracks. Just like we saw around the burn pile of the leather boots."

"You're right," I said. "We should search around here for the boat."

Spreading out, we combed the area, lifting branches and digging under fallen leaves.

I walked a few feet from Nellie and her father. As he guided her on his arm, she kept her chin raised as if she were listening for clues.

Nellie halted. "That sounded different."

"What do you mean?" asked her father.

She spun around, paced two steps, and hopped. "The ground below me is hollow. Whatever I'm standing on isn't just dirt. It's firm. Like a board." She bent down, combing leaves aside with her fingers.

He stomped with his shoe. "I think you're right, Nellie."

Dropping beside them, I helped brush aside a layer of leaves and dirt uncovering a length of plywood. Pulling up the board, we found a deep hole housing a dinghy. "You did it, Nellie!" I called out to our group. "It's here! Nellie found the boat. This is the proof!" I pointed at the Whitaker mansion. "My mother is in there!"

"We need to inform the police immediately," said Nellie's dad. "They must handle this."

"I'm not waiting for the police," I said. "I'm going in there now."

"You can't go barging into that house," said Sal. "It's too dangerous."

Nellie's dad agreed. "The Sheriff and his men will take care of this. We need to inform the station."

Sal clapped a hand on Nellie's dad's shoulder. "Mr. Mott,

you and the scouts should go to the station, while I keep a lookout here, in case anyone enters or exits."

"Very good," he agreed. "Come on, girls."

"I'm not leaving," I said, squaring my shoulders in a firm stance. "I am going into that house."

Sal's forehead creased in frustration. "Listen Alice, I know you're worried. We all are. But you don't know what you'll find in there. It's time for you and your friends to report to the Sheriff."

"What if she's in trouble? What if the police arrive too late, while we could have done something? I could never forgive myself."

"What are you gonna do? Use your umbrella?" He gestured to it.

Heat flooded up my neck, flushing my face. "You bet I will and—" my words dropped off at the sound of twigs snapping. My head darted toward the noise. "Elex?"

He hurried our way, weaving between the trees and brush.

"Grand so, now ya show up," huffed Etta.

Elex's chest heaved from running. "What's the story? Why yous standin' out here?"

"My mother's been taken," I exclaimed. "Where were you last night?"

His face went grim. "She's gone?"

"Yes."

"Where've you been?" Sal said with an air of accusation.

"I done been in New Paltz, huntin' down a clue." He turned to me, looking stricken. "I be ever sorry, Alice. I shoulda come back sooner. If I had—"

"Well you weren't here." Sal crossed his arms. "What did you find in New Paltz?"

"I located Irena's mother. She be kind enough to speak with me. I returned this mornin' to tell June what I discovered. Then I found yous cars parked outside, but no one be in the house, so I came searchin'."

"What did Irena's mother tell you?" I asked.

"Irena done has a twin brother named Ivon. I be positive that he be the one behind this."

Sal exhaled a heavy breath. "Yes, yes. We've already learned that much. If you'd been here, you'd have known that too."

"Keep yer knickers on, would ya," Etta shot at Sal. "We didn't know Ivon was a twin as it were." She turned to Elex. "We found a tie tack with the initials ILJ. It done be the same signature as Alice's house documents. So, we be thinkin' the letters stand for Ivon Jansen."

"True enough but," Elex lifted a finger, "There be somethin' about Ivon that ya don't know. He done been livin' in Saugerties. Watchin' us. Gainin' information and plottin' this whole thing. Last week, Mrs. Jansen received a letter from him sayin' all would be made right now. She didn't know what he meant by that. But, I think I do." He exhaled. "Ivon is reachin' the end of his plot. If June be in that house, she be in real trouble. Which means, I gotta get in there."

"If you're going in, then so am I," said Sal.

I gripped my umbrella tighter. "I am too."

The other troop members echoed me.

"No." Elex held up his hand. "Ya ladies be stayin' here. Ya don't know what yer dealin' with. Ivon is willin' to risk it all."

"Please Elex," I beseeched him. "Let me come. I can help."

"I say we all go," said Myrtle. "There is power in numbers."

"My daughter is blind," said Nellie's dad. "She's not going in that house."

"Dad, I can help," said Nellie, holding her head high. "I have keen senses, they need me."

"No, Nellie. This is a job for the police."

"There might'nt be time fer the police." Elex took off in a limp-run toward the house.

Sal hustled after him. "Are you armed?"

"I have a gun," said Elex.

I chased after them with my troop hot on our heels.

JUNE

CHAPTER THIRTY-EIGHT

Saturday, May 17
8:45 AM

"You see it now? James thought you would figure it out with the portrait. He was wrong." He set the oil lamp on a table, turning up the flame. A yellow glow permeated the small room.

I'd looked at him so many times and yet, never realized the resemblance. "Your beard covered your face."

"True, but I always thought our eyes were quite similar."

My hands fisted. All this time, he'd been coming around, pretending to care. Pretending to be helpful. Since the first day he showed me the Krall house, I knew I didn't like him. Now I knew why. He was a fraud. "Tell me Lloyd, is your real name Ivon Jansen?"

He gave a cynical laugh and clapped. "Well done, June. You've finally solved the case. Irena was my twin. When I crafted this plan, eighteen years ago, I never dreamed that a widow from Manhattan would nearly ruin it."

As I looked into his dark eyes, I couldn't believe I hadn't seen it before. While Irena's hair was far more blond and her skin more fair, they had the same eyes—except Ivon's were full of hate. If James wasn't lying, and he didn't plant the portrait by the creek, then who else knew Ivon's true identity? "If you didn't want me involved, why did you sell me your sister's house?"

"When I listed the house, I never thought someone would buy it. It was only meant to be a ruse—something to make people think that my sister's ghost was awakened. I never dreamed you would buy it. But desperation makes people do crazy things." He paused, sneering at me with the same half-hearted smile I'd seen many times before.

I wanted to smack it off his face.

"Since I could see you weren't going to back down, I sold you the house. It served my purpose because the town blamed you for angering Irena's ghost. I figured that you'd abandon the place once you heard of the disappearances. But no. You didn't do that, did you?" His smile vanished. "You're a single mother. You should have been afraid. You should have let the police handle it. Instead you chose to interfere." He shook his head. "I have worked meticulously. Planning, researching, and hunting down each and every relative in Charles Whitaker's bloodline."

My top lip curled back in disgust. "That's demented."

"No," he snapped. "It's loyal. My sister had a beautiful heart. She deserved a good life. A happy life. And it was stolen from her. I had to repay the injustice." Ivon walked to the man lying closest to me. Squatting down, he yanked the burlap sack off his head and lifted him up by his hair. The man dangled limp in his grasp. His face was bruised and bloodied.

My body trembled at the sight.

"The punishment had to fit the crime," continued Ivon. "The Whitakers took my sister's life and the life of her unborn child. They stole her chance to have a generational legacy, which is why I chose to end theirs." Letting the man's hair go, his head fell to the floor. "When James found out that Irena's death was not a suicide, we devised the plan. I carefully curated each death, beginning with Charles' newborn child. Easy poison scenario. Then it was a matter of the next two sons—unfortunate accidents. One a drowning. One a terrible fall from a tree. Both by Esopus Creek." He lifted a finger. "You see, people will believe what you lead them to believe. The rumor spread through town that Irena was seeking revenge on the Whitaker family. Stricken with grief and fear, Mrs. Whitaker ended up in the asylum. She found her fate there."

My stomach churned as he spoke of their deaths like they meant nothing.

"Then it was time for Charles." His features twisted with wicked amusement. "I took my time with him. A quick death was too gracious. Instead, I added traces of strychnine to his tincture of medicine. He grew more sick by the day. By the fourth, his breathing stopped, and he died in a pool of his own vomit. The maids said he cried out in agony until his final breath. With Charles dead, Felix was terrified. He and his sister Julianne were the only children left. They fled to an estate in Kingston belonging to Charles' brother." Ivon paused, crossing to a nearby table, he uncorked a crystal decanter of whiskey.

With his back to me, I wrestled against the ropes binding my wrists. James watched me without uttering a word.

Taking a drink, Ivon wiped his mouth. "I followed them, of course. After the sudden deaths of Charles' brother and his son, Felix was mad with fear. He was convinced that Irena's ghost had trailed him. When he made to flee, yet again, I caught him alone in his carriage. Here I revealed myself and told him that he was next. He begged for his life, saying he'd give me anything I wanted. I told him to sign over the rights of his manor. He agreed. Returning to the Whitaker Estate, he signed over the deed. Then James and I dragged him to Stony Point, pushing him under the water until he no longer writhed in our grasp." He took another drink of his whiskey, looking pleased.

I swallowed against the knot of fear in my throat.

"James thought we should be done after Felix, but I disagreed." Ivon swished the brown liquid in his glass. "If I was going to wipe out the Whitaker name, then every male in Charles' bloodline had to be eliminated—brothers, uncles, cousins. So, we hunted down each and every relation." Ivon tugged the sack off the second man.

He looked at me with weary eyes. I guessed this was Rhett.

"Each relative led to the next," said Ivon. "Ultimately, it was the Whitakers who failed each other. A little pain, and they gave up the next name."

I shuttered. How were they able to complete such a ruthless plan without being caught? How did the police never find out?

James sighed. "But June isn't a Whitaker."

"She's a loose end." Ivon sniffed. "Don't forget, James, all of this could have been avoided if you hadn't messed up."

James' shoulders sagged like a man laden with a yoke.

"Go on, tell June what you did. Tell her how you failed my sister."

James sighed. "I grew up with the Jansens. I was the same age as Ivon and Irena's older brother, Otis. I had always viewed Irena as a friend, until I had come home from fighting in the Comanche wars. I was a broken man after what I had seen and done. But Irena's goodness brought me back." His gaze traveled up toward the ceiling as if he were picturing her. "She had this light about her, and I fell in love."

I recalled the portrait from the cellar. There was no light left in her countenance. Only sadness.

"Before I could confess my feelings, Irena ran away with Albin. So I went searching for her. I found her a few towns north in Saugerties, working for the Whitakers." James exhaled a sad breath. "I begged Irena to leave him, but she was loyal. In order to keep an eye on her, I took up residence at The Exchange Hotel and found a job at The Saugerties Daily Journal. After a year, I could see that Irena was unhappy with her marriage and the demands of Charles and his wife. Once again, I asked her to leave Albin. I told her that I loved her, and I would take care of her. But she refused me. She said that everything would be okay once she and Albin had a child. Up until this time, Charles' son Felix had been away. I learned later that he'd been sent to live with a Great Aunt in Pennsylvania after a moral indiscretion." He glanced at Rhett. "That was you, I later discovered. However, once that problem had been resolved by a marriage between Mr. Mills and Rhett's mother, Charles allowed Felix to come home. It didn't take long for Felix to notice Irena. Everyone noticed Irena. She was beautiful." His voice cracked. He pressed a hand to his mouth, turning away.

Ivon listened while drinking his whiskey. His expression remained hard, unmoved. "Stop weeping and get on with it, James."

James inhaled. "After three years of trying, Irena finally announced that she was pregnant. She looked happy, and though I disliked Albin, I was happy that her dream had come true. Then one day, she showed up at my house to say goodbye. She told me that the baby was Felix's, and they planned to run away together. Two days later, Irena's body was found dead in Esopus Creek." He shook his head. "Charles said that she drowned herself. I didn't believe him. One of the maids told me to talk to Amara. She had witnessed the truth. When she was leaving the manor, Amara saw Charles and Irena by the creek. She saw him drag Irena under. But because she was a black woman, the police didn't believe her word." His hands clenched into fists. "Charles killed Irena to cover up his son's actions yet again. Felix did nothing to stop it. He didn't care that it was his own child in her womb! I was furious. I thought that Ivon and I had to do this. I thought this was the right thing...but we've gone too far." His hands released, hanging limp at his sides. "You remind me of her, June. You are bright and beautiful like she was. I'm sorry. I never wanted to see you get hurt."

Ivon set his glass on a table. "June never had to be involved, but you chose to plant clues for her. So, I had no choice but to clean up after you. Fact is I never would have returned to Saugerties if you had upheld your part."

"I did my part," retorted James. "The plan was finished 16 years ago."

"Well it wasn't done, was it? If it had been, Henry would have been dead, along with Stuart and Rhett. Some reporter you are. Missing the important details."

James' face reddened. "Henry and Stuart were infants."

"They are Whitakers," Ivon snapped. "When you discovered their relation, you should have dealt with it. Instead, you allowed them to grow. To live. To have a life my sister never did! Alas," he spun around to face me, his eyes alight with a wild frenzy, "the plan I thought I had completed 16 years ago had to reopen when Henry Brickmore's big wedding announcement made the paper. In the article, it mentioned his lineage, and I knew I couldn't leave it alone. I had to end the line once and for all. Then I thought, if one man had slipped through the cracks under James' *watchful* eye, who else was missed? So, I returned to Saugerties, positioning myself as a broker, gaining information, and planning how to finish my plot. That's when it occurred to me, I had to resurrect Irena's story. By listing the Krall house, I could once again use my sister's ghost as my cover. Being the cattle they are, this town believed the ruse."

I huffed. "The police don't believe it. They are searching for answers."

"If they were truly searching, June, they'd have made a better effort. As it is, they've done nothing. They've discovered nothing. Even with James being careless." Ivon cast him another scowl. "Nevertheless, my plan is finally coming to an end. Henry led to Stuart, who led to Rhett. While Rhett gave James and I a good fight at the creek, it was Stuart who was the toughest to break." He cast a look at Rhett. "He didn't give you up easily. But everyone has a breaking point."

I cringed. "How did Stuart know about Rhett's identity, when Rhett himself didn't know?"

"Ah, that's right, you paid Dorothy a little visit." Ivon

nodded. "Yes, unfortunately, Dorothy might have kept the secret from her brother, but she did tell her husband, who in turn told Stuart. Funny how secrets don't stay a secret." His lips twisted into a smirk.

A shiver rippled through my body. "If Irena was the good person, you say she was, I doubt she'd be proud of your actions."

Ivon moved like a flash, the back of his hand striking my face. "All I have done has been out of love for my sister. I'm vindicating her!"

Pain seared through my head. Through gritted teeth, I whispered, "Legacies don't die with people."

He let out an angry grunt. "Don't you ever quit? You're tied up, June! You're done. Why are you still talking?"

His shouting reverberated through my pounding head. Swallowing, I opened my eyes. "Because before Irena died, she lived. That is her legacy. Her legacy didn't die. It lives on. The same as the Whitakers. It lives on in the stories. In the pictures. In the memories. You can kill as many people as you like, and yet, they still live on."

"No, no, no!" He pressed trembling hands to his head. "I've been meticulous. See. I've traveled and searched. I've done it. It's taken 18 years. But I've done it. No thanks to you, and no thanks to James." He spat. "The part that James left out of his retelling is that he should have saved my sister. He saw what was happening, and he did nothing. It is his guilt that forced him to commit to my mission. James failed my sister when she was 18 years old, and now, 18 years later, he's failed again." Ivon turned a hard set of eyes on James. "I always keep the tie tack pinned inside my jacket pocket. It didn't fall out on its own. You took it and probably threw it in the woods. You want us to get caught. Well, you failed me for the last time." Pulling a gun from his jacket, he pulled the trigger. The bullet blew through James' stomach.

I screamed.

James fell to the ground, blood pouring from his abdomen.

"Today, I will fully end the Whitaker bloodline, and my sister's life will be avenged." He walked out of view.

I heard the sound of a cap being unscrewed. Liquid spilled on the floor as he walked around the room. As he circled, I saw the gasoline can in his hands. My heart jolted in my chest. He was going to burn us alive.

ALICE

CHAPTER THIRTY-NINE

Saturday, May 17
9:30 AM

Lifting the outside doors, we hurried down the steps into the mansion's cellar. We heard a muffled scream coming through the walls.

Geraldine jumped. "Who was that?"

"It sounds like a woman." I spun toward Elex. "It has to be my mom!"

Nellie sniffed the air. "I smell gasoline."

"Gasoline?" asked Sal. "You sure?"

"Positive." She nudged her cane along, walking toward the wall, sniffing. "It's stronger over here. Do you see a doorway?"

"No, there isn't a door." I hit the cement, yelling, "Mom! Where are you?!"

Nellie tapped her cane on the wall. "The smell wouldn't be this strong if it wasn't escaping from a crack or something. I think this wall might be connected to another room."

Elex shot up a staircase that led from the cellar into the house. "There be a kitchen up here."

Our troop hustled after him.

We heard the scream more clearly now.

"The smell is coming from over here." Nellie swung her cane side-to-side, hurrying toward the back of the kitchen.

Elex threw open the doors of a walk-in pantry.

I could hear the words, "Help me! Help me!"

Nellie entered the pantry. "The smell is stronger inside here."

"There must be a hidden room." Sal peered inside. "That's why Clyde didn't find anything before."

"I think it's connected to this pantry." Elex tossed bags of flour, searching the floor and walls for an entry point.

My eyes traced the shelves lining the pantry's back wall. On the top shelf, tucked beside a bag of onions, I spotted a cord. Pulling it, the adjacent wall slid into a hidden pocket. As it opened, a scene unfolded before my eyes. In the middle of a dim room, my mother sat bound on the floor. Near her were two men, also tied up. Another man lay dead on the floor. Standing next to the body was a man holding a gun toward us and in his other hand was a lit match. Though he was shaven, the man's face registered in my mind. It was Lloyd Ennis. Then it dawned on me, Lloyd was Ivon.

"You're just in time." He threw the match into the gasoline. It caught aflame in a stream of liquid that snaked around the room.

"Mom!" I screamed.

Elex charged Ivon as he fired his gun. The bullet hit Elex. He jerked backward with the blow. Sal pulled out his own pistol, shooting Ivon in the chest. Ivon looked shocked as he sank to the floor.

Nellie yelled, "What's burning?"

Geraldine grabbed her arm. "Come on, we have to get out of here."

The flames rose quickly.

Sal hoisted my mom into his arms and ran from the room. Mr. Davis and Cora lifted one man, while Myrtle, Elex, and Etta carried out the other. I raced outside with them. Emerging from the cellar, we drew farther from the house as smoke billowed out after us.

Sal set my mom on the grass.

I dropped down beside her, throwing my arms around her. "You're safe now. We found you."

Elex pulled a knife from his boot and knelt down. As he cut off my mother's ropes, blood flowed down his arm. "I cannot tell ya how sorry I be. I shoulda been there last night. I shoulda kept ya safe."

"You're hurt," she said to him in a hoarse voice.

"I done deserve it." He shook his head, looking miserable. "I shoulda been there."

"You're here now," she whispered.

With her wrists and ankles freed, she tried to stand, but her knees buckled. Before she toppled to the ground, Elex and I caught her. Her body trembled as we lowered her back down.

Sirens sounded in the distance. Mr. Mott had gone to the police, but they would have been too late. If it wasn't for Elex charging inside…

Mom stared at the burning house. "How did you find me?"

"We followed the signs like you and Captain Parker taught us."

Slowly she faced me. "I can't believe it worked. Following the signs."

Tears flowed down my face. "Yes, Mom. Just like you taught us."

"It worked." Her eyes glossed with tears. "Thank you. Thank you for coming after me."

"I wouldn't stop 'till I found you. None of us would." I gestured to our troop.

She looked up. "Thank you, girls."

Etta dropped to her knees, wrapping her arms around my mother and me. Then, Cora embraced us, followed by Geraldine and Nellie.

I glanced at Myrtle. Her whole body was shaking, but she remained standing with her hands clenched at her sides.

—

Inside the police station, my eyes drifted around the room as Sheriff Bretton talked about what had happened. Each scout and her parents were spread around the room, some sat in chairs while others stood, anxiously tapping a foot. My mother sipped a cold cup of coffee, while I held a wet handkerchief between my hands. We were all struggling to process. None of us had ever experienced something like that before. Seeing my mother bound with ropes while flames lined the room would forever be seared in my mind. We would never forget what we saw. I exhaled a slow breath.

But maybe that was okay.

In the same way that we had faced our fears to enter that burning room, we would face our fears in order to live on.

Since that first day in the library, I knew that our troop was different. Each of us had felt the sting of rejection. But being rejected taught us how to be strong. Taught us how to think for ourselves. Taught us how to hold up under pressure. Today, Cora, Etta, Geraldine, Nellie, Myrtle and I learned what we were truly made of, and we discovered… it was the stuff of heroes.

JUNE

CHAPTER FORTY

Saturday, May 17
7:00 PM

Never in my life had I experienced such fear. It was the kind of fear that numbed the pain of the ropes cutting my wrists as I pulled and tugged to free them. The kind of fear that kept my eyes from crying though I knew I was about to die. It was the fear that made me beg and plead with a man who didn't possess a heart. As I watched Ivon douse the floor, I knew that I would be leaving my daughter just like her father had left us. But a miracle came in the form of six young scouts.

It had been nine hours since my rescue, and I still felt numb. In my mind, I saw the flames rising from the Whitaker mansion. My throat still ached from the smoke. My heart might always feel the horror of watching James die.

But I was safe. I was alive. I had my daughter, and she had me. That was enough assurance to know that we would be okay.

After an evaluation at the hospital to check out our lungs and bandage my wrists and ankles, Sal checked Alice and me into a room at The Maxwell Hotel. Alice held my hand as we sat on the hotel's porch chairs, watching the sun descend. We were tired, worn down, and didn't have words to speak. So instead, we watched the sun.

CHAPTER FORTY-ONE

Tuesday, June 17
6:00 PM

It had been a month since I had faced death. Reporters from all the surrounding papers had poured into town to cover the story, printing the picture of my troop and me on their front page. They dubbed us heroes, and suddenly the whole town of Saugerties gushed with gratitude. Rhett had been discharged from the hospital, and the doctors predicted that Stuart would make a full recovery. Dorothy Hollis had sent bouquets of flowers, and Gladys Ellsworth, Stuart's little sister, had shown up in person to apologize. Alice had accepted without any form of "I told you so." Even Beulah brought us a pie and gave begrudging thanks. I suspected that she'd pegged me for the seamstress ad, but she wouldn't admit it. Especially because we were now, as Alice put it, practically famous. Left and right, families asked if their daughters could join our troop. (How interesting the sudden change of heart.)

In the aftermath and uproar, life continued, but it wasn't the same. It would never be the same. For that, I was glad. I'd realized something as I watched the match hit the gasoline—I didn't want to die, because I hadn't fully lived.

Since Niall passed away a year ago, I had lived with one foot in the present and one in the past. I struggled to move forward.

I struggled to be free. I struggled to know if it was okay to let go. But feeling the flames had awakened me. It showed me that sorrow had clouded my view of the sun, making me think it wasn't shining. I was done living under the weight of loss and living in fear of letting Alice down. I was done blaming Niall for leaving.

He hadn't left *me*.

He had only left.

Dousing the new glass pane in my front window, I wiped it clean with a rag. Elex had installed the window during the two weeks that Alice and I lived at The Maxwell Hotel. After that time, I was ready to come back. Irena's house had become my home. I was proud of that. I think she would be glad that I had returned. I would continue to shed love on this place, giving it the attention it deserved. Rubbing away the smudges from the glass, I looked up at the sky. It was the middle of June, and the sun shined brighter, or maybe that was only my perception.

"What do you think?" Alice exited our bedroom, dressed in her khaki uniform.

I released an exhale of admiration. "Don't you look smart."

"I feel like a real scout now." She spun around, showing off her snazzy skirt and jacket.

"I'm proud of you, sweetheart." I kissed her forehead. "I better put on my uniform before the troop arrives." Slipping off my work trousers and blouse, I donned my own belted jacket and skirt. As I tied the black scarf below the collar, I heard a knock on the front door.

"Myrtle's here," Alice called from the living room.

"I'll be right out." Checking my reflection in my bedroom mirror, I straightened my jacket and went out to greet her. She stood by the door talking with Alice.

"I apologize for coming early," said Myrtle. "I had hoped to talk to Captain Flynn for a moment before the ceremony."

"Hello, dear," I said walking to her. "You look sharp in your uniform."

"Captain Flynn." She saluted me. "Thank you for the compliment. I wondered if I could speak to you for a moment?"

Diplomatic Myrtle. "Of course." I gestured to the kitchen table and chairs. "Shall we sit?"

She took a seat, looking down at the tabletop.

I waited for her to speak. When she didn't, I asked, "What was it you wanted to tell me?"

She inhaled. "When you disappeared, I was scared. I thought I might never see you again. I couldn't bear that thought. I couldn't lose another…" She swallowed.

I waited, wondering if she was going to say *mother*.

Myrtle drew in a breath. "A man dressed in flowy clothes came to town one day. He called himself a gypsy. My mother fell in love with him and when his caravan left, she went with him. About a year passed, and I got a letter from her. All it said was, "Myrtle, my spirit is finally free. Nature is now my home. This is the life I was destined to live."' Her shoulders slouched. "That's all it said. She didn't say she loved me or that she missed me. I wondered if I had done something to make her leave." She sniffed back tears. "Every night, I would kneel by my bed and pray that she'd come home. I decided to learn everything I could about nature. That way if she did come back, I'd be able to make her proud. Maybe then, she'd stay." She wiped a quick hand below her eyes.

My heart broke. This is why she'd been guarded. She had wanted to be close to me and yet, she was afraid that I would abandon her too. Under Myrtle's tough exterior rested a wounded little girl, wanting to be loved.

"I joined the Girl Scouts because I thought it would make my mother proud of me." She lifted her chin, meeting my eyes. "But the Girl Scouts gave me something I didn't expect. It gave me you. I've watched other girls with their moms, wishing I could be them. That's why being in your troop has meant everything to me. You've made me feel smart and needed." She paused, noticeably swallowing. "You made me feel loved.

That's why, when you disappeared…I was so scared. I couldn't bear to lose you. I couldn't bear it." Tears filled her eyes, and she covered her face.

I rose from my chair, kneeling at her feet. I pulled her into my arms. "I'm here, and I'm not leaving. I love you, darling. You are a wonderful girl."

Her body shook as she cried tears she'd probably been holding since she was five. "Thank you, Captain Flynn. Thank you for loving me."

In my kitchen, holding my crying scout, I knew that this was why I was supposed to come to Saugerties. I was meant to meet Myrtle. I was meant to meet Etta, Cora, Nellie, and Geraldine. I was meant to be their leader, not because they needed me, but because we needed each other. Alice and I were broken, but with the love and help of our troop, we were healing. We were all healing.

We exited the house, carrying my kitchen table for the ceremony. Today, my troop would be sworn in as official Girl Scouts. We were holding the occasion on my front "lawn." (Elex had mowed the weeds down, making it presentable enough.) We set the table down, and I laid out six Tenderfoot Pins.

"My, those are beautiful, aren't they," said Myrtle.

"I'll say." Alice smiled.

As parents and their scouts arrived, I thanked everyone for coming and positioned my original six scouts in a horizontal line before our audience. "I am proud to have you hereby witnesses to attest to the ceremony this day." I blew my whistle.

The scouts marched into a horseshoe formation, which we had practiced at our last meeting. Each scout had passed her Tenderfoot Test with flying colors. Well, almost every scout. Geraldine struggled through most of it, but she was one of us, and we wouldn't let her fail.

I turned my back to our audience and faced the scouts. "I stand before you today with great pride. I am proud of the ladies you are, and the ladies you continue to become. Each of you have faced hardships. Each of you have known pain, hurt, and loss. And still, each of you have prevailed. You are strong young women. It is my honor to officially swear you in today as a Girl Scout for you all possess the characteristics of a scout,"—my eyes moved from face to face—"brave, trustworthy, helpful, courteous, loyal, resilient. As a Girl Scout of the United States, what do you promise?"

The scouts saluted as they spoke, "On my honor, I will try to do my duty to God and my country, to help other people at all times, and to obey the Scout Laws."

One by one, I presented each scout to the audience and pinned the Tenderfoot badge on their uniforms. When I presented Etta, Elex whistled and Imogen stared with an expression of awe.

I nearly chuckled when I presented Geraldine. Never did I think she'd stick it out. She didn't possess an ounce of physical agility, and she seemed more interested in complaining than learning, and yet, when we needed her most, Geraldine had risen to the occasion. As I pinned on her badge, she beamed at the one person who had come to watch, Mrs. Florence Lockwood. It didn't take long for the Saugerties' gossips to spread the news of Clyde's affair and the fact that he'd been turned out from his residence.

After presenting Myrtle, I noticed a man place a hand to his forehead and salute her. I had never seen or met him before, but from the look of surprise and supreme joy on Myrtle's face—I knew it was her father.

As Alice stepped forward to receive her pin, my throat knotted with emotion. I've always been proud of her, but now, there was so much more to it. I admired her. I wished Niall could have been here to see this.

Blowing my whistle three times, my troop and I formed a

line. "The customary tradition is for a Girl Scout troop to be named after a flower. During the last several weeks, I've pondered what flower would adequately define us. Today, I know I've chosen the correct one. It is a flower that represents new beginnings and hope for the future. We are The Daffodil Troop." As we saluted the crowd, the audience broke into applause. Standing before them, my heart swelled with joy.

Following the ceremony, we enjoyed punch and cookies. The scouts exchanged laughs and stories, while parents exchanged pleasantries. When I stepped back into the house to refresh the punch, Elex joined me.

"Twas a grand ceremony," he said.

"It was, wasn't it?" I released a contented sigh. "Those six girls are pretty amazing."

"Their captain be amazin' too." The side of his mouth lifted.

I waved my hand. "Go on."

"I think I be stayin'," his grin widened, "the view here is rather fine."

"Elex O'Keefe," I gave his arm a push.

He winced.

My eyes bulged. "Oh my, that's your bad arm, isn't it! I'm so sorry, I didn't mean to—"

"Don't ya worry."

"Are you sure?" I put a hand to my cheek. "I wasn't thinking about the bullet and the wound and—"

"It do be okay, love." He took my hand. "I'd take a hundred bullets more for ya."

That moment, the world fell away, and all I saw was him. "Thank you."

"Ya don't need to thank—"

I leaned in and kissed him.

He stood stock still, not kissing me back.

"What's wrong?" I said against his lips.

"Kissin' ya hasn't gone well fer me in the past."

"Okay. Then let's live in the present."

"Will the present reject me?"

"Not anymore."

"Holy mother full of grace." He uttered before wrapping an arm around my waist and kissing me with the fervency of a man who'd been waiting, hoping, and finally getting the answer to his prayer.

When we parted, he smiled. "I done take it back. I be acceptin' yer thanks as often as ya want to give it."

"Well you're in luck, because I have more thanks to give." I winked at him.

"Talk like that and I might die after all."

I beamed at him. "We better leave this kitchen before we both perish."

Chuckling, we exited the house to rejoin the party.

"Oh June!" Florence waved a hand at me. "I must talk to you."

As I headed in her direction, I stole another look at Elex, who was looking back at me. I felt a rush of heat. It seemed silly now that I hadn't seen it sooner. I liked him. I liked him a lot. And when you have something genuine in front of you, it makes it easier to spot the fake.

CHAPTER FORTY-TWO

Friday, June 20
7:00 PM

Tonight needed to go perfect.

I had draped a white linen cloth on the dining table, adorning it with white porcelain plates, crystal goblets, and lit candlesticks. I'd even bought a bottle of red wine for the occasion. With my developing knowledge of fire-building, I was able to cook a real meal on the stove. Sauteed onions and steaks, mashed potatoes, and a waldorf salad on the side.

I had my gramophone displayed on the cabinet counter. Though it had to be cranked every four minutes, I thought it might be nice for a dance or two to Marion Harris' sultry voice.

Spraying another spritz of perfume, I rechecked my reflection. I'd chosen the black dress.

A knock sounded on the door.

Inhaling a breath, I raced to the gramophone, wound it up and swung open the door while Marion sang, "Now won't you listen honey, while I say, how could you tell me that you're goin' away?"

Standing in a pinstripe five-piece suit was the ever gorgeous, Salvatore Saviano. His lips parted into a brilliant smile. "Good evening."

"Evening." I stepped back, gesturing for him to come in.

As he entered, his eyes remained fixed on me. "June…" he shook his head. "Just when I think you can't get any lovelier, you surprise me." He swept up my hand, kissing it. "Never thought I'd be one for short hair, but it suits you."

I reached up, patting the side of my new bob. Ever since Irene Castle cut off her long locks, I've longed to be brave enough to do the same. Then I faced off with Ivon Jansen, the devil incarnate. After that, nothing seemed scary anymore. "Thank you. I wanted to do something bold."

He ran a light hand along the edge of my blond bob. "I'd say you already did that. I don't know a single woman who'd go looking for trouble like you."

"I wouldn't say I looked for it, I simply didn't shy away." I grinned, running a hand down his lapel. "I didn't properly thank you for saving me that day."

He stepped closer to me. "You never needed to."

Just as he lowered his lips in my direction, I spun on my heel toward the kitchen. "I hope you're hungry."

I heard a husky chuckle escape his throat. "Famished."

"Good." I glanced over my shoulder, sending him another grin. "I made plenty."

He looked over the table and lit candles. "Fancy."

"I wanted to show you my appreciation. Why don't you open the wine, while I serve the meal."

"Gladly." He uncorked the bottle, pouring us each a full glass.

Seated together, I watched him cut his steak and pop in a bite.

"Mmm," he said as he chewed. "This is delicious. Didn't know you were such a cook."

"There's a lot you don't know about me." I lowered my lashes demurely.

His brows rose with delight. "Perhaps I need to study more."

"Perhaps." I nibbled on the salad.

He guzzled down half his glass. "How's it been living here again?"

Taking in the room, I tipped my head, considering. "I thought it would be harder. But for some reason, I find it comforting. This house is a part of me now. It feels right."

His blank expression said he didn't understand at all. "Well, that's good."

I nodded, taking a sip of wine.

Conversation drifted on as the food left our plates, well mostly his. I refilled Sal's goblet a third time.

"Care for more music?" I asked.

"That'd be swell."

I spun the crank several times and another song played.

He stood to his feet, extending a hand to me. "Shall we?"

I entered his arms, swaying to the languid tune, allowing him to draw me close. I could smell the alcohol on his breath and feel the loose rhythm of his movements. "Sal, can I ask you a question?"

"Anything."

I shifted in his embrace to meet his gaze. "Do you like me?"

He tilted his head, looking incredulous. "I thought you already knew?"

"Tell me anyway."

A warm smile softened his features. "I like you, June Flynn. I've liked you since the day we first met."

"Then why did you lie to me?"

His steps faltered, but he quickly recovered. "What do you mean?"

"You said that you didn't know who planted the portrait at the creek, but I don't know how that could be," I paused, staring intently at him, "when you were the one who did it."

He sniffed. "What makes you say such a thing?"

"Because three men entered a boat the night Rhett was abducted."

"I know. I was there, I told you that."

"You said that you tried to save him. Which would mean that only James or Ivon had abducted Rhett solely that eve. But as Ivon told me whilst I was tied up, Rhett put up a great fight. It took all their strength to detain him. If you had tried to save Rhett, I would have seen four figures in the tousle by the creek. I didn't though. I only saw Ivon, James and Rhett. Which means you lied to me."

The song stopped playing, leaving the room silent.

His arms fell from my waist.

I faced him, eye to eye, with only a mere gap of space dividing us.

His shoulders tensed under his beautiful jacket. "As I told you before, Clyde and I were taking turns staking out the creek because we'd been receiving tips. I was there that night. But Ivon punched me. You didn't see me because I was laid on the ground."

"Oh I believe you were there. But you didn't try to intervene. You watched from the shadows. You watched them row away, and then you planted the portrait for the police to find." I lifted my finger. "A portrait that was being stored in the cellar of the Whitaker mansion."

He shrugged. "Fine, I planted the portrait. Clyde discovered it that day he and Florence searched the mansion. I thought it would help emphasize the story of Irena's ghost renewing her revenge. I have papers to sell. Sometimes, certain methods have to be taken."

"I see," I nodded slowly, "well then there was the matter of James' combat boots. The day I found my home ransacked, those boot prints were tracked through my house. My scouts and I later discovered the boots burned behind the Whitaker property. James denied any involvement in the destruction of my house. He was adamant. Though Ivon too believed that James was leaving me clues, trying to get them caught. Nevertheless, I felt James was being honest. Which meant that someone else knew of Ivon and James' plot. Who do you think that was?"

Sal huffed, rocking a slight step backward. "How should I know?"

"You should." My face hardened. "Because it's you."

He flinched. "You have no proof of that."

"Actually, I do. See, after you broke into my home, I figured it only fair that I do the same to you." I strode to the kitchen cabinet, pulling out a stack of documents. "Everyone needs a motive. I found yours." I donned a glinting smile. Fanning page after page on the floor as I said, "Bills. Bills, Bills. You spend money frivolously on your lavish lifestyle and yet, your newspaper isn't bringing in enough revenue, and the bank isn't happy. Not to mention, you're behind on payments for your father's medical treatment." I waved the next document in the air. "Memorial Hospital is on the verge of dismissing your father."

Sal's jaw twitched with repressed anger. "You have no right—"

"Oh but I do. I was right from the beginning, but you made me doubt myself." I pulled out a worn copy of the Hound of Baskervilles. Walking toward him, I flipped through the dog-eared pages with his notes scrawled in the margins. "The ghost. The legend. The portrait. The perfect blueprint." I tossed the book at his feet. "You knew the whole time."

"You're misunderstanding. It's not what it looks like."

"Oh I think it is." I turned back to the cabinet, extracting a LIFE magazine. I flipped through the pages revealing missing letters from various spots. "Every tip that magically appeared in Clyde's mailbox was delivered by you. You created the messages as a way to absolve yourself from the spotlight. But behind the scenes, you knew who was going to be taken and when. You knew I was in the Whitaker house and did nothing. I would have died in there, if it wasn't for my troop! You knew, but you lied to me over and over again!"

"It wasn't like that," he snapped. "You were never supposed to be hurt. I told him. I told him, but that idiot deviated. He was insane, see. When Alice told me you were taken, I was sick inside. Truly. I was gonna save you, I swear, but Alice wouldn't leave. She begged for my help, and I couldn't say what I knew or else the police would blame me. But it wasn't my fault, see." He opened his hands. "I'd been trailing Lloyd for months after he listed the Krall house, because he wouldn't tell me who owned the property. He said the owner was private, but I said to him, 'the town deserves to know.' This was an important story. I could see the headline: "Identity Of Whitaker Estate Owner Finally Revealed." But that stupid plonker wasn't being helpful. So I trailed him. Then one night, I watched him go into the Whitaker mansion. That's when I found the hidden room with Henry Brickmore tied to a chair. I pulled a gun on Lloyd, forcing him to tell me everything. He spilled his sordid tale of avenging his sister. While I thought him a few cards short of a deck, I understood the duty to family. Family is everything. Besides, self-righteous men like Charles Whitaker and Henry Brickmore deserved what came to them." He sniffed like the mention of them produced a foul smell. "I saw an opportunity. Lloyd, well Ivon, wanted his revenge, and I needed to sell stories. I told him we could help each other. I could print stories that would make his sister's ghost story believable, and he'd tip me off before each abduction. We'd go to print before any other paper. So we'd sell out." Sal stepped toward me, his eyes alight with fervor. "I saw my chance to fix my families' problems and took it. How can that be so bad?"

"Because men died in the process!" I snapped. "I almost became a casualty as well, and you are an accomplice to that!"

His composure vanished into fury. "No, I only printed stories! That's all. And when I saw Ivon going off the rails, I tried to warn you. I planted the picture of Irena. I went to the lengths of upturning your home as a warning. I gave you James' boots as a clue. Can't you see, I was trying to help you! I wanted to see justice served."

I glared at him. "Well, now it will be."

My bedroom door flung open and Sheriff Bretton, three

other officers, and Elex ran out. The officers trained their weapons on Sal, whose eyes flashed with shock before lifting his hands in surrender.

Sheriff Bretton yanked Sal's hands down, clapping handcuffs on him.

"June, come on," Sal protested. "I helped you fix your house. Supported your troop. I saved you from the fire!"

My eyes narrowed. "You almost got me killed."

He continued to plead as the sheriff pushed him out the door. The other officers followed.

I released the breath caught in my chest.

Sometimes villains hide in plain sight. That's what makes them hard to sniff out. They could be your grocer, they could be your postman, they could be your neighbor. You don't really know. You never really know. Unless you observe them carefully. Look for the clues. Look for the peculiarities. Look for the things that go against the role they're supposed to be playing.

That's what I did. I looked for the oddities. Sal always included pieces of truth, which made it hard to detect his lies. But it was the small oddities that gave him away.

Elex placed a gentle hand on my shoulder. "Are ya okay?"

"I am now."

"I be awfully proud of ya. That took courage."

"I'm glad it's over." I shuddered. "I hated the pretense, but I had to make him comfortable in order to get him talking."

"I know it." He nodded. "Course I coulda done without the dancin' and the touchin', and, well, basically the whole scenario, but I be glad it worked."

"I could have done without it too." I leaned closer to him. "I'd much rather be dancing with you."

"Now, that could be arranged." He wound up the gramophone and held out a hand.

I placed mine into his, and he pulled me against his chest. Tucked into his embrace, I felt my tension fall away.

CHAPTER FORTY-THREE

Thursday, June 26
8:00 AM

"On behalf of everyone here at The Telegraph, I say, 'Welcome.'"

"Thank you," I said, shaking the hand of my new boss. "I can't tell you how excited I am about this opportunity."

"Well," he said, "if the recent events have shown us anything, you're going to be a fine reporter."

Thanking him again, I exited the building with a smile that spread cheek to cheek. I was the first female reporter for The Telegraph. I had things to prove, but I wasn't scared. I knew I could do it. I knew I was meant to do it. Whatever the journey ahead had in store, I welcomed it.

Entering the nearby park, I found Alice reading a book.

She looked at me with hopeful eyes. "So?"

I tossed my hands in the air. "I got the job!"

She leapt to her feet, throwing her arms around me. "I knew you would! When do you start?"

"On Monday."

"Well, it sounds like we have some celebrating to do."

"I know five scouts who just might like to join us."

"I know a handsomely rugged man who'd probably like to come as well."

"Who might that be?" I asked with bewildered innocence.

Alice rolled her eyes. "Oh please. You and Elex are practically inseparable these days."

"That's a bit of an exaggeration."

"It ain't far off." She dusted a piece of grass off her skirt. "Now that you and Elex are courting, do you think I can ask him to show me his prosthetic leg?"

I blinked in rapid succession. "You want to see his prosthetic?"

"I sure do. I haven't been able to get it out of my mind ever since you told me part of his leg got blown off."

Her strange obsession struck me as peculiar, but also particularly hilarious. I found myself laughing. "Oh my goodness, Alice Flynn. I don't know if we can simply ask him to show you his fake leg."

"Why not?"

Hmmm. That was a good question.

She crossed her arms. "He showed you."

"That's true. And I had just met him."

"Great." She linked her arm with me. "Now that that's settled. Let's see a man about a leg."

Made in the USA
Monee, IL
21 January 2024

51730143R00171